To a dazzling new vampire series for fans of Bella Forrest's SHADE OF VAM-

PIRE.

Introducing:

THE VAMPIRE GIFT SERIES

by E.M. Knight

www.EMKnight.com

www.facebook.com/AuthorEMKnight

EM@EMKnight.com

tVG 03 - Version 5

Books by E.M. Knight

THE VAMPIRE GIFT:

Currently Available:

The Vampire Gift 1: Wards of Night

The Vampire Gift 2: Kingdom of Ash

The Vampire Gift 3: Throne of Dust

Coming Soon:

The Vampire Gift 4

The Vampire Gift 5

For an updated list of books, and to see the latest dates for my upcoming releases, check out my website:

www.EMKnight.com

Or Facebook:

www.Facebook.com/AuthorEMKnight

You can also sign up for my **New Releases Newsletter** (http://eepurl.com/bYCp41) to get a notification the day a new book comes out! That way you don't miss anything new. And don't worry – I never send any spam.

The Vampire Gift 3: Throne of Dust

By E. M. Knight

Cover art by B. Wagner

First Edition: August 2016

Chapter One

RAUL

DEEP BENEATH THE HAVEN

There is a moment, right before you face your death, that time slows. For a flicker of a second, the world goes still, peace descends upon you, and all is quiet.

Then the roar of the imminent avalanche rips you back to reality and you know that peace was an illusion.

As I look across the cavern floor, I see the snarling faces of The Convicted army opposite me. My coven's vampires are at my sides. The scent of blood and death is heavy in the air. The rock is stained red.

Behind me, the human women are crying, the children are screaming, and their fear is like a palpable thing.

I am not afraid to die. Now is not my time. But the humans who are being protected by the very vampires who've preyed on them their whole existence, they are all terrified of the Final Sleep.

I chance a glance back. The men have collected the women and children in a tight circle. They stay around them, bruised and bloodied and weaponless, but determined to protect their own.

I feel a flicker of admiration for those men. If The Convicted break through, it'll be a slaughter. Hell, many of my own vampires must be tempted by the fresh, succulent meals behind them.

My influence keeps them in line.

For now. Who knows how long it will last?

"Last chance," the leader of The Convicted, the one possessed by The Ancient, snarls. "Step aside and give us the humans. Then, if I'm feeling generous, *some* of you might be spared." He smacks his lips together in a hideous motion. "I will take care not to kill the strongest. Logan would unite our best. He does not want—"

The Convicted's head suddenly twists, and a violent spasm goes through him. Blood spurts from a hole in his neck. He reaches up to touch the spot—and falls flat before his hand even gets halfway.

"You will not, *ever*," Morgan announces, "speak of my husband again."

I look at the downed Convicted, and see the silver dagger sticking out from his neck. Mother had flung it at him from her spot of safety on the cliff above us.

That opens the floodgates. The Convicted charge. The mass of bodies crashes into us like a malevolent black wave.

"HOLD!" I scream at my comrades. "Protect the humans at all costs! Don't let any through!"

But my shouts are lost in the uproar. We're not a trained army. The Convicted are operating as a hive mind, directed by The Ancient. Individually they are weaker than we are. Together, as a group...

The shouts of battle fill the air. Two Convicted jump at me as one. I leap out of the way, almost stumbling on an upturned rock, before reclaiming my balance and thrusting my claws through their chests. Both hands find the hearts of my enemies. I rip them out without mercy.

Somebody shouts to my left. My head snaps over. Sarah, one of The Haven's vampires, is flat on her back. Three Convicted are on her. Two are holding her arms and legs, while the third is gripping her face, ready to sink his fangs into her exposed neck.

A flare of rage erupts in me. I lose myself to the vampire instinct as I bolt to her defense. I shoulder slam the first Convicted off, just moments before he would have tasted blood. I spin and kick at the second. My foot catches him across the jaw, making his head snap sideways with the satisfying crunch of breaking bones.

I don't get to do anything about the third. At that moment, two strong hands wrap around my shoulders. I'm picked up, and, in the midst of battle, flung away.

I hit the ground hard. I leap to my feet as bewilderment rushes through me. Who would be strong enough to do that to me...?

And then I see him. He's an absolute behemoth of a vampire. He has to be at least seven feet tall. His whole body is corded with muscle. He's not one of The Convicted, and neither is he one of ours. Then who...?

His attention is only on me. He starts to pick his way over the bodies, approaching with a broad smile. As he walks, The Convicted around him determinately scramble to get out of the way.

I steel myself. I've got a fight on my hands. I don't know who this vampire is, but I know he's not friendly.

My eyes quickly go to where Sarah had been. But the spot's empty—the battle has already moved on.

As the giant gets even closer, a space clears around us. Then it's just me and him in an empty ring. Almost like we've stumbled into a gladiator's arena.

With a start, I realize that all sound has been cut off. I can hear nothing—nothing except my labored breathing and the giant's lumbering footsteps. I do a double-take. Nobody on the outside of the sphere is paying us any attention. It's like he and I do not exist to them.

My eyes narrow. "Magic," I snarl.

The big vampire laughs. He spreads his hands in a gleeful gesture. "What gave it away?"

And then he charges me.

I would not have expected one with his size to move so fast. Before I know it his shoulder rams into my middle. I go hard into the ground. He lands on top of me.

Again I'm staggered, not just by his physical presence, but by his vampiric strength. I can *sense* it, and there's no way it should give him this much of an advantage. We should be near-equals!

But that is just a fleeting thought as his fists start to rain down onto me. I deflect the worst of the blows but still take some in the ribs and abdomen.

I struggle to get him off. Pinned to the ground like this, I lose all advantage.

The punches continue to fall. I feel a rib crack, and then a sharp pain shoots down my back. I'm entirely on the defensive, and I'm fading fast. He is just toying with me. If he gets bored, it'll be all-too-easy to end my life by tearing out my throat or ripping out my heart.

The dome surrounding us filters out all sounds of the battle, and I realize the fight on the outside has been stealing my attention. *That* is what my focus has been on—because all of my concern lies with the humans.

But what good am I to them dead?

Another surge of adrenaline takes me as I commit fully to *my* fight. I catch one of the monster's fists in two hands. He blinks in momentary surprise.

That's all the chance I need. I bring my legs up and kick him off me with all my strength.

He flies not far, but high, and his trajectory is cut off when his body hits the invisible barrier above us. He grunts from the impact and falls straight back to the earth.

By then I'm back on my feet. I race toward him in a blinding rage and attack.

Our positions switch. Now he's on the defensive, barely holding me off, while I give in to all my vampiric darkness to fuel the attack. I channel all the anger, all the hate, all the fury I have to destroy this beast who dared attack me.

Grim determination shows on his face as he attempts to defend himself. He might be strong, but I'm fast. I'm *quicker.* I dart back and forth, in and out, striking at him like a viper. I never stay close enough for him to catch me. Because if this fight goes to the ground, where he can grapple, I'd be done for.

"You've got more guts than your brother. I'll give you that," the giant vampire snarls. I fly at him again, claws going for his neck, but he manages to swat me back. "James would have never fought as hard as you."

Hearing my brother's name throws me off. "What do you know about James?"

"Isn't it obvious?" He grunts as he fends me off. "I was the one brought here to retrieve him for your Father."

I leap at him. He catches me mid-jump and uses my momentum to send me flying. I slam into the barrier and all the breath is knocked out of me.

He advances on me. "Enough of this." He reaches down to withdraw a long, curved dagger from his belt. The blade reflects the light, but also modifies it somehow. The effect is strange—if I didn't know any better, I'd say it was very dully glowing.

But as he gets closer, a strange dizziness—a weakness—washes over my body.

Suddenly I'm seeing double. I try to stand, but my steps are lurching. I'm like a drunk.

The other vampire laughs. "Not so mighty now, are you, Prince of The Haven?" He waves the weapon in front of him, showing it off. "The blade is made of silver, but that is not what's special. The *hilt*, infused with magic, is what gives it its might. A single stab—" He jabs it at me, mockingly. I nearly fall over my feet trying to get away. "—and a vampire will be at its owner's mercy for days. It forms a link, you see, and if this blade tastes your blood—you become my puppet until you die."

With a savage snarl he throws himself at me. I try to get away, but something is drastically wrong with my body. It's almost like—almost like a much stronger vampire is exerting his influence and making me lose control.

The blade slices through my leg. I scream out in utter agony and crash to the floor.

"With that," the vampire announces, "my mission is done. You will receive a message from my King in a matter of days. If you want to live—" he laughs, "—you would do well to heed what he says."

Darkness starts to close in on the outside of my vision. I try to hold on, but I can barely fight the nausea. Convulsions rack my body, stemming from the cut.

I watch, feeling weak and pathetic, as the other vampire retrieves an amulet from around his neck. Vaguely, I recognize it from somewhere. I've seen it, or its like, before.

But I cannot tell where. *Thinking* is becoming difficult.

The vampire holds the amulet out. A second later there's a blue flash. A round portal opens up from behind him. A shorter vampire, somebody I don't know either, steps out.

The smaller vampire looks at me. His eyebrows go up. But whether in surprise or indignation, I cannot tell, because the larger one grips his shoulder and spins him away from me.

"Get us out of here, Riyu," my attacker says. "We've done all we were sent for."

The two vampires step through the portal, and it winks out of existence. The moment they're gone, the force field disappears. All the noises of the surrounding battle crash into me. In my wretched, weakened state, the blast of sound is enough to make my system shut down.

The entire world turns black.

Chapter Two

JAMES

THE WOODS AROUND THE HAVEN

After the darkness that came with Smithson's final blow, I am sure that I will perish. The wounds puncturing my body will not stop bleeding. All the life force is slowly draining out of me.

I have not the strength to fight.

So I close my eyes and surrender to fate.

But as I feel my consciousness fading, and I feel myself being lowered past the precipice of death, there comes a... pull. A pull, a tug, almost as if I am a fish on a line. And something jerks me back and raises me from the darkness and makes me... drift.

I drift on and on amidst an endless sea of black. I am not dead. But I am not quite alive, either. It feels like I am caught somewhere in between.

Which way I go next is entirely out of my control.

I float on that ebbing current until the first bits of sensation come back to my body.

First is pain. Acute, overwhelming pain. Then exhaustion, then a hunger, then fatigue.

And suddenly, I am back in myself, back in the shell of a body that Smithson abandoned. The wounds that were killing me are closed. How...?

I groan and turn over, then push myself up. I open my eyes—and panic flares when I cannot see a thing.

I blink. I rub at them. I blink again.

Nothing.

And yet... with my hands, I can feel the cold rock I am on. My fingers trail through the thick puddles of blood around me. My blood. So much blood that I should be dead.

Yet I am not dead, only... blind.

Again I rub my eyes, in a fury this time. How can I not see? How can I be blind? Has the strength required for my body to heal itself robbed me of my sight?

Or, is it just the dark? Can I no longer see in the dark?

But if I'm a vampire, that is the one environment in which my vision should be strongest.

Yet all around me is pitch black.

I take a long breath. I can still smell the air. I smell the dampness of the underground, the dank moisture of soil beneath the earth. And sounds—I can still hear. There is the faraway drip-drip-drip of falling water. There is—

There is the sound of distant battle.

I stagger to my feet. A wave of dizziness hits me that I struggle to fight off. I fall against one cavern wall. For a few long moments, I just cling onto it, trying to gather myself, trying to regain my strength and thoughts.

Smithson tried to kill me. He'd have succeeded, too, were it not for... not for...

I don't know what. I have not the foggiest clue why I am still standing. The life was draining out of me—literally—and I had failed everybody. I had betrayed The Haven and was used by Father as a pawn. I'd been seduced by the promise of power... and ended with nothing.

The distant sounds continue. If the fight spills this way, and I'm discovered, I will surely meet my end. Whatever miracle has kept me alive will not repeat itself a second time.

I pad my way out of the crevice I was in and start away from all the sounds. My throat is parched. My entire body cries out for blood.

Yet blood I cannot give it. How can a hunter hunt if he is blind?

My other senses may be enhanced, as they became the day I was turned, but that does not help me now. Sight was the one sense I'd always relied on most. With it gone, the accuracy of the others only makes the loss more painful.

Still, through a tremendous effort of will, I force my body to move. I can admit to myself that I am frightened. I have no idea whether my next step will land on solid ground or send me throttling off the side of a cliff.

What a pathetic sight I would make to any who saw me. A mighty vampire, bumbling around in the dark with all the grace of a human. At least my perception of other creatures of the night remains. It will warn me if any are close by.

To my relief, none are.

After a long and trying passage, I find myself near the ruined castle. I get the smallest whiff of blood. My body straightens like an arrow, and I race toward it.

The mad rush meets a humiliating end. My knee collides with a jutting boulder. The unexpected impact sends me to the ground. Pain rushes through my leg, and I curse, hating my futility, hating my pervasive weakness.

It takes a gargantuan effort to pull myself up to hands and knees. I begin to crawl. Pathetic. But it is safer than running, for a blind vampire.

I tilt my head up and take a series of deep breaths, searching for that lingering scent of blood.

It's coming from beneath an enormous pile of rocks. I begin heaving them away. Each one I cast aside makes the scent a little bit stronger.

The promise of blood energizes me. I move with a newfound vitality. Even if I can't see, I begin to form an impression of the place I am in, drawing upon all my remaining senses to do so.

I cast the final stone away and find it. A tiny pool of human blood. Most has leaked through the cracks in the porous earth, but this tiny reservoir remains.

I sniff at it, first, to make sure it isn't tainted. It's not.

Once that reassurance hits, I dive down and begin to suck at it through dry, parched lips.

The first drop hits my tongue, and immediately I know where the blood came from. It was of Mother's private stores. The most valuable blood in all the kingdom...

I finish the last of it. There wasn't much, but what I had immediately makes me stronger. I wait anxiously to see if my useless eyes might pierce the dark once more.

They do not. The entire world remains shielded away from me.

I mutter a curse and haul myself away. I know that the longer I remain, the more I risk. So I stand and taste the air, searching for the hint of a breeze that might lead me out... out and away from battle.

Chapter Three

RAUL

DEEP BENEATH THE HAVEN

I come to with an enormous gasp. My chest feels like it's filled with ice. I have no sensation in any body part below my waist.

Alarm rips through me—but not for myself. For the villagers. For my coven vampires.

For *Eleira.*

"I'm right here," she says.

I turn in surprise. Sitting at the side of the bed is the girl I live for.

Seeing her there, alive and well, makes all the chaos in my head quiet down. For a moment, everything is at peace.

She takes my hand. "You've been muttering my name for days," she tells me with a weary smile.

Wait. *Days?*

"She hasn't left your side once," Phillip adds.

I look past her and see my younger brother. He looks absolutely exhausted. And with that, my mind is back on overdrive, and I grapple with everything that I must have missed.

"The battle!" I exclaim. "What happened?"

"We won," Phillip says grimly. He rubs the side of his face.

There's something he's not telling me. "But?" I ask. I turn to Eleira, who's suddenly taken a great interest in a spot on the floor.

"But…" Phillip exhales. "It came at a cost."

"Cost? What cost?" I try to push myself up and am surprised when my body doesn't immediately respond.

"Your injuries, for one," Phillip says.

"Forget them," I growl. "I'm alive. I will heal. What happened to the humans? The Convicted? And—" I look around the darkened, unfamiliar room. "Where are we?"

"In a palace, carved deep underground." My Mother's voice rings out from the shadows. "One of the last available strongholds of The Haven."

I peer at her. "I didn't know there was such a thing," I say.

"Many do not," is her vague response. "For the longest time, I thought none did, other than me. I was proven wrong."

She sounds even more exhausted than Phillip looks.

"Wait," I say. "This doesn't add up. Why are you all here? I mean, I appreciate the concern—" I squeeze Eleira's hand, "—but if I was out for days, and Phillip is here, and so is –"

"The Queen?" Mother interrupts. She gives a small and fragile laugh. "How can The Haven be ruled if its most powerful vampires are locked underground? Is that what you're asking?"

I try to push myself up again. Apprehension takes hold. "Yes. Exactly that."

Eleira, Phillip, and Mother all look at each other. The silence is deafening.

"What aren't you telling me?" I ask, my voice low and dangerous. I look around the room. "Who else knows about this place?"

"Apparently, Smithson does," Mother says. "After the fight was over, he and his guards—*my* guards—escorted us down here." She waves a hand around the room. "We've been locked away ever since."

My gut clenches. I never have trusted the vampire Mother took in as Captain Commander.

"We're *prisoners?*" I ask, the disbelief filling my voice.

"That's not how they put it," Phillip says. "We're here for our own 'protection.' While The Haven is under threat, its royalty must be kept safe, was the explanation we were given."

"So it's a rebellion," I say. I look at my Mother, "I *warned* you this would happen!"

"Raul..." Eleira says my name, trying to calm me.

"No," I snarl. I point a finger at The Queen. "This is her fault! We've been here for days? Lord! But you said we won the fight. Fill me in. Tell me what happened."

Mother just glares at me but doesn't talk. It falls upon Phillip to give an explanation.

"You rallied The Haven's vampires against The Convicted. That act of bravery gained you respect. It might be the only reason any of us are still alive."

"We fought The Convicted," Eleira steps in. "All of us, until they all fell. But there were casualties on all sides…"

"How many?" I ask.

"Most of the humans are dead," Mother says without emotion. "And nearly forty vampires were killed."

Forty vampires. The number staggers me. I feel like I've been punched in the gut.

"That's nearly a tenth of our coven," I breathe.

"So you can see why the survivors would be unhappy," Phillip says. "Smithson rallied them together when you were found unconscious. He now holds command of the Royal Court.

"They're all eating from the palm of his hand," Mother spits. "It's despicable."

"But you're still Queen," I insist. "The rule is still yours!"

"With the castle fallen? And the wards broken?" She shakes her head. "Being Queen accounts for precious little in the aftermath, I'm sorry to say."

"The wards are broken?" I gasp. "But—but they're the only thing keeping The Haven safe! Without them, we're exposed to the outside world, and, and—"

"Trust me, Raul," Mother says. "We know. *They* know. In fact, we suspect that's the reason Eleira and I are still alive."

"They need us to resurrect the wards," Eleira says. She makes a point of not looking at the Queen. "But I haven't been taught how."

"Girl, it's not as easy as muttering a few special words and flapping your hands around," Morgan snaps. This sounds, like an argument they've had before.

"Well, maybe if you *told* me what to do, I could *try*," Eleira fires back.

"Easy, easy," Phillip says, stepping between the two women. "There's no use turning on each other. They'd *want* to fracture us. We have to stay strong."

"Phillip's right," I say. "Unity is the only thing that will keep us from breaking." For the third time, I try pushing myself up, and—once again—discover my body unwilling to respond.

I grunt. "Why can't I move my legs?"

Mother flows up to me. She takes Eleira's spot at my side. "We were hoping," she says, pulling away the blanket covering my lower body, "that you could tell us exactly that."

My pants have been stripped away and my legs are bare. I suck in a sharp breath when I see my left leg.

There is an angry, pulsing wound running over my quad, from my hip right down to my knee. The skin around it is black and corrupted.

Beside me, Eleira makes a choked sound a lot like a cry.

I bring a hand forward and poke the flesh at the side—I feel nothing. No nerve impulse, no pressure—nothing at all.

Mother swats my hand away before I get another chance. "Don't touch it!" she hisses. "Do you want to make it worse?"

"They found you passed out and bleeding after the battle," Phillip says. "But none could remember seeing what happened—or what did this." He gestures at the wound.

"Raul, listen to me," Mother says. "I've devoted all the magical energy I have to keeping you alive these last few days. This is no ordinary wound. Silver alone could not have done this." She looks me right in the eyes. "We've been waiting for you to wake so you can tell us exactly how you sustained it. If you do not—you will die."

This time there is absolutely no mistaking it: Eleira starts to cry.

Chapter Four

DEEP BENEATH THE HAVEN

I spend the next hour or two relaying as much as I can about the fight with the massive vampire.

I tell them about the weapon. Mother presses me on it, wanting to know every last detail. But no matter how much I tell her, it doesn't seem to be enough.

"There has to be more to it," she stresses. "It was not an ordinary blade."

"I've been telling you as much!" I exclaim. I'm starting to feel extremely frightened. Eleira and Phillip have retreated to whisper together in a far corner of the room. "It glowed *blue*, but just faintly, and—"

"You think that description *helps?*" Morgan hisses. Her impatience is showing, too. "A blue glow is just something the untrained mind imagines it sees in the presence of a spell being cast! It's an illusion, it's not descriptive; it *doesn't help me*. True magic is a swirl of colors and patterns in a pulse of gossamer threads and fantastic shapes. A single spell makes a beautiful kaleidoscope, a wonderful tapestry, in the mind of the witch who casts it." I notice Eleira edging closer, hanging on to every word. "The blue glow is what all others see. So of *course* a spell was cast, of *course* the weapon was cursed, but what I don't understand—" she spins away angrily, and almost slams into Eleira as she does, "—is *how.*"

23

"Well, I've told you everything I know!" I fire back. "You don't think I want my leg to get better?"

"Forget your leg," Mother snaps. "I'd cut it off and make you a cripple if I could be sure it would save your life." Eleira gasps. "But the corruption is worse than that. It's already in your blood. It will spread through your body. I've kept you alive, but these healing spells are not my forte." She curses. "How I wish Xune was still alive today!"

"Who's Xune?" Eleira asks softly.

Mother turns on her. "Never you mind. Shouldn't you be back simpering by my son, or—"

Eleira slaps her. "I do *not*," she announces, standing up to full height, "simper!"

Morgan laughs. "You want to challenge me, little girl?" She draws her lips back to show her fangs. "I could end your life in a second. And I would, too, if it would save my son."

Phillip rushes in before the situation can get out of hand. "Relax, both of you," he says through gritted teeth. "We're not out of the woods yet."

Just at that moment, a distant door opens. A Haven guard—alone, unprotected—comes inside.

"We thought we heard voices." He sees me and gives me a curt nod. "You're up. Good. You've been summoned."

Morgan faces him. "Summoned? By whom? I am your Queen, and I will not stand for my son being taken away from me—"

"Actually," the guard interjects. "You've *all* been summoned."

"Your trial is set to begin before the Royal Court."

Chapter Five

ASSEMBLY ROOM BENEATH THE HAVEN

I walk last in the line of prisoners. The Queen is first, Raul and Eleira are second. My brother struggles on a pair of crutches, while Eleira is ever-at-the-ready to catch him if he falls.

I keep my eyes straight ahead... but that does not stop me from seeing the guards in the shadows from my peripherals. They've been trailing us the whole way.

Does Smithson really think we'd try to escape? None of us would ever leave Raul. And The Haven, for all its faults, is our home.

The passage we take winds deep underground. Eventually we come upon a large meeting room. A silence falls over all the attendants as we're ushered in.

Smithson is at the head of a grand table. He stands when he sees us.

"My Queen," he gives Mother a deep and gracious bow. He has the nerve to smile. "How pleased I am to have you join us."

All the vampires of the Royal Court sit still around the table. They keep their expressions stony as they watch the exchange.

"And your sons, too. Both in excellent shape, I see." Smithson's eyes fall on

Raul. "He looks *vigorous*. And strong."

He walks around the table and clasps Raul on the shoulder. My brother grits his teeth as Smithson applies downward pressure. "Sit," he whispers. "Why don't you?"

"As Prince," Raul hisses, and the disgust in his voice is obvious, "I'd rather stand."

Smithson lets go. I let out a small sigh of relief. That Raul even let Smithson touch him is a measure of how badly the wound is affecting him.

Smithson passes over me with nary a glance. "How many of our kind did you kill during the battle, I wonder?" he asks in a stage-whisper. The words echo through the entire chamber. "The bloodlust must have been impossible to re-strain for one who has so recently been exposed to the wonders of proper feed-ings."

"Enough," Morgan says. Even here her voice carries. "No more of this cha-rade."

Smithson turns to her. He blinks. "Charade? No, no, my Queen. This is no cha-rade. It is simply the new order of things. The Royal Court—" he gestures at the seated vampires, "—has taken strategic control of The Haven in light of your fail-ures."

"And who gave you permission to lead?" Morgan questions. She glares at the impassive vampires. "I am still your Queen! What you are doing is treason. But—" she softens her tone, "—relent now, and stop this *usurper*—" she motions at Smithson, "—and your crimes will be forgiven. *All* of them."

Smithson returns to the head of the table. I notice he's purposely avoided

Eleira.

"What makes you think," he asks softly, "that we have crimes that need forgiveness?" He puts both hands flat on the table. "We are here to discuss the state of affairs that have befallen our sacred sanctuary. For too long you've ruled with no respect for your Royal Court. It's come time to give those vampires a voice."

Mother looks each one of them in the eye. "This is how you challenge me?" she asks. "With an outsider at your helm?"

"An outsider brought in by you!" Tristan, a vampire who's always been prone to fits of passion, exclaims. All heads turn to him. "An outsider who *you* put in control of your guard, when any of us here would do."

"That's what this is about? Your petty jealousy?" Morgan laughs. "None of you were fit to lead. The protection of The Haven had to be charged to the most capable vampire." Her eyes grow dark. "I see, now, that is what has happened."

"Tristan." Smithson gestures at him to settle down. "You will get your turn. You *all* will get your turns. For now, let me do the talking."

Those of the Royal Court who looked ready to jump in sit back instead.

"It's true that I collected these vampires. It's true that I brought them here today. But I am no usurper, my Queen. I have no use for your throne. Only a woman can rule The Haven." His eyes flash to Eleira. "That much is known."

He stands up again. "So here is my suggestion. Why don't you and your sons take your rightful place at the table. I've been sitting in your seat, but only because you were otherwise occupied."

"In rooms that *you* locked me in!" Morgan hisses.

Smithson shrugs. "A necessary precaution, all things considered. In the mayhem going on outside, who could say what harm could befall our Queen. You mistake my purpose if you think I want to steal your power or influence. My only cause is my Queen's protection. Given that you are alive and unharmed today? I'd say, so far, it's been a success."

"Alive because you locked us in a dark room for a chance to spread your vile whispers in the ears of my Court," Morgan snaps.

Smithson shakes his head. "Whispers? No, there have been no whispers. Keeping you locked away while the danger was still high, was a democratic decision reached by all our members here today."

Morgan looks at her Royal Court. "Is this true?" she asks.

One-by-one, they nod their assent.

"Now that The Haven is... *relatively* secure... I am more than willing to step aside," Smithson says. "So take your seat, my Queen. It belongs to you by right."

A nasty feeling of suspicion crawls down my back as Smithson ends his speech. Mother must feel it too, because she hesitates before taking him up on his offer.

The pause is momentary, but from a woman who usually acts with nothing but absolute conviction, it's loud as a thunderclap.

Smithson steps away to give her room to approach. She reaches the seat. He pulls it out for her a fraction of an inch more. She looks at the surrounding vampires... and sits.

As soon as that happens, an uproar of voices explodes from around us.

There are jumbles of angry screams. I look into the shadows—and gasp. Somehow, all the vampires of The Haven have been concealed there the whole time. I did not feel their presence once.

"Cute," Mother says. The word, soft but precise, does a better job silencing the clamor than any shout or demand. "Using my own torrial against me to hide these other vampires." She gestures at the audience I just discovered. "What other tricks do you have up your sleeve, Smithson?"

"I assure you," he smiles. "That was the final one."

"I'll hold you to that," she says, as calming as if she doesn't have all her angry subjects screaming for her head.

"I expect nothing less."

"So." Mother addresses the assembly. "I am still Queen, is that what you've concluded? How nice of you to take your time about it."

"We had to be sure," a beautiful vampire with flowing, raven hair says from the other side of the table, "that it was not you who caused the castle to fall. That it was not you who unleased The Convicted."

Mother stares right back at her. "These are doubts that crossed your mind, Deanna?"

"With the erratic way you've been acting, we couldn't be sure!" Carter, one of the most vocal opponents of the Queen back when she listened to the advice of the Royal Court, accuses. His grey hair and pointed goatee make him look more a fantasy-trope wizard than a sophisticated vampire. "We needed time in the aftermath of the battle to consult, and decide amongst ourselves, what the right way of moving forward would be."

Before Mother can respond, Raul steps forward. "You all are fools," he says, "if you think that cowering here beneath the earth, and locking away the most powerful witch in existence, will help repair the damage that's been done. *Or* if you believe that Morgan is responsible."

"And what about you?" another member of the Royal Court reproaches. "How do we know you're not in league with her? How do we know you didn't conspire to take down The Haven?"

"*That's* what you're accusing me of?" Raul's voice becomes sharp, precise, and dangerous.

"We saw your bravery on the battlefront," another vampire interjects. "But if it wasn't for your Mother, none of this would have happened! *She* was the one who opened the doors of The Haven to a rival coven. You think we're supposed to accept as coincidence that the day they arrived, calamity struck? How many of us were killed in the fight against The Convicted? Look around you, how many seats are empty? How many faces that you've known will never be seen again?"

"Hear, hear!" a voice cries out from the surrounding mass. "The Queen failed to protect us! The death of our own lie at her feet!"

Raul turns toward the assembly. His red eyes flash. "*This* is what you've been discussing with us locked away?" He turns to the Royal Court. "*This* is how you've been spending your time? Not figuring out a recovery, but arguing onto whom to place the blame?"

"The blame is your Mother's!"

"The blame—"

"*SILENCE!*"

Morgan's sudden shriek rings out like a thunderbolt. The air cackles with a cold electricity as her command whips into all the vampires and she exerts her strength.

The room goes completely quiet. But I can feel the discord building in the air. I can feel the tension growing like a giant trap being set. At any moment, the jaws will snap shut and annihilate anyone caught in the snare.

"That's better," the Queen says. She stands up and begins walking around the table. As she does, she brushes a hand over the back of every occupied seat.

Some of the Royal Court ignore it. Others visibly shiver with her so close.

She addresses the vampires on the outside instead of those of the Royal Court. "You all fought valiantly for your kingdom," she tells them. "But you made a mistake when you allowed Smithson to lock me away. How many days have been lost? How many nights have come and gone while you hid down here like cowards, like scheming thieves?"

She pauses as she passes Smithson. He watches her, completely impassive.

She touches his cheek. "This man claims to have put me under guard for my own protection. It is a noble claim. An even bolder act. As a showing of good will, I will not punish him for it—though all of you know it is well within my power, and my right."

"Power?" Deanna sneers. "What power? You've crippled The Haven with all that you've done. When the castle fell, the wards disappeared—our safety is no more! The sun rises above the sanctuary now. Any can come upon us from the Outside. We are exposed; we are vulnerable! Smithson led us down here to safe-ty—"

"Where you could lick your wounds, caring nothing for the future of our sanctuary!" Raul snaps.

"Our *future* would not be under threat were it not for the actions of The Queen," Carter says softly. "She isolated herself in her rule. She did not take council when it was offered. And worse, above all—she locked away the witch!"

With that, he flings a finger right at Eleira. For the first time, all the attention falls on her.

Something clicks in my head. I stand up.

"That's what all this is really about, isn't it?" I ask. Vampires who are unused to me speaking look my way in surprise. "You've been skirting the subject, but it's all about Eleira, isn't it? It's all about the succession. *That's* what frightens you."

"The hell with the succession," Tristan spits. "How do we even know she is who The Queen says she is?" A murmur of agreement comes from the assembled vampires. "Have we once been given proof of her abilities? Do any of us even know if she *is* a witch?" The murmurs grow louder. "All we have to go on is The Queen's word. And as she's proved in recent weeks, it's highly unreliable." The murmurs pick up. "We are supposed to just accept this—this *girl—as* the natural successor to a Queen who led us to ruin? I say, put her to the test! I say, let her prove her worth!"

"If that is what you really think," Raul says, "then you are all bigger fools than I first credited you for. Tell me if you cannot feel Eleira's strength. Tell me if she is not the most powerful vampire here!"

"Power... strength... vampiric ability..." a familiar female voice comes from

33

deep in the shadows. "It is all an illusion. As I have demonstrated to all those here who have been willing to watch."

Victoria steps out to the front of the mass. She's wearing a rich velvet dress, and her hair is perfectly done. She looks nothing like the wretched creature she was last time I saw her.

"You," Mother says.

Victoria gives a keen smile, then a shrug. "Yes, me. Who else? Weren't you the one who warned me that you could take away my borrowed strength? Well—" she gives a little laugh. "I didn't need you to do it. I made the choice myself."

The magnitude of that admission takes a moment to sink in. When it does, I am almost staggered.

That's the source of the discomfort I felt when I first saw the assembled vampires. None showed any signs of injury from the battle. And even though days have passed, they could not have healed so fast—not without fresh human blood providing them energy for the process. And after the fight, there definitely weren't enough of our humans around. The stock in the bloodbanks was destroyed when the castle fell.

So, the question was, how did they all heal?

And the answer is staring right at me. They were given Victoria's blood.

My eyes dart from vampire to vampire in the crowd. Guilty looks pass across many of their faces. Clearly, they weren't ready to admit such a breach of law just yet.

"I'm glad you could find such pretty clothes," Morgan says primly. "It's a shame they do nothing to hide the hideousness of your soul."

34

"Bitch!" Victoria snarls. She rushes forward, but Smithson catches her before she can do anything stupid.

Victoria takes a moment to calm down.

"Smithson," Mother asks. "Why is our prisoner not under lock and key?"

"Because, my Queen, she has proven her worth. The members of the Royal Court did not see that she was fit to remain chained any longer."

Morgan arches an eyebrow. "Even with this display?"

"She was provoked."

A visible tremor passes through Mother. She is obviously unused to being a puppet Queen.

"Very well, then," she says. "What else happened in my absence?"

"I told all of them—every single one—how Eleira was made," Victoria announces. There's victory in her voice. "They know her powers are borrowed. Just as mine were. Just like mine now—" she shrugs, "—are gone."

"Not gone, but lessened," someone notes. "Restored to what they should rightfully be."

"Just as the false witch's will be!" Carter proclaims. "Smithson, get your guards—and seize her! Let's see what happens when *Eleira's* blood is spilled!"

But nobody at all moves, because at that moment, a blue light erupts from around Eleira. It flows out from her and covers her like a shield.

She takes a step forward. Next thing I know, she's *floating*, right up above the table. She speaks in a terrible voice:

"You think I don't know what you think of me?" she asks the assembled vampires. "You think I don't hear your sneers, your japes, your quiet whispers? You think I do not notice the hateful stares, or feel your enmity?"

The glow around her expands, until half the vampires are shielding their eyes. She continues to hover half a foot above the table.

"You think that I asked for this?" Her voice booms. "You think I wanted to be ripped away from my life, from my family, and be cast amongst you as a creature of darkness? You think I wanted never to see the sun again, to never look upon a human being without feeling that insatiable urge to feed?"

In front of her, the light starts to gather. It collects into a roiling cloud, which then soars and rises above her head. Blue sparks of electricity cackle within it like mini lightning bolts.

"But most of all," she continues, the rage clear in her voice, "You think that I *dare* pretend to be a witch? You think that I *dare* play with powers none of you can understand?"

The storm grows larger. Louder. More violent. Some of the vampires start to edge away.

"I could destroy each and every one of you where you sit," she proclaims. This sounds nothing like the Eleira I know. "Do you want a demonstration? Do you want me to prove my might?"

She points at Deanna. "You? Do you wish to die today?" She shifts her gaze onto Carter. "Or you, who dare threaten me?"

"Eleira," Morgan says firmly. "That's enough."

The girl turns on my Mother. "Or you," she screams, gathering a roiling ball of energy in her hands and readying to throw it at her. "Are you the one who will die today?"

In a sudden violent jab, she thrusts her hands out. The ball of energy flies right at the Queen.

None of us can react in time. But just before it hits, Morgan flings an arm up and stops the projectile a hair's breadth from her heart.

And then a second glow erupts from around the Queen. This one is large and powerful, and it swallows up Eleira's like the sun swallowing a candle. Eleira gasps, and her face twists in rage. But Morgan is already on her, and before I know it, the two women are wrestling, as magical energy rages on around them.

They fall as one to the floor. Nobody else moves. It takes me an extra second to realize why: we cannot.

All the occupants of the room, save for the two witches, are locked in place, unable to lift so much as a single finger.

Eleira snarls and hisses as if possessed. Her claws come out and she tries to rip at Mother's heart.

But The Queen is more experienced in hand-to-hand combat. She deflects the attacks easily. They scuffle and roll some more, and then Eleira is pinned to the ground.

Mother roars above her. She screams in a language none should know or speak. It's cruel and harsh and sadistic, and—somehow—it makes Eleira give out.

The glow around her dies. She slumps to the ground. A moment later, Mother's glow winks out, too, and the vampires are all released.

Raul is first on the table beside the pair. "Get away from her!" he screams at Mother. She does not fight him, but simply steps aside.

"She is alive, do not worry," she says, in a voice meant for Raul but reaching the whole assembly. "But once more, she was possessed. The Royal Court is right. I have failed them. But now is not a time to bicker. The wards must be resurrected. Because without them..." she casts a heavy look around, "Without them, the possession can come again. And when it does, Eleira *will* kill."

Chapter Six

DEEP BENEATH THE HAVEN

I open my eyes and discover a strange pounding in my head. It's like my skull has constricted, and my brain is fighting against it with every beat of my heart.

I look around. I'm not in the assembly room anymore. This place is pitch black and smells of mold.

Thanks to my vampire vision, I see I'm not alone. The Queen, Raul, and Phillip are conferring in hushed voices in a corner far away.

How did I get here? I have no recollection of the journey.

Phillip is the first to notice me up. He gives a start and points the others over. He and his brother rush to me. Morgan takes her time behind them.

If it wasn't for Raul's leg, he'd reach me first. I wince when I see how hard it is for him to walk.

"What happened?" I ask when they arrive.

"Eleira," Raul cups my face with his hands. "How much do you remember?"

"We were summoned by the Royal Court. They started saying these horrible things about me. And then—and then nothing."

A grim expression falls over Raul's face. "It's as Mother said," he mutters.

"What did she say?" I ask.

"That you blacked out," Morgan answers as she steps into our little gathering. "You were provoked and angered. You do not have control of your emotions yet. Clearly. You are barely more than a child."

"I'm seventeen," I say through gritted teeth. "Almost an adult."

"Almost," Morgan sighs. "But you will never get there, will you? Not with the gift that you've been given."

The vocalization of that thought makes me shudder.

"You're also newly-made," Phillip says.

"The bloodlust took hold of you at the assembly," Morgan continues. "That is why you don't remember. That, coupled with…"

A horrible realization takes hold. "Possession?" I whisper.

Morgan gives a solemn nod.

"Did I—did I do anything?" In a softer voice, I add, "Did I *kill* anybody?"

The three vampires share a look that does not give me any confidence in my innocence.

"Not quite," Morgan says.

Raul looks at his mother. He seems conflicted. "Let me just tell her!" he says.

She lays a hand on his shoulder. "We agreed to break the news properly."

"What news?" I ask. "Stop playing these guessing games! I'm on your side— it's the whole Royal Court that's turned against you."

"Yes," Morgan says, a slight smile playing on her lips. "That was the situation that we faced. But you helped remedy a large part of that."

I blink. "How?"

"You threatened all the vampires there," Raul says. "After they put your abilities under doubt. You cast a spell—more than one—and frightened them. And then—" the tiniest spark lights up in his eyes, "—you attacked the Queen."

I gasp. "I didn't!"

"With magic, too," Raul says.

"You tried a particularly nasty incantation against me," Morgan says. "Had I even a tenth less ability, you would have killed me."

Shame and regret flood through me. "But why would I attack you?" I say in a small voice. "Am I so lost to the vampiric darkness?" I finger the empty spot on my hand where Raul's ring used to be. I wish I still had it.

"No," Morgan says. "In fact, your recovery proves your resilience. But when the bloodlust took over, your mind became vulnerable. You could not prevent somebody—an enemy—from exploiting the link that was created when you opened the Book of the Dead."

My head starts to spin. Fear takes me. If I don't even have control of my mind...

"What do they want?" I ask quietly. "Why are they using me? Can we... stop it?"

"The pressure you feel in your head," Morgan says. "That is a protection spell I cast around your mind while you were unconscious. It's only a temporary measure, unfortunately. But it protects you for now."

Raul grumbles something under his breath. I don't think anyone's meant to hear, but my superior hearing allows me to pick out his words: "We should have waited to get her permission."

I don't quite understand his concern. If the spell protects me...

"Thank you," I say.

Morgan gives a grim smile. "If only it were that easy," she says.

"There's more?" I ask.

"She's not going to like this," Phillip mutters.

"The spell establishes a connection between our minds," the Queen continues, looking off into the distance. "Not a telepathic one, nothing of the sort you share with Victoria—"

"Share*d*," I cut her off. "Past-tense. It's not there anymore."

Morgan's head snaps to me. "What? Since when?"

"Since the Narwhark attacked," I say. "When Victoria almost died, the connection between us was severed."

"No." Morgan shakes her head. "No, that's impossible. No, that would mean one of you should be dead!"

"I'm still here," I say softly.

"Well I can see that!" she snaps. She starts to pace back and forth. "I should have suspected something when the spell on your mind fell into place so easily. Or when I saw Victoria. She's changed. I thought it was because she gave away her blood, but no—it was because of you.

"That bond must have been passed off to someone else. Yes. Certainly. That is

42

the only thing that makes sense. There *has* to be a bond between you and another being, Eleira. You cannot survive without it. Because of the way you were made..."

"I don't feel like there's any bond," I offer.

"There *is*," Morgan stresses. "There *must be*. It's the only way—"

"And what if there's not?" Raul interrupts. "If Eleira says she doesn't feel another bond, maybe it's because *none such exists.*"

"Don't be a fool," Morgan says dismissively. "You know nothing of magic. How can you have an opinion?"

"Raul might be right," Phillip interjects. "I've been reading about this type of thing, and—"

"So now you're the expert here, too?" Morgan demands. "*I'm* the one who's practiced magic for centuries, let us not forget."

She sounds petty and insecure and entirely unlike herself. She must truly be shaken.

"We're not doubting any of that, Mother," Phillip says thinly. "It's just—"

"Enough of this!" she cries out. "We'll discover the truth in due time. Switch subjects. We have to consider what we say next to the Royal Court. We must present a united front, and—"

"Hold on," I say. "You said there's a connection between me and you?"

"Yes, yes," Morgan says impatiently. "It links you to me in such a manner that you cannot channel magic without my consent. Moving on..."

"What!" I exclaim. "No, wait, you can't just gloss over something like that!

What do you mean, I need your consent?"

The Queen sighs. "Don't fault me. It was the only way to protect you. Before, you drew on the magical energies latent in this world yourself. Now, that ability is linked to me. The reason for it is that magic *exposes* you to possession. If you cannot access it, you cannot be possessed. It's that simple."

"But it's not simple!" I cry. "You can't just—you can't just take the ability away from me!"

"It's the only way I could protect you," she says. "If somebody were to attempt taking hold of your mind again, I would know—and I would stop them, because the core of your magical abilities are now controlled by me."

Indignation races through me. "No, you can't do that!"

"I told you she wouldn't like it," Raul says.

I surge up. "I don't need you to shield me as if I'm some doll! I need you to *teach* me, Morgan! Give me guidance that will let *me* protect myself!"

"Sadly, the world does not revolve around you, *Eleira*," the Queen replies. "I did what I had to do. That is the end of this discussion. The only reason I am entertaining you with this explanation is because your little showing before the Royal Court brought the powers back to my hands. The coven vampires realized that it is I, not Smithson, who can protect them. You were a threat from which I saved them. We couldn't have staged it any better.

"But now? It's beyond time for us to return to the assembly."

Chapter Seven

ASSEMBLY ROOM BENEATH THE HAVEN

The pain in my leg is nearly unbearable, but I hide the discomfort as best as I can. Now is no time to show weakness. Now, it's time for all The Haven vampires to see my strength.

I sit to my Mother's right at the head of the table. Eleira's possession and subsequent fight with Mother forced the assembled vampires to shift their focus away from petty politics and onto more important things.

Namely, restoring the safety of The Haven.

We've already been here for hours. Most of the points discussed have been beaten to death: the destruction of the blood banks, the failure of the wards, the imminent risk of another attack.

At least the showdown between Mother and Eleira restored the vampires' faith in their Queen. They see her as ruler, and me—rightfully—as her second. Now it's up to her to undo the damage that was done in the days Smithson took control.

Plans and strategies are set out and discussed with a lot more civility than the first time we were here. But all of them reek of desperation to me.

"How will we feed if so many of our humans are dead?" A vampire asks from the sidelines. "Who will supply the blood for the next Hunt?"

The casualties from the fight with The Convicted are awful: forty vampires dead—a staggering number—and countless humans. We've never suffered losses that great.

All The Convicted are, of course, eliminated.

"Where are the surviving humans now?" I ask.

One of the guards steps up. "They have been relocated to holding cells nearby."

My hands tighten on the edge of the table. "You locked them away as you did us?"

"It was," Smithson says smoothly, "for their own protection. In the mayhem that followed, many of our kind needed to feed. I took it upon myself to ensure the humans be escorted to a safe location, where they could not be made prey until decisions about their future were properly made."

I eye the Captain Commander warily. I could almost—*almost*—take him at face value when he claims to have kept me, Mother, Eleira, and Phillip locked away as a means of "protection."

Almost...but not quite. While we were there, he'd riled the Royal Court against us. Even if he stepped aside as soon as Mother returned, something about the whole turn of events seems very suspect in my mind.

Phillip, as if reading my thoughts, lays a hand on my shoulder and whispers, "He has the whole of the Royal Court eating from his palm. Be careful. He's gained more power in The Haven faster than anyone ever has before."

I give a solemn nod.

"Thank you, Captain Commander," Mother addresses him formally. "You are right, of course. How many humans still remain?"

"The precise count," Smithson says, "is two-hundred and eighty-four."

A murmur of shock ripples through the assembled vampires. That puts the vampire-human ratio at nearly one-to-one.

"So few cannot sustain us!" a voice cries out.

"We will starve if we remain here!" another echoes.

Mother's head snaps to the dissenter. "Nobody is keeping you," she snarls viciously. "If you want to leave, you know the way."

That proclamation is met with abrupt silence.

And I know why.

So many of The Haven's vampires have grown comfortable under the Queen's rule. The attack jarred them, but none can imagine living without protection of our sanctuary, or the familiarity of the coven.

Vampires are not nomadic creatures. They need a home base, they need a tribe. That's why Smithson is such an oddity. Moreover, that's why, despite all their huffing and puffing, The Haven vampires *do* want their Queen back. They want their lives restored. They want comfort and shelter, not uncertainty and upheaval.

That is the great irony about our race. Despite the darkness lurking within each and every one of us, we are, at our core, fragile creatures.

My eyes go to Eleira. Knowledge of that fact is what makes me believe that not all the good has been extinguished from our kind. And every time I look at the woman I love, I'm reminded of the fact that with a little perseverance, maybe that good can defeat the dark.

But when I catch myself thinking those thoughts, I almost laugh. I sound a bigger idiot than any of the fools who tried to go against Mother.

At least my advantage is that I can keep such romanticized notions to myself.

"Just as I thought," the Queen says into the quiet. "Now, then. The first priority is supplying The Haven with fresh blood." She inclines her head oh-so-slightly to Phillip. "My son has some ideas in that regard."

My brother steps forward. "You are right, of course," he begins, addressing the vampires in the crowd. "The number of humans cannot sustain us all. Not if we are to restore the bloodbanks with their blood. So, from now on, there will be no feedings on The Haven's humans. *None* are to be touched."

His announcement meets with an uproar of angry voices.

"We can't live without blood!"

"What about the Hunt?"

"We are starved already. Victoria's blood wasn't enough!"

"Quiet!" the Queen commands. "Let Phillip finish."

"The bloodbanks provide the lifeline of The Haven," Phillip goes on. "Without them, we have nothing to fall back on in case calamity strikes."

"But this *is* a catastrophe!" someone protests.

"Yes, and in times like this, our most precious resource must be secured. The humans we have will only be used to fill the bloodbanks. They will not be fed on directly, ever."

"That's hardly a solution!" a voice cries out.

"Let me get to my point," Phillip grunts. "With the humans off-limits, we must turn to alternative means. Luckily, there are other options available. The wards are down. But they were originally made to lock the humans in. How many of you remember what kept them from escaping before?" He doesn't wait for a response. "The *predators* surrounding The Haven. They are all still there. And they—"

He's cut off by a sudden, raucous laugh. I glare at Carter, who's making no effort to keep his mirth in.

"Listen to this one!" he says, swinging an arm out to take Phillip in. "He would have all of us become like him, feeding on *animal* blood, operating at half, a third, a *tenth*, of our usual capacity."

"It would only be temporary," Phillip stresses. "Until the bloodbanks are restored—"

"Which will take how long, exactly?" Carter challenges. "Five years? Ten? *Fifteen?*" More disgruntled murmurs wash through the crowd. "Can you imagine—" he turns to the assembly, "—waiting *fifteen* years to taste fresh, human blood again? To be denied the most precious sustenance for a decade and a half? For one like him, who's fasted for so many centuries, it hardly makes a difference. For the rest of us? It would be hell."

"Unless you're proposing an alternative, Carter," Mother begins.

He turns to her. "In fact, I am. One that is so glaringly obvious that I do not see how it is not our first choice."

He flings a finger at Eleira. "*She* was brought in as a human, from the Outside. As have others, over the years, to expand the human genetic pool. Well, we are creatures of the night. We are *hunters!* I say, let us unleash our basal instincts. Let us run into the world and feast upon humans as we were designed to! Let us not restrain ourselves, but let us rise up, and conquer!" His gestures grow maniacal. "Let us be loosed, and let us *kill!*"

Shouts of agreement rain down from the sidelines.

"And then, when we are fully satiated, when we are fully fed—let us bring more humans here!" Carter continues. "Let us make new slaves. We will capture them and we will gather them and we will make them *ours.* We have two-hundred-and-eighty-four now? Let us bring the number up! Let us bring it to *ten* thousand! Twenty thousand!! And then, with so many humans, none of us would ever go hungry again!"

The cries of agreement come louder and louder.

"Why does the Queen let us feed once a month? We should have a Hunt every week! Every day! We should be unleashed and fully embrace the powers that have been given to us. Do you not agree? Do you not agree?"

"Yes, yes, YES!" come the shouts.

The frenzy rises until it hits a boiling point.

Ever-so-calmly, Mother raises her hand.

"A nice fantasy," she tells Carter, "but one that is utterly incompatible with reality. Tell me. When was the last time *you've* been Outside?"

At that, Carter falters. "I hardly see the relevance—"

"It's been two hundred years, if not more, for you," I say softly. All heads turn to me. "The world that you know out there is gone. A whole new one exists. If you think ten *thousand* humans can go missing in this day and age without anybody batting an eye, you are delusional. If you think our coven's vampires can be unleashed, and can run and feed on the men and women of California without anybody noticing, without an alarm being raised, without a *war* being fought…"

I force my bad leg out in front of me and make my way to Carter one agonizing step at a time. "I *have* been out there, Carter. My brothers and I were the ones who found Eleira. We were the ones who brought her back. Just because vampires have extra powers does not mean we can be careless. If you start bringing more humans here, you won't just attract attention from the other covens. The humans will notice. Their governments will notice. Their armies will notice. They will strike at us. What you are suggesting risks sparking a whole war between the two races. A war," I finish, "that we cannot hope to win."

"You're weak," Carter snarls, standing up to challenge me. "Oh, you might have the advantage of time, being made before me, but your mentality is weak. What progress has ever been made without taking risks?"

"There are necessary risks," I remind him, "and there are reckless ones. It's easy to see where yours fall on the spectrum."

"So you would have us crippled, like your younger brother was?"

I've had enough. I grab him by the front of his shirt. "Do not," I hiss in his face, "speak of my brother like that again."

I release him. He falls back in his seat, clearly shocked.

With as much grace as I can, I hobble to my place at the front.

"Well done," Mother whispers to me as I pass. "That was a grand display of conviction. They needed to see that from you."

She turns to address everybody else.

"Even if Carter's ideas were feasible," she says, "we cannot draw unnecessary attention to The Haven while the wards are down. Let's say we bring more humans in from the Outside. Despite our best precautions, there *will be* a chance of their escape. With the wards up, that becomes impossible. The Haven becomes invisible to the outside world. Until then, while we are exposed and vulnerable, I do not wish to invite more uncertainty in."

"Then you should be working to restore the wards, not wasting time with us!" Deanna says. "Forget the bloodbanks. They are not the highest priority. Re-establishing our security is!"

"There's something all of you are forgetting," Eleira says quietly. All eyes turn to her. She's been so subdued this whole time that they're probably surprised she would speak.

But I know that her reservation is not a sign of meekness, but intelligence. She's trying to take in as much of her new life as possible before voicing her opinion.

"And what may that be, *Princess*?" Deanna sneers.

"If you bring new humans in—" Eleira fights down a grimace, "—you will be taking them from a world in which they've seen the sun. They won't survive for long in eternal darkness. Depression and despair will take them."

"How do you know this?"

"I'm the one who was most recently human here," she says. "I have the best understanding of their psyche."

"What do we care if they are depressed?" a weak vampire asks from the outskirts of the gathering. "They will be prisoners—they matter not!"

"Besides," Deanna scoffs, "that's not exactly a problem. With the wards down, the sun shines on The Haven just as it does anywhere else."

Smithson, who's been uncharacteristically quiet this whole time, suddenly speaks.

"The Queen and her sons are right," he says. "Bringing in new humans is too risky. We cannot do it."

Just like that, he settles the debate. I'm astounded by how easily the vampires accept his advice.

I make a mental note never to underestimate him. His influence over our coven is greater than I first thought.

"The Haven's strength," Smithson continues, "lies with eternal night. It allows you to enjoy the full hours of every day. As things stand currently, half our time we are bound underground. So bringing back the wards—" he looks at the Queen, "—must be the absolute priority."

She acknowledges him with the most miniscule nod.

A new thought occurs to me. "The humans who still live," I say, "have spent their entire lives without seeing the sun. They cannot be allowed to now. It would only confuse them. So, until the wards are back..." I look at Eleira, and hope she can understand, "...they must be kept locked away where they are. They know we fought for them. In a way, they know we are on their side. So it falls upon us, now, to learn how to coexist with them.

"Speak plainly!" Carter exclaims. "I know the meaning behind your words. You would cripple us with animal blood, too." He sneers. "As expected. At a time that we need strength, our leaders make us weak on purpose. If that is the will of the council, I cannot remain."

He stands and makes a show of glaring at all of us. "Who's with me?"

None utter a single sound.

"Fine," he says, and storms out the room.

A pair of guards start to follow him, but Smithson tempers them with his hand. "Let him be," he says. He turns to the Queen. "How long until you restore the wards?"

A flash of uncertainty crosses Mother's face. It's quickly hidden. "That is difficult to say," she admits. "First, I need to assess the damage. Thanks to somebody's *orders*," she gives him a thin smile, "I have not yet had the opportunity to go above ground."

"Then this meeting is adjourned." Smithson announces. "We will reconvene tomorrow, after the Queen has seen the state of The Haven for herself.

"Of course," he gives a nasty, predatory grin, "she will not go anywhere without a personal escort of my best guards. Unless the Royal Court objects?"

One-by-one, the vampires at the table shake their heads.

Smithson stands. "Night comes in an hour," he says. "We will go above ground then."

Chapter Eight

ELEIRA

THE HAVEN

I huddle into myself and shiver as an icy wind blows down my back. It's not the cold that troubles me.

It's the absolute silence of The Haven.

I follow Morgan around the edge of the crater where her castle once stood. The ground is still unstable. I don't trust it. I'm reluctant to come close enough to the edge to peer all the way down.

But what I do see is ghastly. It's like a wound has been ripped in the earth right where the castle stood. The drop to the bottom is long and perilous. It's a wonder any of us survived the fall.

I look at the Queen. Now I can truly appreciate that it was only by her protective spell that we still live.

Smithson's guards follow a safe distance behind us. They're far enough away to give the illusion of privacy. But I know with their vampire senses, they can hear every word we speak.

Raul had wanted to come up with us but his mother forbade it. In a whisper that only I heard, she confided that the more stress he put on his body, the quicker her healing spell would fade. He argued against staying put, but in the end saw reason: he would be no good to anybody dead.

I hate that that thought even crossed his mind. Vampires aren't supposed to die, not from a knife wound. Raul stood for me when I was in trouble. I want to do the same for him.

But the thing is, I feel utterly helpless to affect anything.

Phillip and Smithson remained at the edge of the woods. Once Morgan and I complete a circle of the crater, we rejoin them.

"Are all the vampires from the Wyvern Coven gone?" Morgan asks.

Smithson nods curtly. "They deserted when the castle fell. They took advantage of your generosity for sanctuary, but they would not fight."

"And now word of The Haven's weakness will spread," Morgan sighs. "Soon vampires the world over will know of our failure. Of our vulnerability." She turns on Smithson and pulls herself up to full height. Her voice rises. "If you thought you were doing this coven a *favor* by locking me away...! How many days have been lost? While our enemies have been gathering their strength, we've been hiding, *trembling* underground because of you!"

The guards see the looming confrontation and run closer. Smithson gestures for them to stand down.

"My priority in all of this has been to ensure your safety, my Queen," he says. "Until I was certain another attack would not come, I had to keep you there. You are the only one who can restore the wards. If you fell in a secondary assault, what would happen to The Haven then?" He looks her up and down. "I am your man, as I have always said. But in this decision I had the support of the Royal

Court."

"Don't speak to me about them," she hisses. "They are frightened and cowardly, just like—"

Morgan stops when she notices how close the surrounding guards have come.
She softens her voice.

"Of course, the Court's wishes must be respected," she says.

Smithson gives a toady smile. "I'm so glad you and I see eye-to-eye. Shall I
show you the rest?"

We begin our trek toward the village. "With the casualties sustained by The
Haven's vampires," Smithson says as we walk, "the Royal Court has also mo-
tioned to bar the creation of any more Convicted. Not that you would consider
turning any of your remaining vampires into one of those horrible creatures, of
course."

"Of course," Morgan says tightly. For half a second, I see past the mask of
eternal youth on her face, and glimpse the tired, old woman underneath. But a
breath later, it is gone.

We walk a while longer. Another creeping silence falls.

"I trust you have other guards posted at the outskirts of The Haven?" Morgan
asks. "To alert you of any potential intruders?"

Smithson shakes his head. "I'm afraid I do not have sufficient numbers for
that, my Queen. But worry not. The entrances to the underground stronghold are
properly guarded."

"So while all of our vampires are locked underground, the rest of The Haven is completely exposed?" Morgan asks. "Anybody could just walk in and ransack us."

"With all due respect," Smithson continues, "the lives of The Haven's vampires take priority over material possessions."

"Hm," she says. "And the Royal Court...?"

"Agrees with me completely," Smithson finishes.

"No." Morgan shakes her head. "This is wrong. The Haven is no longer a safe place. I will not resurrect the wards until you know the area has been swept. I need to know there are no stragglers remaining from the Wyvern Coven. And if you argue against *that*, Smithson, it will prove to the Royal Court how misaligned your loyalties are."

He bows his head. "I am here only to serve and obey."

"I, for one," Phillip says all of a sudden, "find it hard to believe that our vampires would give up the luxuries of their usual residences above the trees so readily. Or," he continues, "that they would stay underground once it's been established that the threat has been eliminated. The Convicted are all gone. Who else would attack? And if, let's just say, another coven decided to go against us, would we not be better served readying our defenses?"

"What are you suggesting?" Smithson asks.

"Allow the vampires to return above ground. They need to go back to their regular lives. We *won* the battle against our enemies. That should be a cause for triumph, not fright."

"That is a proposition you will have to bring before the Royal Court," Smithson says smoothly. "I am not one to decide such things."

Phillip scoffs. "You hold enough influence to—"

Morgan stops and places a hand on his shoulder. "Now is not the time for us to bicker," she says.

Phillip glares at her. I've never seen such aggression in him before.

"He's using you," he spits at his mother, then turns and strides off, breaking through the ring of guards as if they don't exist.

"Do we follow him?"

The Captain Commander considers... and shakes his head. "The Queen is whom we need to protect," he says. "Her son is less important."

I don't know if it's my imagination, but at that moment, I think I see a black speck float across the white of Smithson's left eye.

I blink, and it's gone.

"Important or not," Morgan says, "you will have to answer to the Royal Court if harm befalls him. I would send your guards to follow. Just in case."

Smithson hesitates. He could easily reject the request. But why would Morgan want Phillip to be watched?

Smithson grunts. "Go," he tells two of his men. "But if he wanders past the boundaries of The Haven, he's on his own."

The Queen smiles. "Thank you for granting my request."

"It was a wise one," Smithson tells her.

"Now," she says. "I want to see our humans."

Chapter Nine

PHILLIP

THE HAVEN

As soon as I'm out of the line of sight, I take off at a blistering run. I race through the familiar trees of The Haven's wooded forest.

It feels good to simply move. To feel the wind against my face. To escape the suffocation brought upon me by being held prisoner, first by my Mother, then by Smithson, over these last few weeks.

But no sooner do I get half a mile away than I hear the sound of pursuit. I slow down. I should have known better than to expect to be left alone.

I look back and see two vampire guards trailing me. I hail them with a salute.

What can I do other than to acknowledge their presence?

They stop a long way off. Neither of them raises his hand.

For the first time, I realize that I don't recognize these two. Obviously, I know all the usual residents of The Haven.

That means these guards came from somewhere else. I've been so preoccupied with the thoughts raging through my mind that I didn't notice it earlier.

Quickly, I expand my mind to judge their strength. They are both stronger than I. Did they become so after sharing Victoria's blood? Or is it something else?

Where did they come from? Are they—

A black blur suddenly streaks out from amongst the trees. It moves so fast toward the guards that they cannot react before it strikes.

The Narwhark leaps at the first and tears out his throat. He goes down in a gurgle of blood. It might just be me, but the demon seems... bigger, somehow. More solid. More *menacing*, than the first time I'd glimpsed it.

I react without thinking. No matter what some of the coven's vampires think, I am not a coward. My legs start to pump as I run to help the remaining guard.

But I don't get even a quarter of the way there before he's down, too. The Narwhark sits on his chest, sinking its jagged teeth into the fleshy part beside his collarbone.

The vampire screams and struggles to fling the demon off. But he has no idea what he's up against. The malicious black beast lifts its head up and roars, making a sound like a sheet of metal being ripped in two. Then it rips down and crunches the vampire's vocal cords.

The screams die on the wind. The Narwhark takes another bite of the dead vampire's flesh.

Then, to my horror, it digs its claws into his chest and feasts on his heart.

This time there's no mistaking it. The Narwhark visibly becomes more solid. As it eats the heart, the blackness of its body thickens, swirling around and into it like gathering storm clouds. Its leathery skin seems to harden.

It swallows the last bit. The air surrounding the demon actually shimmers, then starts to tighten and constrict as if the demon is pulling in the energy of this world to strengthen itself.

The self-preservative part of my mind tells me to run. I saw what the creature did to these two vampires, both of whom were more capable of fighting it than I.

And yet I can't look away. Something about the display is so visceral, so gruesomely fascinating, that, despite all sense and logic, the dark part of my vampire psyche is drawn to it.

I cannot fight that feeling. Seeing the demon feed is vicariously exciting. It's almost like reliving my first experience of taking blood. There is a level of transcendence that falls upon me from watching the affair.

The pint-sized demon tosses its head back and makes that awful metal-ripping sound again. Then it jumps to the other mutilated body and starts to feed on the second heart.

Run, Phillip! a pressing voice tells me. *Run while you can still get away!*

But both my feet are rooted to the spot.

The Narwhark finishes its second meal. Slowly, and with absolutely no urgency on its part, it turns toward me.

My body tenses. But... I don't feel threatened. Ironic, given all I've seen. Logically, I know I will meet my end. When the Narwhark attacks, it *will* kill me.

The only thing to do is to go down fighting. I ease on the tight hold I always maintain on my vampiric darkness.

The moment I do, it surges through me in a sudden rush of power. My body's instincts flood into me. Adrenaline pumps through my veins, blood fills my muscles, and my mind goes blank.

I only know one thing, and that is the insatiable urge to fight. To *kill.*

To feed.

But the Narwhark does not move from its spot. It simply stares at me, as if I'm an oddity on display in a museum.

I think I see a spark of intelligence in its eyes.

And then, before anything else can happen, it dashes off into the trees.

I nearly stagger backward from shock. It didn't attack me.

Why?

I have precious little time to consider the reasons. The sound of running feet reaches my ears. I turn around and see Smithson and his guards, plus Eleira and Mother, rushing toward me.

Smithson is the first to reach the clearing. His eyes fall on the two downed men. Then they come to me.

Rage as I've never seen it explodes on his face.

"*YOU!*" he screams, pointing at me, doing nothing to hide his hatred. "*YOU KILLED THEM!*"

With a snarl he throws himself at me.

A surge of madness takes hold, because the moment he attacks, I start to laugh. I was ready to face the Narwhark. What threat could a vampire possibly be in comparison?

I crash with him to the ground. His fangs are out and his claws are extended. We grapple with each other for position, and I keep laughing and laughing. I see the surprise flash in his eyes as he finds me a more capable combatant than he first assumed.

The laughter pours out of me as I fend off his attacks. I'm not even trying to strike back. I just take perverted delight in the struggle. The vampiric darkness makes me feel more alive than I have in ages.

Seeing the Narwhark feed somehow freed the last of my inhibitions about being who I am. I've resisted for so long, but what Mother told me when she made me drink April's blood resonates with full force now:

"'You were always the intelligent one. You sensed the same darkness inside you that I did when you were made. You knew it could overtake you, if you only let it, and you knew that its power would be unrivalled by any in our coven. You knew that had you embraced it, you would have risen in power, and, eventually, stood above even me.'"

If I don't hold back, I could be her most powerful son.

Smithson yells obscenities at me as he tries to claw his way past my defenses. My mad laughter fills the air. Even though I'm on my back, I fend him off with relative ease. He's strong, no doubt, but I'm quick—or at least, I discover myself to be now that my restraint is gone.

He strikes at my shoulder and gets past my guard. My blood pours free. I cry out in delight—I'm too far gone to feel pain. The fool doesn't know what he's doing. He doesn't know who he's up against, or what I'm capable of... should I turn my mind to it.

The time to do that is now. Enough play. The madness spreads, the darkness grows. With all the force in my arms, I push him off. As Smithson stumbles back I jump to my feet. I ready myself to leap at him and tear *his* throat out, to feed on *his* heart, just as I'd seen the Narwhark do—

I do not get the chance. From the sidelines, a blue glow flashes like a thunderbolt. Silver chains streak out from under Mother's sleeve.

Next thing I know, they are wrapped around Smithson, holding him tight.

"How dare you?" he rages at her. "Release me! Release me now!"

"I will do no such thing," Mother says calmly. She steps to my side and softly touches my arm.

The contact brings me back to myself. I realize my chest is heaving, my body is lined with sweat. All my muscles feel as if I've been submerged in an icy bath.

She squeezes once. At that moment, all the fury drains out of me. It's like a valve has been turned loose and eased all the pressure.

Realization of what I was doing hits me. Sudden alarm rips through me at my recklessness. What was I thinking? What—

"You were just witnessed attacking another member of the Royal Court," Mother tells Smithson. "An unprovoked attack, not in self-defense, but in a blind rage." She motions at my bleeding shoulder. "You drew blood. By the look of it, you intended it to be a killing blow. You aimed for his neck. You are lucky Phillip was able to deflect it, else you would be tried, found guilty of, and executed for murder.

"As it stands," she faces the guards, "Captain Commander Smithson went against a direct edict of the Royal Court. No vampiric blood is allowed to be spilled. The edict was passed to prevent such heedless violence. Passed, I might add—" she smiles, "—while I was locked away.

"As such, it is fully within my right to take the Captain Commander into custody."

"You cannot do this!" Smithson roars. "Guards—apprehend her! Get these chains off!"

His men do not move.

"I think," Morgan says quietly, "that you will find these men not loyal to me or you, but to the letter of the law. That is how you intended things to be while I was gone. Wasn't it?"

"Phillip killed two guards!" Smithson screams. "The bodies are right there!"

"And yet his hands are clean," Mother says to the entourage. "When we arrived, he stood a dozen feet away. Their murder does not fall upon Phillip." She steps towards Smithson. "Come now. You and I both know the type of creature capable of doing this. But you haven't told the other vampires of the threat, have you? The surprise on the faces of these guards," she gestures at them, "tells the whole story. You did not tell anybody about the Narwhark. You hoped to use it to rally more of my vampires against me. Yet that plan has backfired on you now, hasn't it?"

Mother moves to stand near the two mutilated bodies. "This," she says to all the vampires now watching her, "was the result of a demon attack." She tosses her end of the chain to the nearest guard. "Take Captain Commander Smithson to the stronghold's prisons. Inform the Royal Court of what happened here. Assemble all the coven's vampires and let them know... that their Queen is back."

Chapter Ten

RAUL

DEEP BENEATH THE HAVEN

News of the Narwhark attack spreads like wildfire through the underground stronghold.

Whereas before, vampires were fine going anywhere alone, now they only travel in twos and threes. A pervading sense of fear has taken root. Dread has settled into every heart. If there is a creature out there, a *demon*, who can destroy two vampires so easily, then all the security Smithson promised is scarcely more than one extra illusion.

Mother has successfully taken back control of the Royal Court. Still she answers to them, but no longer are their decisions influenced by Smithson's desires.

It took just one meeting to dismiss Smithson from his post and anoint Phillip as his successor. Carter and Deanna argued against it, as expected, but the rest of the Court members were persuaded by both Phillip's rational, level-headed nature, and the guard's depiction of how well he handled himself in the fight against Smithson.

Surviving the Narwhark attack also gave him a little bit of a mythical status.

"I never asked to be Captain Commander," Phillip gripes to me in private. "But

Mother was dead-set on the nomination. Once she made her opinion known… the others quickly fell in line."

I wasn't there at the meeting where it happened. I'd been stuck in my rooms, nursing my leg.

Phillip gives an uneasy laugh and scrubs a hand through his hair. "What a reversal of fortune, huh? From prisoner to Captain of the Guard."

"Mother trusts you now," I tell him. "That is what counts the most."

His worried eyes fall on me. "It should be you, you know," he says softly. "You're the one who should have this position. Not me."

I gesture at my leg in disgust. "With this lingering injury?"

For days I'd tried to play off the severity of the wound. But the warning of the giant vampire echoes in my head:

"It forms a link, you see, and if this blade tastes your blood—you become my puppet until you die."

"Has it improved?" Phillip asks.

"Of course not!" I snap. "Look at it!"

Phillip flinches at my outburst.

"Sorry," I say. "I'm sorry. I'm not used to being weak. It's making me… testy."

"That's understandable," Phillip says. "What has Mother told you?"

"As much as she's told you. Her spell is keeping me alive. But she cannot heal me. The corruption is in my blood. If the spell goes out…"

I don't finish the dreadful thought.

Phillip casts worried eyes upon me. "We'll find a way to fix it," he says. "I've been looking up as much information as I can. I'll work harder. There's precious little in the computer archives, but maybe I can discover something if I hack into—"

"Phillip." I say his name firmly. "You are Captain Commander now. Your duties lie with securing The Haven. *That* should be your focus. Not me."

"I can't just stand by and watch my brother die!"

"Hey. Hey, look at me. I'm right here, aren't I? It'll take more than a flesh wound to kill me."

Phillip frowns and pushes his glasses up.

"You have other responsibilities now. You have to guarantee order within The Haven. Have you gone through the guards as we'd discussed?"

Phillip sighs. "You know it's only before you I can display this type of uncertainty? Out there—" he gestures in the direction of the door, "—they all look at me like some sort of hero, for having survived the Narwhark attack." He shakes his head. "A week ago, few could hide their distaste for me. A *month* ago, I was little more than that eccentric, unwanted youngest son. The Elite tolerated my presence, but none of them respected me. Not like they did you and James. Now...?"

"I know what it's like to always have to show a brave face," I tell him.

Phillip gives a weak smile. "Imagine how Mother must feel."

"She's been doing it her whole life," I remind him. "She thrives on having rule."

"Yes, we know that."

"So?" I remind him. "What about the guards?"

Phillip told me how the two vampire guards who were killed were not of our coven. The only explanation we could come up with was that Smithson brought them in during the upheaval following the attack.

That also helps explain his lapse in judgment when attacking Phillip. He wouldn't have risked so much, or acted so instinctively, were the dead guards not his own.

Phillip stands taller, regaining the conviction required of the Captain Commander. "Once it came out that Smithson was made prisoner, more of the guards abandoned."

"How many?" I ask.

"Eleven in all," he says.

"So Smithson brought thirteen." I grunt. "An interesting number."

"Do you think it means anything?"

I fix my brother with a grim look. "You and I both study the stars. There are no coincidences in this world." I look away. "How is it they were not noticed?"

"Smithson kept a tight rein on the guards. The Haven vampires do not like to mix with them. There's a fraternity amongst the soldiers, so it was easy to keep it a secret. Besides—" Phillip sits on the edge of my bed. "Mother brought Smithson in to replace Andrey. But he wasn't the only one you killed in the fires."

"No," I say darkly. "There were three more."

"Well, replacements had to be made. With an Outsider as Captain Commander, why would our regular guards be alarmed when others were brought in?"

"Yes, that's fine," I grumble. "What I don't understand is how—or why—*we* didn't notice. How you and I didn't see them in our midst."

"We're as guilty of dismissing the guards as any of the Elite," Phillip says softly.

A silence descends on the room. "And Mother?" I ask. "Did she know?"

"I haven't brought the issue up."

"Good. Let's keep it that way. Smithson's betrayal hit her hard enough. I suspect they were intimate together, did you know?"

"I assumed as much." Phillip shrugs. "That was why she took news of Andrey so poorly. He was her lover, too."

"One of many." I shudder as I think of the countless advances she'd made on *me* over the years.

At least there's been a stop to that.

"The guards who remain," Phillip continues, "are all Haven vampires. I made sure of that. They're angry, too. Angry that they let Smithson's cronies infiltrate their ranks. Angry that they took them in as brothers so quickly. Angry that they ran when the going got tough."

"Then why would these eleven run?"

"Maybe they didn't feel safe," Phillip offers. "Maybe this was part of some ploy. Maybe they had orders from Smithson to leave should his position be compromised."

"There's only one person who can tell you the truth."

Phillip nods. "Yes. I know... and he is under interrogation now."

Chapter Eleven

TORTURE CELL UNDERNEATH THE HAVEN

I scream as the whip of silver cuts deeply into my back for the fifth time.

The wounds aren't healing. How could they? When inflicted by a silver weapon, cuts on our bodies do not close the regular way.

The muscles surrounding my spine feel like they're being ripped from the bone. Thirteen lashes, that's what I'd earned. Thirteen lashes, one for each of the traitorous vampires I snuck into The Haven's guards.

Of course, none knew of their true purpose... or intentions. When the Queen apprehended me and turned the Royal Court against me, they knew they had to get away. But she didn't know about them. No, it was only her troublesome youngest son who found out... and who sentenced me to this punishment.

Another lash of the whip strikes me. I grit my teeth and try to keep the scream in.

It's ripped from my throat anyway.

Blood pours past my waist and down my legs in thick rivulets. My whole body tenses and heaves with every breath I take as I try to control at least some of the agony.

Six lashes, I think to myself. *Six done, seven to go. Half left to endure.*

My labored breathing is the only sound that fills the chamber between strikes. I swear revenge on the vampire wielding the whip. When I get free, he will be the first to die.

I wait for the next lash. But it doesn't come. My arms, bound around the thick redwood stump, which had been brought down here from above ground, are stretched from their sockets. I lean into the remains of the tree and try to block my mind from the pain, to enter a transcendent zone where the agony from the silver weapon is not quite so acute...

Just when I let up the smallest bit, the whip cracks and strikes my back. Another tortured scream comes from my throat. The pain, I could deal with—even if it's stronger than any I've experienced since being left in the sun my first day as a vampire.

It's the sickening feeling of my back being torn open, being ripped to shreds, that I cannot abide.

Six left, I tell myself. I focus on the number. *Six left, only six, just six...*

"I think... that he's had enough," a sweet female voice rings out.

I gasp. *Victoria!* What's she doing here?

Lucas, the vampire charged with executing the punishment, snorts a laugh. "Who are you to command me?" he asks imperiously. "I answer only to the Queen and the Royal Court."

I hear Victoria flutter toward him. I try to turn my head—but the stiffness in my neck is too great to overcome. I cannot.

"I'm glad you say that," Victoria tells him sweetly. "Because right here I have a letter from the Royal Court granting me power to exercise their rule… when it comes to issues of any *prisoners* held in our midst."

Lucas takes the paper and reads it. He grumbles something incomprehensible but angry.

A second later, I hear him storm out of the room.

Victoria walks toward me. I suck in a breath when I feel her hand trail over my back.

"Oh, Smithson," she says sadly. "What have they done to you?"

I absolutely hate the pity I hear in her voice.

"Unchain me," I demand. "Let me down. If you've come to—"

"But you have no idea why I've come," she says. Her fingers find the edge of a particularly nasty wound.

She presses them into it. I gasp.

"Not so invincible now, are you?" she murmurs. "What your underlings in the Vorcellian Order would think if they saw you like this now."

My gut clenches. "What did you say?"

She gives a soft, feminine laugh. "What, did you think you could keep your connection to the Vorcellian Order hidden? No, no." She trails her hand down my ruined back. "I know all about it. I know all about *you*… even if you think I don't."

My first instinct is to deny everything, every link and every connection. If Victoria can be convinced that she's wrong…

But then again. I cannot tell how much she knows. And the mere fact that she's *aware* of the Order tells me that this whole time, I have underestimated her.

A grave mistake, that. One that I can only fix by giving her the respect she's due now.

"Who sent you?" I say. "Do you come on behalf of the Queen?"

"The Queen and I aren't yet on speaking terms," she informs me. "She would not be pleased if she discovered me here. Neither would her youngest son, the one who took your position away from you. Come to think of it..." she taps her lips, "...neither would the Royal Court, or any of the Elite..."

"The letter—"

"A forgery. You don't really think me *that* capable, do you? Sure, I gained your trust... before that, I gained James's trust... and before even that, I gained the trust of Logan, the greatest vampire King ever known. But even I have my limits."

Her hands move to the shackles binding my arms. I feel her fingers dance along the surface.

"What are you doing?" I hiss.

"Freeing you. Helping you escape. Isn't it obvious?" She works the final latch and the mechanism springs free. My left arm falls to my side. "It would help if you weren't such a bloody mess."

She moves to work on the second shackle. But before she can get to it, I whip around and grab her by the throat.

She gasps. Her eyes go wide in horrified surprise.

"What makes you think," I growl, "that I need your help?" My fingers dig deep into her flesh. The fool vampire let me catch her unguarded—and that's all the proof I need to call her on her bluff.

She doesn't know jack about the Vorcellian Order. If she has even a tenth of the knowledge she professes, she would have realized—or at least considered—that my true strength is cloaked.

"You said," she gasps. "You said when you rescued me, when you gave me your blood and let me live, you said that we would be allies!"

"Allies in the dark," I hiss at her. "Allies with a common purpose, a common goal, but allies whose allegiance was hidden from others!" My claws protract and push into the flesh of her neck. "What you've done here is to give both of us away! There is no going back from this."

"And who says I want to go back?" she snarls, the fight coming back to her after she'd overcome her momentary shock. "To be threatened and hated by all those around me?"

"They don't hate you," I say. I can hardly believe her paranoia. "You shared with them your blood. They owe their recovery to you."

"And how long will that gratitude last, huh? How long? Until the Queen remembers why she locked me away in the first place and decides to do it again?" She looks down at my arm. "Release me, Smithson. If they find my body next to you, you'll be executed. You're not going to risk that. And if you want to run, to escape, you'll need me with you. Cut the charade and let go. I know you're not about to kill me."

I glower at her... and relax my grip.

She takes a step back, rubbing her throat. "That's better," she says.

"So now what happens?" I snarl. "You forged a letter. You tried to free me.

You'll be found out—you can't remain." I curse. "You can't start to imagine how much you've screwed everything up! When the guards come..."

"When they come, you'll tell them exactly what happened. I came to free you because I wanted your help. You refused, and I left."

I scoff. "You think anybody will buy that story?"

"With the wards down, a Narwhark on the loose, the blood banks gone, and the humans nearly all dead?" She forces a laugh. "I doubt many will consider *this* a priority."

She takes a quick step to me, plants an unexpected kiss on my cheek, and darts into the shadows, quick as a fox.

Chapter Twelve

JAMES

THE WOODS AROUND THE HAVEN

The sun's dying rays filter through the branches of the evergreens above. When the last of them disappear, I know it's time to move.

I emerge from my makeshift, hastily dug grave in the ground and stagger toward the nearest tree. It's not fully night yet. Some light remains, and it affects me.

But, after enduring an entire day beneath the sun's harsh rays in Father's prison, I'm not so afraid of it as I once was.

That, perhaps, is the only reason I'm still alive.

I hear movement in the bush. I go absolutely still. My nostrils flare as I take a deep, cautious breath.

It's a hare.

My mouth salivates at the prospect of fresh blood. Even if it comes from an animal. Even if it comes from one that is so easy to kill.

I wait for the hare to get close. It is unafraid of me—or rather, it is unaware of me. Riyu's cloaking spell still has not worn off.

Another contributing factor to my survival.

The animal comes closer. When it's less than five feet away, I crouch, jump, and grab it.

But the little thing is ferocious. It sinks tiny little teeth into my hand. The bite makes me let go in surprise.

My prey scampers away.

A great sense of defeat, of failure, crashes into me. This is what has become of the once-great vampire James Soren.

Pathetic. Pitiful. Nine times out of ten I fail to capture the prey I am going for. I am not worthy to be called a vampire. I am not worthy to be called a hunter or a predator. I am not worthy to be known, or feared, or even acknowledged to be alive.

Not in the state I am in now.

That self-pity is something afflicted on me by my Father. It was while in his care that the first tendrils of such poisonous thoughts came into my mind. It was while in his care that all of my shortcomings were revealed to me.

It was in his care that I lost myself.

A branch cracks behind me. I spin around.

There, coming away from the nearby creek, is a frail, elderly moose.

The animal looks to be on its last legs. Its eyes are white with cataracts and unseeing. Its legs shake under its bulk. A day, maybe two—that's all it has left to live.

Usually the sight of a beast so weakened would fill me with disgust. The idea of feeding on such a creature would be reprehensible. Disgusting. The blood would be so thin, so tired, so tasteless…

It would not be blood that can sustain. The blood can barely even keep the animal alive.

Yet now, what choice do I have?

I make no effort to conceal myself as I approach. It makes no effort to run away. It knows its time is near. It has nothing to fear.

I step right up to it. I put one hand on its neck. "Look at us, two wretched things," I say. I bring my face close to its ear. "I'm sorry," I whisper, and with a great twist, break the animal's neck.

It falls to the ground, immobilized but not dead. I drop to my knees with it. I tear a slash in its throat, bring my lips to the wound, and start to drink. The blood is disgusting. It is putrid and old and stinking. But I force it past my lips anyway, knowing that my body will make some use of it. The human blood I had earlier from Mother's stores was hardly enough.

Whatever sustenance *this* blood has left, my body will exploit, and that, in turn, will make *me* a little bit stronger.

It will bring me closer to the vampire I should be.

I think on the stories of Lestat that once appealed to me so. I think of the way he dug himself beneath the earth, of how he had to recover by feeding on worms and insects and bugs after being burned and left for dead by those closest to him. I think of those trials and consider my own, and think that maybe I don't have it so bad.

"Ah, but Lestat, you are only fiction," I murmur through a mouthful of foul blood. "Your agony cannot compare to the real agony of the world."

And with that, I stand and wipe the remaining drops of blood from my lips. There's nothing I can do with the moose's body. I have not the strength nor inclination to hide it. If it leads a trail to me, so be it—but I think that were anybody really looking, I'd already be found.

Most, I imagine, consider me dead.

Chapter Thirteen

SMITHSON

DEEP BENEATH THE HAVEN

Mere moments after the fool girl is gone, the doors to my torture chamber open... and Carter steps inside.

He has the letter Victoria presented in one hand. "What is this?" he begins. "A mockery—"

He stops short when he realizes I am alone and half-bound, yet making no move to escape.

He approaches me, eyes narrowed and cautious. He shoves the letter in my face. "Were you behind this?"

I snort a laugh. The jerky movement makes all the wounds in my back feel like they're going to rip open. "Me? How could I be? While locked away? Of course not."

"The woman you brought to us, Victoria. Lucas said she was the one who brought him this forgery."

"You confuse me with James. I did not know Victoria prior to my arrival. The Soren prince was the one who brought her from The Crypts."

"She was the Queen's prisoner. You freed her in the aftermath of the battle."

"And she shared her blood with all of you, letting you heal," I say. "Had I not freed her, The Haven's casualties would have been greater. You welcomed her as your own."

"And she spat in our faces trying to run with you," Carter growls. "It's a good thing Lucas came to me first. If any others of the Royal Court had intercepted him..."

"I wanted no part of running. My place is here. With the Queen, as part of her guard."

He sniffs. "You say that as if you still have influence. Look around, Smithson. You've lost it all. Your command has been stripped from you. Much like..." His upper lip curls up in a nasty sneer. "Much like the skin on your back."

I give a too-casual shrug, refusing to take the bait. "Wounds heal."

"What did Victoria want?"

"For me to go with her."

"Why?"

"I assume she no longer felt safe."

"And you refused?"

"As I said, my place is here."

Carter brings a hand up to stroke his pointed goatee. "What game are you playing at, Smithson?" he asks softly. "I would have thought that any who rose to power, then lost everything, would be eager to leave."

"Where would I go? If I left, I'd spend the rest of my life hiding. I'd spend every day in fear of an assassin with a silver dagger, sent after me by the Queen." I lower my voice. "If you think Morgan would simply forget about me, then *I* have greatly overestimated your intellect. I thought you were one of the sharper members of the Royal Court."

"Praise will not get you far with me," Carter notes.

"What about honesty?" I ask. "Would you appreciate that?"

"I would," he says. "If I could trust the source."

He walks back to pick up a ragged brown robe and tosses it to me. "Put that on. The remainder of your punishment can be administered later."

I glance at my still-shackled arm. "Hard to do in chains," I say.

Carter grumbles but walks over and opens the lock. My arm falls free. I rub my wrist, then throw the robe over my back. I try to hide the spasm of agony that takes me when the heavy material makes contact with the open wounds.

Carter watches me with a clinical eye.

He's searching for weakness, I think. *He wants to use me.*

I need to play that up as much as I can. If he considers me malleable and weak...

Well, that will give me the perfect opportunity to weasel my way back to where I need to be.

"The Captain Commander sentenced me to thirteen lashes," I say. "Going against him now is not the smartest move for you."

"You will be given the rest in due time," Carter says. "For now... here." He tosses a small vial to me. "Drink."

I snatch it from the air. The moment I pull out the stopper, the fresh aroma of potent blood greets me. I salivate. This is a rare mix indeed.

"A portion from my personal collection," Carter explains. "All of the Elite have their own stores. Mine is amongst the best. That blood is from the strongest humans, the ones who were deemed most robust. It is the finest you will find in The Haven."

"And you're offering it to me," I state. I want badly to gulp it down, but I don't want to reveal my desperation yet.

"Phillip did not say you couldn't be fed."

My grip on the vial tightens. The blood calls to me.

I ignore the temptation. "So you are here on his command."

Carter snorts a laugh. "Hardly. I'm here because… because I think that you and I can help each other. Now hurry up. Drink, before I change my mind."

I see no further reason to hold back. I bring the vial to my lips and tip my head back.

The thick, life-giving nectar flows down my throat. My wounds start to heal. As they close, the skin on my back stitches itself up. Strength returns to my body. Sharpness comes to my mind.

"Much better," Carter says when the vial is empty. "And now we can talk."

"What is there to talk about?" I ask.

"The Queen, for one," Carter answers. "Your position with us. Your influence, here, and in the outside world. The power either of us might wield over the Royal Court."

My interest perks up. This is… intriguing.

"I'm listening," I say.

"First, we forget the incident with Victoria ever took place." Carter walks to the burning brazier and holds the letter out over the flames. The paper catches fire and turns to ash in a matter of seconds.

"There," he says. "Now, only you, I, and Lucas know of the forgery she attempted. Lucas is not of the Elite, so his say hardly matters. If you keep Victoria's betrayal a secret, I will too."

I nod slowly. Carter has been one of the Queen's most vocal opponents, but I never considered him to be this wily.

"If the new *Captain Commander*—" Carter does not hide his disgust, "raises issue with you being set free early, you will tell him that I sanctioned it. He can take up the grievance with me."

"Why are you helping me?" I wonder.

Carter gestures toward the door instead of answering. "Walk with me?"

I nod.

Together, we proceed through the underground tunnels of The Haven's one and only stronghold.

"Thanks to you, the Royal Court regained prominence," Carter says. "We would never have accomplished that alone. And I grow tired of the Elite being shackled by the Queen's rule. *You* gave us all a voice, and for that, I will not forsake you."

I lower my head in an attempt at meekness as we near a group of four vampires. Their conversation dies the moment we're within hearing distance. They

86

look at me—and Carter—with open suspicion as we pass.

"You see?" Carter sighs. "There used to be harmony here. Now, all that is ruined. Yet some things that have changed... have changed for the better."

"Such as?"

"The Queen feels accountable to us," Carter says. "Her decisions are no longer absolute. She needs the Royal Court's approval."

"I don't see how this involves me," I say. "Without my position in the guard, I don't belong to the Court."

Carter stops and faces me. He grips my shoulder. "Let us be frank," he says. The torches on the walls make shadows dance across his face. "Even if you were ousted from your position, anyone with half a brain can tell that you were the most capable Captain Commander The Haven has ever had. Phillip is no match."

"Phillip is what you have now. I'm not going to be reclaiming the post any time soon."

"No," Carter's eyes glimmer. "But it is power you seek, is it not? It is power that you truly want."

I eye the empty hallway. My vampire senses tell me we are alone. Still, it is difficult to feel like I can speak freely.

"All that I *truly* want," I say carefully, "is to serve my Queen."

Carter snorts in disbelief. He steps back and gives a great laugh.

"How quaint," he tells me after he's calmed down. "And here I was, thinking you a man of ambition."

"Ambition can take many forms," I say cryptically.

"Very well. This is my offer to you. Mull it over for a day, maybe two, and get back to me."

"Tell me."

"You claim you want to serve the Queen. Fine. I can help you get back into her good graces."

My eyes narrow in suspicion. "How?"

"The Royal Court can be made to believe that she... overreached... when stripping you of your post. I can see to that. If you, in turn, make peace with her sons..."

I stop short. "Raul? Or Phillip?"

"Both," Carter says. "If you gain both their trust... the Queen will be like putty in our hands. You influence them... I influence the Royal Court... and together, we can work from the shadows, you and I, to turn The Haven into something truly marvelous!"

There is a frenetic zeal that carries just on the edge of Carter's voice. I catch the undercurrent easily, but only because I am so used to dealing with men like him when in my natural position of power in the Order.

"You set me on an arduous path," I tell him. "Peace with the Soren brothers is an impossibility. They both hate me. If you remember, I nearly *killed* one."

And I did destroy the eldest, I think, with no small degree of satisfaction.

Carter spreads his hands. "Peace with them is what I require. It will not happen overnight, I understand. But if you extend the olive branch..."

I shake my head. "It will do little good."

"So you would rather remain like this, stripped of any power, imprisoned, and lacking your former influence?"

"Of course not," I growl.

"Then take me up on my offer," he says. "The Haven is in turmoil. The wards are down. We are exposed to the world. But our coven will rise again. A Queen has always ruled this sanctuary. I will not pretend to be able to change that. But there is an enormous difference between an absolute monarch... and a puppet Queen."

Chapter Fourteen

PHILLIP

THE HAVEN

I storm into Carter's rooms, not bothering to hide the fury that distorts my face.

"You set him *free*?" I demand.

Carter looks up from the book he is reading. He blinks at being disturbed.

"Set who free?" he asks, an absolute picture of innocence.

"You set—" I slam two fists on his desk, "—my prisoner... *free*... without consulting me, or the Royal Court, or the Queen, or anybody else!"

"Oh you must mean Smithson," Carter says casually. He turns back to his book. "Yes. I did that. Why?"

"You undermined a direct order," I hiss. "A direct order *I* gave."

"Is this how the Captain Commander deals with problems that arise?" he asks. "By throwing a childish fit?"

He's trying to rankle me. I know it. But all the peace I once felt inside me, all the patience—all of it has been abolished in the recent series of calamities.

I used to be calm. I used to be steady. Now, I find myself giving way to my emotions more and more. I find myself falling into fits of rage and anger at the smallest provocation. I find the animal inside, the vampire, fighting harder and harder to be set free—and I find myself less and less willing to resist.

I force myself to take a deep breath. "Smithson was in the middle of receiving thirteen lashes when you stopped it. His sentence was not concluded. Why did you interfere?"

"Thirteen lashes was excessive," Carter says. "I have a decree, somewhere in here..." he rummages through his desk and pulls out a crumbled sheet of paper. He straightens it against his leg and hands it to me. "Look at that."

I read it quickly. It's an order signed by the majority of the Royal Court, authorizing the release of Smithson.

"The Queen's name is not here," I state.

"The Queen was not aware of the punishment Smithson received."

"Without her signature," I say, "this order is void."

Carter laughs. "You really think so? My, but you have a lot to learn." He leans forward. "Life is harder now that Mommy's word isn't absolute law, is it not?

A growl comes from deep in my throat.

With a gargantuan effort I force my emotions down.

"I had full authorization to act as I did," Carter says. "So if you came to trouble me for that, I suggest you leave. I know you have other, more pertinent matters to attend to," he sneers. "Such as, for example, how to get our entire coven to acquire your taste for animal blood."

Chapter Fifteen

RAUL

DEEP BENEATH THE HAVEN

Light from a distant torch casts my room in an eerie red. I sit behind my desk, considering, thinking...

Then, with a grimace, I pull away the fleece blanket and look at my leg.

The wound looks awful. It hasn't changed from this morning. Just as it hasn't changed since yesterday, or the day before that, or the day before *that*...

The worst thing is that I cannot even feel my leg. The entire limb is numb, useless, as if it's asleep.

And the smell... nothing can mask the horrific smell.

The wound reeks of corruption and blackness and disease. It's a sickly-sweet stench that reaches deep into my nostrils and lingers for far longer than it should. It sticks to the back of my throat, beneath the vile layers of that murky horrible odor of my infected blood.

Maybe I should be grateful it's not getting worse. At least Mother's spell seems to be working to ward off the infection.

But I am unused to having such a crippling affliction for so long. Every hour that passes brings me closer to the inevitable.

There is a confrontation looming in the background. I know it. I can feel it. The massive vampire who gave me this wound said his blade formed a link between us. A link he could use to take control of me.

So far, there has been no attempt. But is any of that because of Mother's spell? Or is it simply because that beast has not yet exerted the blade's proper power over me?

The door to my room comes open. Hastily, I drop the blanket and look up.

Eleira lingers on the threshold.

I start to rise. But, in my excitement to see her, I place too much weight on my bad leg. It gives out. I have to clutch at the table to keep from falling.

She rushes to my side. "Are you okay?" she asks, concern painting her voice.

"Fine," I grumble. My excitement has been replaced by a nasty irritation. She shouldn't have to see me like this—shouldn't have to see me weak and fragile and *ruined.*

She shouldn't have to worry about the vampire who is supposed to be her bastion of strength.

"Let me help you," she murmurs. She starts to move to place her arm under my shoulder...

"I'm fine." I rip away. "Get me my walking stick."

Eleira looks around the room, finds it propped up on the opposite wall, and retrieves it. When she gives it to me, her eyes are dark and impossible to read.

"What?" I snap. I know I'm short-tempered, but dammit, how can I help it? It's humiliating, being seen like this.

Especially after spending six-hundred years impervious to the regular afflictions of the world.

"I'm... worried about you," she admits. "You haven't left this room for days. Whenever I ask Morgan what she thinks, she gives a cryptic non-answer." Eleira hesitates, then reaches out and takes my hand. "Why don't you let me help you?"

It's all I can do not to sneer. This wound is turning me nasty. Eleira is the girl—the woman—I love.

I should not be taking any of this out on her.

So instead of pulling my hand away, as was my first instinct, I turn it over and twine my fingers through hers.

"You cannot help me," I say softly. "Not in the way you want."

Again the brute vampire's message echoes in my mind:

"*You will receive a message from my King in a matter of days.*"

But days have already passed. I've heard nothing.

She envelops my hand with both of hers. "You're not even letting me *try*," she protests.

"Enough." I spin away. I feel an anger rising. The last thing I want to do is lash out at Eleira.

I do not want to give her reason to hate me more.

"Raul..." for a second, she sounds empty, destitute, helpless. She sounds like a girl caught up in an adventure—a nightmare—much greater than herself.

But then her voice takes on an inflection of strength, and love flares in my heart at her bravery.

"Raul Soren." She walks right up to me, easily overtaking me with her quick strides. "It does not bode well for the Prince of The Haven to stay locked up in his rooms like some sickly child. The other vampires are whispering. They sense something is wrong."

I laugh. "They sense? They *sense*? Of course they sense it, Eleira. They've *seen* me hobbling around the perimeter of the Royal Court's assembled table. You think they don't know? Of course they know. What we cannot tell them—what we must do everything to hide—is the *severity* of this damned paper cut!"

My voice gets louder and louder as I continue my spiel. By the end, I am shouting.

"It's not a 'paper cut.' You and I both know that," she fires back. Her passion has been evoked, and she's staring at me with hard, determined eyes. "The Queen is keeping the worst of it at bay. But you heard what she said—healing spells are not her forte! So let *me* try, let *me* probe you, let *me* see what I can find."

"You?" For a second, incredulity at the suggestion staggers me.

"Yes, me." Eleira stands up to full height. "I am more than capable, you know."

"Look, I know you want to help..." I temper my tone, "...but you've hardly had any training. You mean well, Eleira, but..."

I trail off. This is more difficult than it should be.

"But you don't think I know enough, is that it?" she asks.

I grunt and nod. "You've only been aware of your powers for a very short time."

Her expression becomes steely and determined. A spark shines in her eyes. "That doesn't mean I'm incapable—"

"I didn't say that," I interrupt. "All I mean is this. If the greatest witch alive couldn't help me, how could—"

"How could I, right?" Eleira's voice is icy. "I'm not blind to who I am, you know. Neither am I blind to what I can do. I know my capabilities, Raul, just as I know my limitations! You think I haven't been practicing? You think I haven't been using every spare moment of my time to try to *understand* this gift? To discover who I am, what I can do, the things I'm capable of?"

I grimace. "I didn't mean it that way—"

Her eyes flash. "Then how *did* you mean it? Please, do tell me. Because from where I'm standing, you sound like a pompous brat—the Brat Prince." She gives a quick, harsh laugh. "Oh yes. Tell James I've read The Vampire Lestat too. I know all of Anne Rice's fictions. Phillip's been giving me books—"

"So you're cozying up to Phillip now?" I demand. I hate how petty I sound, how jealous and bitter, but there's little I can do to stop those feelings.

"Why?" she asks. "Do you not want me to?"

"I could care less what you do in your spare time—or who you spend it with," I snap.

Eleira gasps. For a brief second, her face falls.

And then she steels herself and marches straight for the exit.

"No, wait...!" I begin, but by then it's too late. She's already slammed the door on me.

"Dammit!" I curse. My fist hits the table and nearly cracks it in two.

I'm breathing hard. My body is hot all over. Why did I have to be so stupid? Why did I have to bicker with her? Now she's gone, and angry, and I'm angry, too, and the frustration grows—

A sudden chill takes me. It washes through my body and down my leg.

I shudder and grit my teeth. I try fighting it off—

Without warning, my bad leg goes out. One moment I'm standing, the next I'm hobbled over, clinging onto the side of my desk. A spasm of horrendous pain rocks me. I clench my jaw hard to stop from crying out.

Pressure is building beneath the wound. Alternative waves of hot and cold take me. My whole body breaks out in a sweat that coats my back, my neck, my chest, and my arms...

Another jolt of sharp pain. One more all-consuming effort to stop from crying out. My vision swims. The room starts to move and warp as if underwater.

My grip on reality is fading. I lose hold of the desk and fall down. Black shadows crowd the outside of my sight. My mind drifts, and my body feels so far away, as if it's no longer my own. Whatever happens to it does not happen to *me*, but a distant replica of me, a replica I cannot touch or reach or even influence...

Just before the shadows take over, I hear the door open... and a sharp, quick, female gasp.

Chapter Sixteen

ELEIRA

DEEP BENEATH THE HAVEN

I stroll briskly through the tunnel leading away from Raul's room. The fight with Raul has put me in a sour mood. I came, just to check on him, after feeling guilty for neglecting him for the past few days. I thought he'd be happy to see me.

Instead, he was... nasty.

Maybe I should give him more leeway. But he's not the only one dealing with problems. All the vampires of The Haven have troubles on their minds. With all the recent upheaval that surrounds us...

I'm so absorbed in my own thoughts that I barely pay attention to where I'm going—or if anyone's around me.

That's why I nearly jump out of my skin when I turn a corner and see a human woman walking toward me. Alone.

She spares only the briefest glance before hurrying on. But I recognize her face. She was the one I caught looking at Raul when we were searching the village for April.

And now she's heading toward his room?

For a second, I debate following her. What is she up to...?

But I quickly decide against it. Raul can do what he wants. He's done exactly what he wants, for a very long time, before I was around.

Besides, it's not like he and I are even *officially* in a relationship.

A pang of guilt takes me at that thought. We haven't exactly been given time to discuss such things, given everything else that has been going on around us. Discuss, or even *consider*...

God. I catch myself thinking those thoughts and stomp them down mercilessly. I sound like a petty teenage girl. I have more important matters to deal with!

So I put the woman out of my mind and continue on to see the Queen. After Phillip's replacement of Smithson as Captain Commander, she's been more willing to give me time—and patience. Maybe it was the shock of the Royal Court going against her that made her realize I really was on her side, and that she should treat me as such.

Whatever the cause, the fact of the matter is that I've learned more about magic in the last few days than I had in the preceding *weeks*.

But no sooner do I turn into the hallway leading to her room than the sound of commotion comes rippling out. A second later, a stream of vampires race out of her rooms. Phillip is leading the guard, but Morgan is right there beside him. They see me and stop just long enough to exclaim, "The Narwhark has broken through! It's been sighted underground!"

"What?" I gasp. Morgan had put up a series of small guard spells up that would alert her to the demon's presence. "Where?"

"Somewhere in the vicinity of Raul's room," the Queen answers.

I gasp. "I was just there!"

Morgan's eyes pierce into me. She grips my arm. "Did you see anything?"

I shake my head. "I—no. I spoke to Raul. That's it."

She narrows her eyes. "There's something you're not telling me," she says.

I look down. "We had… a fight," I admit.

The Queen searches my face. "Is that it?"

I hesitate before voicing my concern. "Raul wasn't like himself. I think the wound is affecting him. He said some things—"

"That you undoubtedly found hurtful," Morgan interrupts hastily. "Yes, yes. Anything else?"

I bite my lip… and shake my head.

"Mother, we *have* to go," Phillip insists. "If the Narwhark is running loose underground, if it attacks anybody, madness will ensue!"

She nods and releases me. "Come with us, Eleira. If we find the demon—you will be needed."

Chapter Seventeen

PHILLIP

DEEP BENEATH THE HAVEN

I get the first inclination that something is wrong when my brother does not answer the door.

"Raul!" I pound on it. "Raul. Open this door! Open it now!"

I try the handle, but it's locked. He never locks his door.

"Raul!" I try again. "If you don't open it *now*, we will tear it down!"

"Oh, step aside," Mother mutters. She shoulders me away and puts one palm against the middle of the door. There's a flash of blue, and all of a sudden, it's torn off its hinges.

Inside I find a scene unlike I could expect.

A beautiful human woman is kneeling over Raul's unconscious form. There's a small slit in her wrist that leaks out blood. She holds it to Raul's lips, trying to feed him.

At our entrance she gasps and spins away. Eleira stiffens beside me.

"You!" she exclaims.

The Queen takes one look at things and—for some reason—instantly dismisses her son. She hurries around the perimeter of the room, tracing one arm over the walls. She completes a full circle in blinding speed before returning to us.

"The Narwhark isn't here," she says. Still she hasn't so much as acknowledged Raul's miserable state. "Send the rest of the guards to sweep this quarter of the stronghold. If the Narwhark returns, they will find it—though I suspect it's already long gone."

"What?" I exclaim. "You *said* you only just felt it. You told me your guard spells were triggered—"

"Triggered, yes," she responds soberly, keeping her voice low so that only I can hear. "But the spells aren't specific. They could have been set off by something *else*."

She casts a meaningful look at Raul and the human woman. I don't quite understand what she means, but I order my guards out as she instructed.

They leave the room in a rush, each eager to prove his worth and loyalty to the Queen.

Then it is just Eleira, Mother, Raul, the human woman, and me.

"Close the door," Mother tells me softly. "What happens next must not to leave this room."

"Um..." I hesitate, looking at the splintered remains of the door on the floor. She mutters something under her breath. A blue light emits from her. It sweeps toward the opening and seals it in a soundproof barrier.

She looks at Eleira. "Do you think you can duplicate that?"

The younger girl nods. Her eyes, however, don't once leave Raul. Her hands make tight fists at her sides.

"Then do it," Morgan says. "All around the room. You have my permission to."

Eleira takes a deep breath, focuses, and closes her eyes...

A moment later a blinding blue flash erupts from around her. This time the light sinks into every surface of the room. It does so even quicker than Mother's had.

Eleira's eyes open. "It's done."

Our attention turns to Raul... and the woman still beside him.

She's glaring at us. Her wrist continues to leak blood.

Raul, on the ground beside her, is barely breathing.

I take a step toward them, ready to go to my brother's aid—but Mother stops me by placing a hand on my shoulder.

"We need to be extremely careful," she says. "Either one of them might be possessed."

My stomach sinks on hearing those words. But then I realize why Eleira did not rush to Raul's side right away:

She understood the same thing.

"I'm not possessed!" the woman exclaims.

"Really," Morgan says. She does not move from her spot. "Then why are you willingly feeding this vampire your blood?"

"To save his life," she says, both defiant and angry. "As he did mine."

Eleira sucks in a breath. But Mother nods. "You must be the one he spared in

103

the fires," she says without emotion. "The one I lost Andrey for."

The woman doesn't respond. She only glares at the Queen.

"Step away from my son," the Queen commands. "It is not your blood that he requires. It will do him no good—"

Raul sputters, coughs, and opens his eyes.

Eleira rushes to his side right away. She drops down and cradles his head. "I'm sorry," she says, running her fingers through his hair, "for all those things I said. I'm truly sorry."

Raul offers her a weak smile. "I'm the one," he says, "who should be apologizing."

Mother makes a nasty, sneering sound of disbelief as she approaches. She shoulders Eleira out of the way and takes Raul's head in both hands.

"Tell me what you remember," she demands of him. She gestures to the human. "How did this wench get here?"

"I can speak for myself, thank you very much," the woman says. "I came to give Raul my gratitude for sparing my life. This was the first opportunity I've had to do so."

Raul coughs and pulls himself up. He brings a hand to his head. "Gods, I feel awful. How am I..."

"Still alive?" Mother finishes for him.

He grimaces and nods.

"I don't know. By all accounts, you should be dead."

Shock runs through me. Eleira gasps.

"The disturbance I felt wasn't the demon," Morgan continues, undeterred. "But it *did* come from something dark and sinister. An external, malicious force penetrated the stronghold."

She looks around the room. "My guess is that whoever gave you the wound created a link between you and it. Oh, don't look so surprised, Raul. I know you know, and I know you've held that knowledge from me. There are few weapons in this world that can harm a vampire as you've been harmed. The weapons are part torrial. I've seen mention of them in my ancient texts."

Raul avoids looking directly at the Queen. Eleira holds onto his shoulder tightly.

"It's true," he admits.

Mother nods. "I've been holding off the worst of the corruption. But I've been unable to reverse it. There is only one who can, and that is the vampire who holds the blade that made the cut. But he is an enemy, which means—"

She cuts off suddenly, and looks at the human. "I believe you've heard enough. It's time for you to return to your kind. It's safer there."

"Cassandra stays," Raul says firmly. "I owe her my life."

"I'm not so sure about that," Morgan murmurs.

"What do you mean you're not sure?" Eleira exclaims. "He's alive now, isn't he? He's conscious and breathing and—"

"Eleira." Morgan cuts her off firmly. "I know you care for him. But you must hold your emotions in check. Especially now."

Her voice is stern yet gentle.

I eye Mother from the side. She's the same vampire I've always known, and yet...

And yet I feel like she has become more capable of real empathy.

Eleira clamps her lips shut. Determination glints in her eyes. "Whatever Raul needs," she says, "I will give."

"An admirable sentiment," Mother says. "One that is mirrored in him, I think. But that's beside the point. Cassandra, if you are to stay now, you will become bound to him—" she nods at Raul, "—forever."

Realization dawns on me about what Mother means. There's only one way for a human to become bound to a vampire *forever*.

"You want him to convert her," I breathe. "You want to make Cassandra one of us. You want to give her the Dark Gift!"

Morgan nods, considering. "It's either that, or destroy her. She has heard too much to simply be let free."

Raul pulls Cassandra to his side. "I won't let you harm her," he snarls.

Morgan spreads her hands. "The choice is hers," she says. "Be made into a creature of the night... or die."

The human woman stands. The blood trailing down her wrist has slowed to a trickle.

"Vampires destroyed all that I had," she says. I admire her courage for facing the Queen without backing down. "Why would I want to be made into one of you? If you're going to kill me, then do it now. Don't drag out the inevitable. But if you share some gratitude for your son's life—give me a day to say goodbye to my family."

"Stupid woman," Morgan says. "You don't *have* a day. You think I'd release you into the midst of the stronghold, given all that you've witnessed? Even if we could trust you—and that's a big if—you know nothing of the vampire hierarchy, or what things are important to be kept secret, and what things aren't."

"I have a brain, don't I?" Cassandra fires back. "I'm not completely dumb!"

"And yet here we found you, feeding your blood to a vampire. *Willingly*."

"She's more than proven her worth..." Raul begins.

"Quiet," Morgan snaps. "Unless you want to take the choice out of her hands and have me make it. For what it's worth, I think it would be a great shame to waste a life such as hers. She's brash but resilient. And—" Morgan's eyes shine, "—she worships you."

That elicits a tiny gasp from Eleira. She pulls Raul closer.

At the same time, Cassandra's chin juts up. "I do not."

"I see the way you look at him. We *all* do," the Queen says. She casts an impatient glance around the room. "We're wasting time."

"Yes," Eleira agrees. "Yes, we definitely are! We need to help Raul, to make sure *this* won't happen again."

"No," Morgan says. "We need to figure out how it is that this woman's blood actually saved him. I have a suspicion..."

Without warning she grabs Cassandra's arm and jerks her toward her. Her fangs flash. Next thing I know, Mother has pierced that woman's neck and taken the Little Drink.

Morgan is off her before Cassandra has a chance to react.

"Yes," Mother says softly, tasting the blood. "It's exactly as I thought."

"What?" Cassandra exclaims.

Mother stabs a finger at Raul. "He," she says ominously, "has given her his blood."

Chapter Eighteen

PHILLIP

DEEP BENEATH THE HAVEN

A wave of shock rips through me. Sharing vampiric blood with a human is one of The Haven's most grievous crimes.

But my brother does not deny it. He just stares at the Queen, eyes blazing with inequitable defiance.

"Is it true?" Eleira asks softly beside him.

Raul nods. "It was the only way I could save her life." He glares at Morgan. "After I found her being *toyed with* by your guards."

"Former guards," Mother corrects. She looks at Cassandra in great triumph. "So," she says. "It looks like the choice has been taken out of your hands, anyway."

"What do you mean?" she asks.

"Once your blood has been transfused with that of a vampire," Mother explains, "the transformation will take you whether you will it or not. Now, it is not the most *pleasant* way of being made—in fact, it carries a high degree of risk— but before the vampiric serum was discovered, such an exchange of blood was the only way we made newborns."

Eleira gapes at Raul. "You knew this?" she asks.

He gives a grim nod. "Yes." He turns toward her. "But I had no choice."

"Is that what you did to me?" Eleira asks. "When you first brought me to The Haven?"

"James fed you a small drop of his blood infused with the vampiric serum when you were taken," Raul admits. "Just enough to prime your body for the transformation, which was expedited at The Crypts."

"This is different. This time there was no serum injected. Vampire blood does heal humans. At first." The Queen narrows her eyes at Cassandra. "While it is true Raul's blood will begin to transform her, it's more likely to *kill* her. Any amount of vampiric blood sloshing around in a human body will initiate the transformation, but without the serum there to aid the process, when the transformation actually hits, most humans do not survive. Except for a rare few."

Cassandra gasps and backs away. She hits a shelf and holds onto its sides as if fighting for her life.

"You mean… you mean, if I don't die, I'm going to become one of *you?*" she asks, breathless.

"Yes," Morgan says. Suddenly a silver dagger appears in her hands. "Unless you'd rather be a corpse now?"

Faced with the imminent prospect of her death, Cassandra gulps and shakes her head. She is not quite so resolute as she was before.

The dagger is gone in a flash. "The fact that you have my son's blood running through your veins explains why we find you here now. It was not coincidence that brought you to his chamber when he needed you. A type of link is created between a vampire and his spawn that lasts until the full conversion takes place.

It is in the blood.

"Right now, Cassandra, your body is thriving on a mix of your own human blood... and Raul's superior vampire blood. Your body knows that Raul's is stronger, that it provided more sustenance. It is also linked to its source. If Raul were to die before the transformation took hold of you—before vampiric and human blood fused together to make *you* into a vampire of your own standing— then the blood fueling your body would lose its potency. Its link to Raul would be eliminated. It would lose its transformative power. It would lose *all* of its power, and if that were to happen, it would be as if a crippling disease struck you. Your body, which is becoming reliant upon Raul's vampiric blood, would crumble. You would break. Oh, you might come out of the sickness, if you had the requisite strength, but the odds of that happening are not very high." Mother pauses, and meets the eyes of everyone in the room. "Not very high at all."

I step in to help the others make sense of the convoluted explanation. "What she means," I say, "is that any human who is fed vampire blood becomes aware of the condition of the vampire who it belongs to, on a subconscious level. The same essence that animates us and makes us immune to sickness and disease is responsible for the phenomenon. It is why feeding humans our blood is prohibited," I add, looking at Eleira. "The link that forms ensures the human will do everything she or he can to guarantee the vampire's survival, until the conversion is complete. Of course," I gesture at my brother's leg, "most vampires don't suffer afflictions such as that."

"The stars tell us that everything happens for a reason," Mother continues. "Raul, you know this. It is what brought Eleira to us."

He grunts in response.

"There was a reason, then, too, that you killed Andrey. There was a reason that you spared this woman's life. For that, I can no longer hold you accountable for Andrey's death. Because had you not killed him, you would not have saved Cassandra… and, in turn, she would not have been able to save you."

Eleira looks at the Queen, then over at Cassandra, who is taking all of this in with wide, owlish eyes. "But I don't understand why *her* blood was able to help him now," she says.

"Think, girl!" Morgan emphasizes. "The wound Raul sustained in battle poisoned his entire body. It began a corruption his system could not fight on its own. I was able to halt its progress with my spell, but I could do nothing to *cleanse* the blood. Cassandra, however—" she gestures at the woman, "—is the only vessel on this earth to hold a store of Raul's *un*tainted blood. When she gave him her wrist, it was not her human blood that saved him—but the clean, unsullied blood he fed her that gave him strength."

A dark expression forms on Eleira's face. "But now the store is emptied," she says. "Raul will not be given another chance. Am I right?"

Mother hesitates… and finally nods.

"Cassandra bought him time," she says. "How much time, I cannot say."

Chapter Nineteen

JAMES

THE WOODS AROUND THE HAVEN

Days pass slowly as I recover my strength. I feed on the weakest, most damnable creatures. Old, decrepit beasts with scarcely enough life force to sustain them. Hobbled, pitiful things whose blood tastes of soil and dirt.

But every time I *do* feed, I come a little bit more into myself.

I stay away from the predators surrounding The Haven. I don't trouble them, and they don't trouble me. Sometimes I cross paths with one. They never attack.

There's only one reason for that: they all consider me too weak, too paltry, to even be worth the effort of the kill.

If I were in their position I would feel the same. I still disgust myself. Feeding on creatures which are the lowest of the low? It's repulsive.

But what choice do I have?

None.

At least my eyesight has returned. I think on the horrible days I spent wandering about, completely lost, stumbling over rocks and roots and bashing into tree-trunks. I could have avoided them. I could have navigated my surroundings with more dexterity... but in those initial days, I had not the inclination to try.

I felt miserable, and so I acted miserably. Something drove me to continue on, to not completely give up faith.

But faith in what? I believe in no gods. The only thing I believe in is my own vampire nature—and for a good long time, I thought even that had been lost to me.

How could I be a creature of the night if I could not see? The thrill of being a vampire *comes* from the hunt, it *comes* from being able to navigate where others cannot. It comes from owning the night, from owning the darkness, not from being crippled by it.

Maybe it was the vampire inside me that made me persevere. That instinctual longing for life, for continuity... it was not lost to me, no. Not entirely.

It had just been driven down deep inside me.

But now that I'm getting stronger, things are changing. Now, at the very least, I am making an effort to hide my traces. I'm not yet willing to wander far from the boundary of The Haven. This is the safest spot for me. This is the one place where I have the best chance to recover, because I know these grounds.

And yet, there is an eerie emptiness all around me. None have come to search for me. It helps that I am still cloaked, of course. But still. I would have thought that when Smithson discovered my body missing, or when Mother found me gone, more of an effort would have been made to find me.

Apparently, I thought wrong.

I haven't sensed a vampire in my vicinity even once. Where are they? I don't dare wander in past the border of The Haven. But even I know there should be *someone* there, on the other side. Either the guards patrolling their territory.

Perhaps some of the Elite, checking on the ruined wards themselves.

But there have been none.

I tense when a small mountain lion, almost a cub, makes its way through the bush near me. I go still. It cannot sense me, not with the cloaking spell, but it can still hear me—it can still smell me. Even if I've spent the sun-drenched hours of each day buried beneath the earth, protected by dirt from those awful rays, even if my body reeks of earthworms and moisture and the damp of the under-ground—

The cat stops. Its ears twitch. It hears something in the distance.

Something that I do not.

It turns its head in that direction, away from me. My body should be attuned to danger—but I feel no threat. Whatever caught the animal's attention is not something that should trouble me.

But with its head turned, the cub has given me the opportunity of a lifetime. My nostrils flare as I allow myself to pick up the fresh whiff of strong animal blood. It is nothing compared to human blood, of course. But against the back-drop of the feeble beasts I've been feeding on, it makes a world of difference.

My body needs blood. So the choice is made for me.

The hunter's instincts erupt. Even if they're subdued, even if they are a tenth of what I am accustomed to, they guide me with a single-minded purpose. I pounce from my spot and descend on the cat.

It has scarcely a second to react before I crash into it and take it to the ground. It turns over and swipes at me, those muscular legs pumping furiously. Its claws draw blood, but that only enlivens me. I feel the cat tear through my skin, feel my own hot blood pour out. It stinks, my blood does, because it is tainted by all I've been feeding on, by the pathetic scraps and small remains of whatever I've been able to scavenge.

Yet it will not be this weak for long. My fangs come out. I sink them into the animal's neck. I wasn't aiming, but my teeth cut right into the thick, pulsing carotenoid artery. Immediately, my mouth fills with blood. Hot, red, lush, life-giving blood.

In my near-depraved state I find that it tastes almost as good as a human's. I draw deep, so deep, and drink it all, until the cat stops kicking and its body lies as an empty shell beneath me. My new wounds quickly close, and I feel an energy—a revitalization—take hold of me. It washes through me and fortifies my limbs, gives strength to my bones.

Why had I denied myself this? I wonder. *From whence came the hesitation before the kill?*

I had forgotten my true nature. And now, with this beast lying dead at my feet with its blood coursing through my veins, I have regained a small part of it once again.

And, suddenly, I am so much more aware of the forest. I hear the eagles in the treetops, the owls sitting on their perches. I feel the exuberance of life all around me—from the trees, from the water, from the rain. I spread my arms and breathe in deep, tasting the night air as I have forgotten I can taste. There are squirrels in the closest redwood, there's a fox in a hollow underground. Nearby, resting, is a small pack of wolves.

Suddenly, I'm reminded of the wolf I killed right before I stole Eleira. A cruel smile forms on my face. A sort of hunger opens up inside, not for blood, but for *power*. I want to feel powerful. I want to be feared. I want to revel in my vampire nature and let the world know once more that I am James Soren, eldest of the Soren brothers and rightful heir to the throne of The Crypts—

And then the madness of my thoughts crashes into me, and I stagger back. I trip and fall, not caring if I am graceless, completely indifferent to how I look.

One feeding, I think in alarm. *One feeding is all it took to restore those feelings of euphoria, of mania. One feeding... and it wasn't even on human blood.*

A sound in the distance catches my attention.

It's like... a cough. It is a cough from somebody—from a person. A human.

I bolt upright. All my senses go on high alert. I focus on the sound. I see the world around The Haven spread in my mind, and...

There!

From right over there, the sound comes again. Except this time, it's not a cough, but a whisper.

And it's answered soon after by the whisper of another.

Rashness takes hold. I race through the trees. My mouth salivates even before my nose can pick up the human scent of blood.

And there, tight together in a clearing... I see them.

A group of humans. A poor, disheveled lot. There's a woman with red, fraying hair peering out into the darkness. A tall man, bald and unattractive, confers with her.

Theirs are the voices I heard.

117

But there are more. I do a count of the group. There are twenty of them in all, including the lead man and woman. Some have backpacks open at their feet. Others are munching on dried meat. They look like lost mountaineers – definitely not part of The Haven's villagers.

"Well? How much farther?" the man asks. "We've been walking in circles for days."

"Yes, but that is because we need to be careful," says the red-haired woman. "We have to be absolutely sure the vampires know we mean them no harm."

I freeze. The woman speaks as if she knows we exist! But then the ludicrousness of the rest of her statement takes me. *Harm?* She thinks that this ragtag bunch of humans can be seen as a threat?

I cannot help it. I start to laugh.

Immediately the man and the woman whip to me. "Who goes there?" she calls out. "Show yourself!"

I bite down my laughter, but I do not move.

"Who are you?" the woman yells. Excited murmurs come from the people behind her. "Friend, or foe?"

And then, on a whim, I decide to toy with her. I'll play her little game.

Let's see how they react when they see a *true* vampire walk into their midst.

I waltz out from my hiding space. Moonlight streams through gaps in the trees.

Gasps sound from the humans when they see me. As they should, as I look like a veritable monster. My clothes are soiled and ragged, my hair is unkempt, and—most of all—my mouth is red with the blood of my latest prey.

"Neither friend nor foe," I say loftily. "But *vampire.*"

At that I expect them to run, or shriek, or scream. They do none of those things. As soon as my pronouncement is made, the woman and man, together as one, drop prostrate to the forest floor.

"Forgive us for not recognizing you, Master," the woman mumbles. "We are not gifted with the same sort of vision you are. The moonlight is pitifully weak, and we dare not use our flashlights."

Their response stops me in my tracks. The people behind her—the rest of the strange ensemble—immediately follow suit. They also throw themselves to the ground as if kneeling before a king.

Is this some mockery? Who are these people? The woman at the front is the only female I see in their whole company.

I step closer. They should be frightened. They should be scampering away. But I smell precious little fear on them. Only... excitement.

"Who are you?" I demand. "How did you get here? Do you know where you are?"

"Oh, yes," the woman answers. "We've been searching for your sanctuary for years. The Haven calls to us all. We are but your humble servants, if you will have us."

Curiosity ripples through me. "You know of The Haven?" I ask.

"We know of The Haven," she answers. "Because you have one of ours."

My eyes narrow in suspicion. "One of your *what?*"

"One of our members." The woman dares a peek up. "You have April."

Chapter Twenty

CARTER

A CAVE BENEATH THE HAVEN

I sneak past the guards who are supposed to be watching The Haven's humans. It helps immensely that they are lazy from the drink I gave them hours before. They were hungry, as are all The Haven's vampires, and a treat of blood from one of the Elite's personal stores was not a gift they could refuse.

Of course, they had no idea it had been tainted with a special mix of herbs known to make vampires sleepy. I'd only put in the slightest amount, just a drop, so they would not be able to detect the taint.

And then I waited... and when the concoction took hold, I knew I was in the clear.

I raise my hand against the burning torchlight that surrounds the human's little space. They are all contained on a relatively small, flat piece of rock inside a cave, with only one way in and one way out.

The humans all remain close to the entrance. They do not want to go past the circle of torches. Rightfully so. Even though they know that, for now, they are protected, and for now, no vampire would dare take their blood, they are smart enough to stay away from the dark places where little... *accidents...* have been known to occur.

A few of them take note of me when I appear. They give no sound of alarm. They are used to the presence of vampires, even if they are not entirely comforted by it. Some of them, in fact, look upon me with a grudging sort of respect.

They know that without The Haven's vampires, they would not have survived the massacre.

I drop down from the cliff edge and walk amongst them. Many are huddled in groups, speaking in low whispers. Those whispers go quiet when I pass. Not that it really matters—if I so wished, I could focus my hearing and listen in on any conversation going on around me.

But I am not here to eavesdrop on the pitiful complaints they are likely making to each other. No, I am here to find one particular girl.

I find her sitting alone, on an uneven rock, far away from everybody else. She tenses as I approach, but does not look up.

"Come to kill me, have you?" she asks when I stop by her side. Her voice is full of resignation and defeat. "Figures. I knew my time was short when we made the deal."

I have no idea what she's talking about—but the information is valuable. I tuck it away into a pocket of my mind.

"No," I tell her soothingly. "That is not why I am here."

She gasps and looks up. Clearly, she was expecting someone else.

I kneel down beside her. "You're April," I say. "Aren't you? We haven't met, but I am—"

"Carter. I know."

A flicker of surprise shows on my face.

"James made sure I knew the names of all the Elite when I was his—"

She coughs and breaks off.

"I understand." I place a hand on her shoulder. "You needn't say more."

To my surprise, she doesn't flinch away. *Tougher than she looks.* I think.

"What do you want?" she asks, point-blank.

"I'm not sure if you're aware of what happened to Captain Commander Smithson," I begin.

She shrugs. "Word spreads, even amongst the humans. I hear he was stripped of his post."

"That's right," I say. "But in talking to him, your name came up… more than once."

She meets my eyes. "So?"

"He said that you are a friend of Eleira's. That you are one of the few humans she trusts. Or maybe—one of the few humans who trusts *her*."

"I knew her before her conversion." April tries to shrug it off. "It's no big deal."

"I recall how you were introduced alongside her at the ceremony."

April gives a quick, bitter laugh. "You think I had a choice in that? It was all the Queen's doing." She looks around. "Anyway, look at me now. It's not like the connection has been much help."

"You're alive," I say. "Surely that counts for something."

She doesn't answer. After a moment, she asks again, "What do you want?"

"I want to help you," I say. "Just as I've been trying to help Smithson."

Her eyes narrow in suspicion. "I don't need your help."

"Are you sure?" I ask. "The former Captain Commander could be put under interrogation." I run a hand through the young girl's hair before forming a fist. I pull her head to me and hiss in her ear, "Who knows what sort of secrets might escape his lips."

She jerks free of my grip. She has definite spunk, this one. "I don't see how that concerns me."

I sigh, and stand up. "Fine," I say. "If you want to be obstinate, be obstinate. But I cannot be the only one who noticed the time you and Captain Commander disappeared, together, underground. Nor am I the only one—" a cruel smile plays on my lips, "—who might be looking for any sort of *information*... that might help my position with the new Captain Commander of the guard."

April looks at me with hard eyes. "And who is that?"

"Phillip Soren," I say.

She gasps.

"You didn't know? I don't fault you." I shrug. "It only happened a day or two ago."

"That's when Phillip brought me here," she whispers. "He didn't say anything about that."

"Yours was the first blood he tasted, was it not?" I shake my head. "Don't bother answering that. It's common knowledge amongst the Elite."

Again she stares at me. "Why did you come, Carter?"

124

"To offer you friendship. That is all."

"What makes you think I need the friendship of another vampire?"

"Is that a no?"

"I don't know you," she says. "I certainly don't trust you. How can I tell if you're not just planning on using me for your own gain?"

I chortle a laugh. "That, dear April, is the one thing you can absolutely rely on." I stand. "But my gain, and yours... do not have to be two mutually exclusive things."

I wink and turn away. "Consider my offer before turning it down. One more ally in a pit full of enemies can never hurt." I gesture at the other humans, all far, far away from us. "I can tell you have few enough friends here."

And then I walk away.

But a moment later I hear her voice. "Carter—wait."

I turn around. She runs up to me.

"Tell me what you want," she says, exhaling. "And I will see what I can do."

I smile. "For now? Just keep your ears open and *listen*." I lower my voice and cast a long look around us. "Not all humans hold as much tolerance for my kind as you do. If you can be my eyes and ears on ground level... I will see that you are properly taken care of. You will be protected."

"It's not protection that I need," she begins.

My eyes twinkle. "Of that, dear girl," I say, "I wouldn't be too sure. I will visit you again when the time is right. Have a pleasant night."

Chapter Twenty-One

RAUL

DEEP BENEATH THE HAVEN

"The Royal Court has been called to order," a messenger informs me from the doorway. "Your presence is requested."

"I'm sure it is," I growl.

The vampire takes a step back. He can sense that I'm not in a pleasant mood.

"How long do I have?" I ask.

"They're gathering right now," he replies.

"Mother knows?"

"The Queen is the one who called the assembly."

"Fine," I say, dismissing the weaker vampire. "Tell them I'm on my way."

He ducks a hasty bow and hurries out of my room.

I look at Eleira, sitting cross-legged on the bed. Her eyes are closed, her face a perfect mask of concentration.

She is so beautiful, I think. And then: *I do not deserve her.*

There is a set of thick playing cards spread out in front of her. There are symbols on the front, of the same sort that I saw in The Book of the Dead.

Morgan gave those cards to Eleira and told her they would help channel her magical abilities. She did it right before taking Cassandra and Phillip out of my room.

I remember the confused look Eleira gave me in the aftermath. "I don't know what she expects me to do with these," she'd said. But then she'd propped herself up in the spot she's in now and started to study them. A light went off in her eyes, and she murmured, "I can't read them... but it's almost like I *know* what these symbols mean."

Ever since then, she's been absolutely quiet, picking a card up, examining it, studying the marks, and then setting it back down before turning to the next.

I did not want to interrupt her, so I left her to it. After our fight, I've been trying my best to keep my temper down.

The wound is causing me more pain than ever. Since Cassandra rescued me, the wound has been throbbing non-stop. Every second I'm awake is spent in absolute agony. The pain is acute, it's pervasive, and I can do absolutely nothing to lessen it.

It makes me feel, somehow, like less of a man.

That is why I've kept my mouth shut. The only comfort I have is Eleira's presence. I do not want to screw anything up by snapping at her—and I'm liable to do so if we engage in conversation.

Suddenly, her eyes pop open. She finds me looking at her. I start to look away, but the smile that spreads across her face makes it impossible.

"What?" I ask.

"The way you look at me," she answers. Her voice hitches. "It's like... like I can sense your love."

Sudden hope blooms in my chest. *Maybe I'm not so far gone as to be unredeemable.*

"You truly think so?" I ask.

She nods and stifles a giggle. "I *know* I'm not imaging things."

I limp to the bed, using the walking stick to support the majority of my weight. Eleira is like a beam of pure, white light in the darkness. Seeing her smile, hearing her laugh—it chases all the heaviness away.

"It's true," I say when I reach her. I crawl onto the mattress. "I *do* love you, Eleira. Even if I've done a crappy job of showing it."

I lean over the playing cards and slowly bring my lips to hers.

The kiss is sweet and sensual. She lets out an adorable sigh when I finally pull away. It tugs on the very strings of my heart.

"When I saw you on the floor," she says, taking my hand and gripping it tight, "I wasn't sure if you were going to wake again. I wasn't sure—wasn't sure if I would ever hear your voice, or look into your wonderful green eyes again." Her grip becomes even tighter. "It scared me."

"Hey. Hey," I promise. "I'm here now, aren't I? Cassandra's given me another chance. This time, I won't blow it."

"She's given you *time*," Eleira clarifies. "But we don't know how much. What happens when that runs out? We don't have a cure."

I shush her by placing my lips on her mouth again. "I will *not* go softly into the night," I vow. I hesitate for a brief second, then make up my mind. "There's something I need to tell you. Something I haven't told anybody else."

"Yes?" she asks, inquisitive.

"The vampire who cut me with the blade. He said that there would be a mess—"

But I'm cut off when the door slams open, and Phillip rushes inside.

"You're still here!" he exclaims. "The Court is getting angry. They're all assembled—they are all waiting for *you*!"

I curse. "Can't they start without me?"

Phillip looks at me like he's never seen me before. "You are the Queen's eldest remaining son," he says. "You are second only beneath her. You cannot skimp your responsibilities to the Court again!"

"Again?" I demand. "You say that as if I've done it before."

"You know what I mean," Phillip grouses.

With a disgruntled sound, I shove off the bed. "Fine," I say. "But I can't say I like it."

"You don't have to like it," Phillip reminds me. "It is your duty to be seen there."

"To be seen weak and hobbled, like this?" I kick out my bad leg.

"Raul..." Phillip says. "This isn't like you. Look, I know things are difficult. But—"

My harsh laugh cuts him off. "Do you, now? Are you the one who almost died?" I can't stop the bitterness from bubbling out of me. "Are you the one who hasn't been given even a second's reprieve since? You talk to me about duty as if you know what it means. What do you really know, Phillip?"

"Raul," Eleira tries to cut in. I snarl right over her.

'You are the Captain Commander now, and how much have you done? What have you changed? Is The Haven safer now, with you at the helm, than it was before? I don't think so!"

"Raul, that's hardly fair!" Eleira exclaims. "He's only had the position for a few days. What do you expect him to do?"

"The Narwhark is still on the loose," I say. "No vampire is safe with it there. And—"

"This is a discussion," Phillip interjects, "that should take place before the Royal Court."

He shares a look with Eleira. I don't like it.

She nods. "Phillip is right."

"Fine!" I say. "Fine, fine. Let's go, then. Let's show all the Haven vampires exactly what their Prince looks like right now."

Chapter Twenty-Two

ELEIRA

DEEP BENEATH THE HAVEN

I've never seen Raul in as bad a mood as he is now.

It's understandable, of course. Going through everything he's gone through in such a short span of time...

Still, the darkness I glimpse beyond his eyes is frightening. It's like something else took hold of him after having been revived with Cassandra's blood.

I know he's fighting it. I know he's worried. I just wish there was something I could do to help.

Raul, Phillip, and I reach the enormous chamber where the Royal Court sits assembled. All conversation dies down when we enter.

Carter, the grey-haired vampire I can't help but have bad feelings about, sneers the minute he sees us. "Took you long enough," he says.

Raul and Phillip walk around to take their spots on either side of the Queen. I stand back on the sidelines.

I hear some of the vampires behind me give snarky remarks about my relationship to the Soren brothers. I ignore it. Their japes can't hurt me now.

"Now that we're all here...?" Morgan starts. "The session of the Royal Court can begin. Last time we were gathered—"

"You left to assess the damage done to The Haven," Deanna cuts in. She looks around at the Royal Court and all the other vampires in the audience. "So? We are all anxious for your verdict."

"The damage is extensive, as you no doubt know," Morgan replies. "For now, it is safer for us to remain underground."

"Yes, but for how long?" Deanna asks. "What steps have you taken to allow us to return to our homes?"

"Are you so anxious to go," the Queen replies, "before the wards are back up?"

"And how long will that take?" Carter demands. "We are wasting away down here, subsisting on *nothing*—while doing nothing to ensure the future looks brighter than it does now!"

"And there's the Narwhark!" somebody else cries out. "The demon has to be contained. It has to be caught and killed—"

"You cannot just *kill* a demon," a vampire pipes in. "The two guards it killed were our most capable fighting men."

"Then we need to hunt it! All of us, banded together as one!"

"Whoever unleashed The Convicted can strike at us again!" a worried female vampire says. The meeting is quickly descending into utter chaos. "What assurance does our Queen give us that another strike will not come?"

"None!" a vampire across the assembly exclaims. "She's done nothing for us since the wards fell!"

Morgan stands. The movement is smooth, but it's enough to draw everybody's attention. The frantic voices quiet down.

"It is true that I have not done as much as I would have liked," she begins. "But it is not for lack of effort. If you remember, it was this court that agreed to keep me locked away while Smithson took control. The days we lost cannot be recovered. Luckily—some things can."

She meets the eyes of two guards standing behind me. They are posted at the second pair of doors leading into the room. She gives the slightest nod.

On her cue, they pull the heavy doors open. They pick up two heavy, black chains from within, put them over their shoulders and start to pull.

There comes a deep groan. And then, from out of the darkness, sitting atop a short trolley, the Queen's massive crystal throne appears.

The guards grunt with effort as they roll it all the way into the room. It comes to a grinding stop not far from the Royal Court's table.

"This," Morgan announces, "was excavated from the rubble of the castle. You all know what it is. You've seen it in the throne room. What you don't know—" her dark eyes sparkle, "—is how lucky we are to have found it undamaged."

Morgan steps away from the table. As she does, I feel, just for a flicker of a second, a wave of great power come from the throne.

I suck in a breath. My heart starts to beat a little bit faster. Now that I have experience with magic, I can tell what the throne *really* is:

A great and powerful torrial.

Carter surges up and bangs an open hand on the table. "Did you forget that you answer to the Royal Court now?" he demands. "The throne is a symbol of who you were—who you *used* to be. There is democracy in The Haven now!" Murmurs of agreement float down from the watching vampires. "There is accountability. You do not rule alone. And you insult us—" Carter turns a circle, and gestures at every single vampire in the room, "—you insult all of us by bringing it back? I say, let the throne be buried! I say, let it remain in the ruins of the castle—exactly where it belongs!"

"Hear, hear!" a voice cries out. Dozens more take up the rallying call.

Carter sits back down and crosses his arms, smug as a cat.

Morgan looks vaguely amused. "You must think I have the memory of a five year old and all the cunning of a blind fish." Now it's her turn to sneer. "I did not bring the throne here to remind you of the past. Carter, you prove your ignorance with that *riling* speech. The throne is an object of magic. It is a torrial, though the meaning of the word is lost on you.

"It is what permits maintenance of the wards. Without it, they would never have been sustained for all the long centuries of my rule. They require a constant stream of magic. The crystal throne is key to that. Even a witch as strong as I am cannot do that without such help.

"Now, here is the key. I've used the throne to maintain the wards for hundreds of years. It can only be linked to one witch at a time. When the castle fell, my link to the throne was broken. It cannot easily be restored. The throne answers only to the Queen of The Haven... and as we all know, time is nigh for a new Queen."

Morgan looks straight at me. "The real reason I called this assembly?" she asks. "Was to begin the process of succession."

Chapter Twenty-Three

ELEIRA

DEEP BENEATH THE HAVEN

On the Queen's pronouncement a chorus of voices rings out. The cries range from offended to incredulous. Mostly, the vampires are confused.

"The succession can only take place under light of the full moon," Morgan continues. "That is when the throne's magic can be passed on to another. That gives us approximately two weeks. Two weeks in which the proper arrangements must be made, and—"

"This is ludicrous!" Deanna exclaims. "The girl you'd have as Queen knows nothing about us! She is not *one* of us—she does not even have a seat on the Royal Court!"

"Her name," Morgan reminds her. "Is Eleira. And she is the most powerful vampire in this coven. You would do well to remember that."

"I remember, all right," Deanna fires back. "I remember the frightened, anxious child you brought before us at her introduction. I look at her now and see the same girl! Nothing's changed—why should *she* be the one to lead us?"

"If you want The Haven restored to what it once was," Morgan says, "you will see that Eleira is named Queen. It is the only way for us to use the throne and restore the wards."

"So why wait?" a vampire calls out. "Why delay until the next full moon? The throne is back. You are at the helm—*you* can set the wards once more!"

A rush of voices join in agreement.

"Unfortunately, no," the Queen says. "My link to the throne was broken when the castle fell. It is what the enemy wanted. Only through Eleira can we re-establish what has been before. And—" she holds up a hand before more protests can rain down, "—before you ask, a witch can only be linked to it *once*. I am truly sorry," she does not show it at all, "but that is the way of magic. It cannot be changed."

Hushed whispers take hold of the crowd.

"At least," Deanna finally says, "we now have a deadline."

"Wait," Carter says. "You speak without hearing from the girl. I am as guilty of that as the next, I admit—but I say it is beyond time for us to hear from Eleira. Let us see what she thinks! Let us hear her thoughts."

Morgan turns her head to me. At her side, Raul stiffens.

She smiles sweetly. "You and I have discussed this before," she says. "Why don't you tell the Royal Court the conclusion we reached?"

I look out at all the hostile faces. I can feel their enmity pulse through the air.

No matter what's happened, they still view me as an outsider. It's a title I doubt I will soon shake.

I stand up and carefully approach the table. The Royal Court members on my side scoot away from me to give me the smallest bit of space.

Morgan inclines her head in invitation. "Go on," she encourages.

I open my mouth to speak—and find myself blanking.

Morgan and I have never discussed *anything* about this. What she just told the Court is an outright lie.

And, suddenly, I feel very much the seventeen-year-old girl that I am. Doubts and uncertainty start to crowd my mind. Who am I to pretend any sort of influence over creatures who've been alive ten, twenty, *thirty* times longer than I have? I might be one of them, yes, and I might be most *powerful* ... but all of that fades to insignificance in light of what they are tasking me with.

They wait for me to speak. The silence stretches. Somebody coughs.

"Eleira," the Queen's voice is terse. "Tell the Royal Court that you can feel the power contained within the throne. We will begin with that."

I give a jerky nod. The back of my neck starts to break out in a cold sweat. What on earth is happening to me? Why am I so nervous? This is completely unlike who I am!

I take a deep breath. *Just like improv at Stanford,* I think. I clear my throat. "I—"

But just then, a strange, black mist starts to collect in the corners of the room and steals my attention. It pools into a thick, swirling liquid.

None of the other vampires seem to see it. *Their* eyes are all on me.

But I cannot look away from the growing darkness.

From out the corner of my vision I see a small, dark shape dart into the room. My breath catches.

The Narwhark!

I feel a shift in the air, and suddenly, everything *slows*.

Time stretches out before me in an endless sea of discontinuity. A vampire on the other side of the table opens his mouth to speak, but his lips are moving at a snail's pace. It's like watching a video recording playing at one one-hundredth of its usual speed.

The darkness grows. It becomes thicker. The sweat on my back turns into a whole-body chill. I try to find the Narwhark again, but it has disappeared. It moves so fast, faster than I've seen it move before.

I wait for the alarm call to go up. But no vampires have noticed the demon. It wouldn't even matter if they had, because they are still frozen in time. The black in the corners now extends to cover the whole of the ceiling. It seeps down the walls, like an oily paint, and pools onto the floor. It swirls and collects beneath each standing vampire, all of whom are absolutely oblivious to it.

Has time truly slowed, or is my mind operating at hyper-speed?

Carter's lips are still moving, caught in the first syllable of his first word. But no sound reaches me.

Yet the chill from the blackness extends to envelop me. The cold washes through me in angry waves, lashing through my muscles and bone. I want to groan. I want to cry out. But there's nothing I can do, because I, like the rest of the vampires, am caught in some type of time warp. My mind works, but my body is dismally slow in comparison.

The black continues to come, to flow out onto the floor. It's thick like oil but non-reflective. In fact—if anything—it catches and absorbs the light. When I look at it, it's like I'm looking at a space that isn't there. Like I'm looking at an *absence* of reality. It's like the black is not part of this world, but something come to erase it, like a hole punctured through a fine, colored painting.

And then, the demon leaps up from nowhere and lands at the back of Morgan's seat. She is oblivious to it, just like all the vampires are oblivious to everything else. It wags its malformed tail in front of the Queen's eyes and then looks at me, almost in mocking, almost in triumph.

Its small, beady eyes meet mine, and I see a spark of intelligence in them.

It knows I'm the only one who can see it, I think. It's a frantic thought.

And then it dips its tail straight down and pricks Morgan's shoulder.

The touch is soft, even delicate, and when it pulls away, only the smallest bead of blood comes out. If it wasn't for my superior vampire vision, I wouldn't even be able to tell the Narwhark *drew* blood from this distance.

That's all it takes, one tiny jab, and then the demon springs off. It lands in the midst of one of those growing dark pits. It casts one more look at me, wily as a thief, and lets the darkness rise up and wash over its body.

And then it melts into the floor, as the darkness scatters away like water on a hot pan.

As soon as it's gone, time speeds back up to normal.

"—frightened," Carter says. "Look at her, she is not fit to lead, she is *frightened* of us all!"

Morgan swats at her neck, right where the Narwhark pierced her. She brings her hand away and looks at her open palm. Finding nothing there, she frowns. She turns to address me, when, all of a sudden, Raul surges up.

"SILENCE!" he screams, even though only Carter was talking.

All the attention turns to him. I want to speak, to give the Queen warning of what I saw, but my tongue is glued to the roof of my mouth.

"SILENCE!" Raul rages on. "I DEMAND COMPLETE SILENCE!"

Fear quickly takes me. The voice coming from his lips is not his. The speech pattern is not his.

What's worse, even though everybody has returned back to normal, I find that *I* cannot move. I cannot speak. I cannot affect anything at all.

Something is wrong. Something is very, very wrong.

Raul's head jerks up in a spasmodic motion. His whole body twitches as words, not of his own volition, stream from his mouth.

"THIS IS MY MESSAGE TO YOU ALL. YOU HAVE SEEN OUR MIGHT. YOU HAVE SEEN OUR POWER. SUBMIT, JOIN US, AND YOU WILL BE SPARED IN THE WAR TO COME. BUT RESIST..." Raul's arms fly out, and he points directly at his mother, "...AND YOU WILL END UP LIKE HER!"

Two things happen at once.

Morgan falters. Her knees give out, and she falls halfway to the floor. She catches herself on the table at the last possible moment.

At the same time, Raul collapses. He goes convulsing to the ground. Red froth spills from his lips as his body twitches, twitches, twitches, in horrible, jerking movements, like a marionette controlled by a demented child.

A great commotion breaks out. "You will not... have my son," the Queen gasps. A flash of light bursts from her body. I see the tell-tale blue glow, but I also see the fine, individual strands of the spell, the kaleidoscope of colors that can only be glimpsed by those with The Spark. I see them rush like thousands of tiny fireflies toward Raul. They descend upon him and flow into his body. He becomes surrounded by a protective aura.

The convulsion stops. He goes still.

And then the Queen takes her final breath, closes her eyes, and drops to the floor.

Chapter Twenty-Four

PHILLIP

DEEP BENEATH THE HAVEN

It all happened so fast.

I knew something was wrong the moment Eleira stood up. When she took so long to speak, it's like my mind started to splinter. I *felt* a menacing force enter the room.

But I could not pinpoint its source. Before I knew it, that splintering became a hammering at my temples. It would not let up. I seemed to be caught in a vortex, unable to tell exactly *what* was off but keenly aware that there was something.

And then Raul uttered that horrible scream and called for silence and delivered his speech…

I have no doubt in my mind who it came from. The vampires of Father's coven. The vampires of The Crypts.

After Mother uttered that life-giving spell to spare Raul, absolute mayhem broke out. By then, I'd snapped to my senses and took command of the situation as Captain Commander should.

I tell the guards to run and lock down the stronghold. Nobody is to come in or out. I double the sentries on duty before telling all the gathered vampires to return to their rooms.

Carter, as expected, protests loudly. But I think his bravado more ceremonial than real.

Even *he* was shaken when he saw the Queen fall.

Finally, the hall is empty save for Eleira, Raul, Mother, and me. I give voice to the fear plaguing all of us.

"We've been compromised."

Raul is awake, thank the heavens. He claims not to remember anything of what happened, though. My concern, as is Eleira's, lies now with Mother.

"I *saw* the Narwhark," Eleira says. "I saw it, and it looked at me. And I felt like it had... become different. Like it had grown. Like it knows what it's doing, that it's more than a creature of base instinct."

I nod solemnly. "I suspect as much." I go on to explain exactly what I felt when I watched the Narwhark feeding on Smithson's two guards.

Eleira looks truly frightened by the time I'm done. "Morgan said she was the only one who could destroy it," she says. "Because she is a witch. But she never told me what to do. I haven't any idea of how to fight it!"

"Maybe you can't," Raul says darkly.

My head whips to him. "What?"

"If the Narwhark's attack was unprovoked, that would be one thing," my brother says. "But it happened at exactly the same time as the..." he shudders, "...message."

He then proceeds to tell us exactly what the vampire who gave him the flesh

143

wound said. About receiving a message from the King, about the link that he claimed would be formed between the master of the blade and the one it touched.

"But why didn't you say anything before?" Eleira exclaims. She gestures wildly at the body of the queen. "That's *exactly* the sort of information that could have helped her find a cure!"

"You speak as if she's dead!" Raul snarls.

"Easy," I stand between them. It doesn't take much for me to assume my natural role as peace keeper. After all, I've been doing it for my two brothers for hundreds of years. "We don't need to fight."

"Eleira, you said you could probe me, look into the cause of my injury," Raul says. "Do the same for the Queen. Tell us what her condition is."

Eleira shakes her head. "I... cannot," she admits. "I could do it to you because your mind is unguarded. But Morgan is a witch. Hers is closed off to all but the most skillful. And even then..."

"Even then what?" Raul asks.

"Even then, what do you think we would find?" Eleira says. "She's breathing. She's still alive."

"But in a coma," I say.

We'd tried waking her multiple times already, with no success.

"Yes, yes exactly!" Eleira says. "And the spell she cast just before she fainted— she did it to protect you! The only thing I know for sure is that if I try anything, on you, or on her, I risk disrupting it. There's a balance here, a delicate balance, and I will *not* be the one who throws it off!" I see angry tears form in her eyes. "She gave you yet *another* chance, Raul. Do not waste it!"

It shocks me how stoic my brother remains. Here is the woman he claims to love, showing so much passion—and he is all-but-blind to it?

"Is it true?" Raul, ignoring all she said, asks. "What Mother told the assembly about the throne?" The looming crystal structure stands in the background like an enormous elephant in the room. "How it is the object that allowed her to maintain the wards? How it can only be linked to one witch at a time?"

Eleira slumps down. "I don't know," she admits. "This was the first I'd ever heard of it."

"It's like her staff, isn't it?" I ask. "It allows the user to wield greater power?"

"I can sense the magic in it," Eleira replies. "So yes. It is a torrial. But I think it's unlike any other in existence."

"What makes you say that?"

"From everything your Mother taught me—which, admittedly, hasn't been much—torrials are greatly prized and very rare. The amount of magic needed to maintain consistent wards around all of The Haven is enormous. I appreciate that now. I think the throne might be one of the strongest ever created."

I nod. "That makes sense."

"We will need to send a delegation to The Crypts," Raul says under his breath.

I blink. "Excuse me?"

"Somebody needs to talk to Father," Raul says. He looks at me, and then over at Eleira. "We need peace between our covens. If we do not do something now, how many more lives will be lost? How much further uncertainty will we face?" He pauses for a moment and then says, "I will go."

"What!" Eleira and I exclaim at the same time.

"It has to be me," Raul continues. "I understand that, too. The message the vampire gave me in the fight—and the one that was passed through me today— they all point to that being the only choice. Phillip, you are responsible for the entirety of the guard. You cannot go. And Logan won't entertain any but his sons. There is nobody else."

"What about your leg?" I demand. "You're in absolutely no state to go!"

"If I remain, it will only get worse. The Crypts are the one place where may- be—*maybe*—a cure can be found."

I shake my head. "I don't like it," I say. "Not at all. But…"

"*What?*" Eleira demands. Her tears are very visible now. "What? Are you sid- ing with him, too?"

I spread my arm. "Raul is right. What choice do we have?"

My brother gives a grim nod. "I'll have to leave immediately. Before the Royal Court hears of the plan. They will bicker for days without taking action. We can- not afford to wait that long. Not just for me—but for Mother, too. She needs a strong, capable witch to heal her. I know of no other place where one can be found. Father demonstrated what his coven is capable of with the most recent attack. We survived, but he speaks of war as if it's inevitable." His hand tightens into a fist. "We must do all that we can to prevent it."

He turns to Eleira. "You say you saw the demon stab Mother with its tail. But I cannot believe the Narwhark is being controlled in any way by vampires from

Father's coven. Can you?"

Eleira shakes her head. "No. Absolutely not."

"Then it was just coincidence, the timing of it all?" I don't bother hiding the skepticism that fills my voice. "The demon attack, the message from The Crypts? All of it just *happened* to occur concurrently?"

"We have two enemies right now. Both of whom are known to us," Raul says. "Father's coven and the demon. We cannot lump them together and pretend they are one."

"But I do think that something—or someone—was telling the Narwhark what to do," Eleira says.

Both Raul and I turn to her. "What makes you say that?"

"The way it looked at me." Eleira shivers. "It was like it *knew* what was in my mind."

"That doesn't prove anything," Raul continues.

"No, but the demon is made to *kill*. It is a predator, more so than any of us. For it to simply stab the Queen and leave... it had a purpose acting the way it did. The only way I can see that being possible is if it's being manipulated by another entity." Eleira looks uncertain for a moment. "That sounds crazy, doesn't it?"

"Sometimes," I say slowly, "you have to trust your intuition. You are becoming more attuned to it with every passing day. The vampire inside of you is growing stronger. I know," I add, "because I am experiencing exactly the same thing."

"We need to get Mother somewhere safe where she can be looked after," Raul says.

"I'll have her brought to her rooms. A double guard will be posted at her doors."

"No," Raul says. "Make it triple, at least."

I nod grimly. Leave it up to my brother to take up rightful command.

Chapter Twenty-Five

RIYU

THE CRYPTS

"The message has been delivered, my King," Dagan, the leader of my company, reports to Logan. "The Haven has been given its choice."

My Father—no, the *King*. I have to stop thinking of him as family!—gives a curt nod. "How will they respond?"

Dagan is thrown off by the question. "I... cannot say, my Lord." From my vantage point at the far wall of the room, I see the way his huge muscles tighten.

"You were there, weren't you? You were the one who last saw my son? You—" the King steps away from his throne, "—were the one who slashed him with that gruesome weapon."

I am very attuned to the King's moods, and I can feel the bridling anger barely contained beneath his words.

"As you gave me permission to," Dagan counters.

"No," Logan says softly. "I did not *once* give permission to use such a disgusting thing against my own kin!"

Dagan goes absolutely still. "When Beatrice gave it to me, I assumed—"

"I know what you assumed. It doesn't take a brilliant strategist to figure that out! But Beatrice is not *me*, she does not speak for *me*, she does not act for *me*, and she certainly..." the King spits right into Dagan's face, "...does not issue commands to the lieutenant of my First Guard that can be obeyed without first being confirmed with me!"

His anger is rising quickly.

"Where is the blasted woman?" Logan roars. "Who has seen her last? You, there, Riyu. I know she confides in you. Come forth."

Surprise whips through me at being addressed directly. Most of my interactions with the King come from instructions passed down through the chain of command.

I step from my spot and approach. I bow my head in respect. I do not speak.

I learned long ago that it is best, for one as weak as I, to simply observe. Observe, stay quiet, stay in the shadows, remain hidden... remain *unseen*.

Until the proper opportunity presents itself to pounce without hesitation.

"She gave you the weapon and told you to do your..." the King's upper lip twists in disgust, "...*magic* upon it. Is that right?"

I nod. Father—*the King, dammit, I need to get my thoughts in order!*—has never hidden his disdain for a male wielding magic.

Even though he understands the advantage magic can bring, he is of the old school, which believes that magic was only entrusted to women because they are the weaker sex. For a man to be born with The Spark... well, in the King's eyes, it is a sign of that man's inherent weakness.

"And then you gave the weapon to Dagan, who did not hesitate to make use of it. Is that so?"

Once more, I nod.

"And you *also* helped him find my son on the battlefield and isolate him from the rest, so that he could be infected by the twisted blade. So in reality, all fault falls on you!"

I lick my lips but do not speak. I take the tirade in stride.

In fact, in recent weeks, the vampires of The Crypts have grown more and more used to the King's swinging moods. He has been known to go from furious to tranquil in the blink of an eye.

This is simply par for course.

"Enough of this." Beatrice's voice breaks through my thoughts. I feel her approach from behind.

I do not look her way. It would be a grievous mistake for a vampire of my strength to turn away from the King.

"You," Logan grunts. "Where have you been? *You* are the cause of all this, you—"

She shuts him up by stepping up to him and kissing him. Logan has always been a man of stark passions. This woman knows exactly how to incite them... and how to calm them down.

The King goes from barely reserved to ravenously passionate. I dare a quick glimpse at Dagan. He's watching the display with complete apathy. But I cannot help but feel the stirring of some very bad, very unwanted emotions in my gut.

I tear my eye away from the heavily muscled vampire. If anybody even *sus-*

pected my secret…

Quickly, I stem those thoughts. Better not entertain the horrendous possibilities.

Eventually the King lets his woman go. He yanks her to his side and openly gropes her ass. Some of the rage has flowed out of him.

"You should not chastise poor Riyu so," Beatrice says sweetly. "If the fault lies with anyone, it is with me. Yes, I let both your lieutenant and his trusted under servant assume the command came from you. I take the blame." Her voice turns sultry. "So punish *me*, if you're going to punish anyone."

A growl of deep desire comes from the King's throat. I don't know the sort of bedroom games they play, nor do I want to.

"Later," he promises. "When we are in a more suitable space."

"The King can do as he pleases anywhere," Beatrice reminds him. "Dismiss all these men, and have me *now*."

A trickle of discomfort goes down my spine.

"I would, but I am not done with them."

"Then tell them what you want. But be quick about it. My recent *activities* have given me quite the appetite for…"

She leans in and whispers the final word in his ear.

It sounds a lot like "lock."

The atmosphere in the room shifts. Few know exactly the sort of experiments Beatrice runs underground. But all have heard the agonizing screams, the shrieks for mercy, which occasionally drift up from her "laboratories."

Vampires are ruthless killers. None of us shy away from a little blood. But what Beatrice is doing, the mystery surrounding it, and the absolute immunity with which she operates makes even the most hardened vampires just a little bit... tense.

A sound of pleasure comes from the King's throat as Beatrice runs her hand up and down his chest. Once more my gaze flickers to Dagan as that hand dips past Logan's waist and explores the other contours of the King's body.

"This is what I want," the King finally says, once his attention has been brought back to us. "I want The Haven to know the offer of peace is real. There cannot be death on either side while they contemplate it. That means—" the King casts Dagan a hard look, "—that my son cannot be allowed to die. If one of their Elite is struck down while they debate and confer, they will never submit to us. I know the woman who rules that coven very well. She is not the one to stay meek. We have *made* her meek, we have demonstrated our power, we have shattered the safety of her little world. Now that she knows what she is up against, she is more malleable to our suggestions. But make no mistake. Push her more, and she will fight back like a cornered cat."

Dagan goes to one knee. "What would you have me do?"

"The link exists between you and Raul. You will use it to ensure his continued survival. Until we hear back."

"And how long will we wait, my King?"

"We give them a week. That is enough time to contemplate exactly what we are offering."

"A wise decision," Beatrice murmurs.

The King allows himself a self-indulgent smile. "Patience is a great virtue of mine," he says.

Inside my head, I cannot help but scoff.

Dagan hesitates. "The link exists, yes," he says. "But…"

The King's eyes flash. "But what?"

For a glimmer of a moment, I see the black, floating specks swarm in the whites around his pupils.

"But Dagan can do nothing to control how fast the poison spreads," Beatrice finishes for him. "Only I can. And for that, I need the one who enchanted the weapon with me. I need Riyu."

"Have him then," Logan says dismissively. "But woman…" a ragged hardness fills his voice, "if you ever go behind my back like this again, the experiments you conduct beneath the earth will pale in comparison to what I do to you."

At this threat, Beatrice actually falters. "Y—yes, my King," she says.

I think: *And now he's back.*

Chapter Twenty-Six

RAUL

DEEP BENEATH THE HAVEN

"All the arrangements are made," Phillip tells me, only hours after I gave my intentions to leave. "The plane is ready. The guards have been to the airfield and confirmed it's safe."

"And you trust them?" I question.

"*Trust* is a little difficult to conjure up at the moment," he says.

I grunt. It seems after the fight with The Convicted, we've had nothing but a barrage of bad news.

"But I rely on them," Phillip continues. "We both do. And they are of our own coven, not vampires brought here by Smithson."

"Who's to say they haven't been corrupted by his influence?" I ask.

Phillip regards me for a moment. "I haven't seen you this way for a very long time."

"What way?" I ask.

"Dark. Brooding. Suspicious."

I bark a laugh. "No? Don't be surprised. It's in our nature."

Phillip shakes his head. "Not like this. You haven't been like this since Liana."

"Do *not* speak to me of her!" I snap.

Phillip doesn't react to my outburst. His behavior is at odds with what I've come to expect.

Then again, he's changed—grown. Not only from taking April's blood. That was just the initial push.

He's grown leaps and bounds since being made responsible for the guard.

"That proves it," he says. "She's on your mind. Isn't she?"

"Who? Liana? No, of course not—"

"Not Liana. Eleira!"

I turn away. "Eleira is always on my mind," I grumble. I trail a hand over the small marble statue in the room. "Why wouldn't she be?"

"And yet, she's not here," Phillip says. "You sent her away."

"What do you know of it?" I hiss. A hard knot of anger tightens in my stomach. "When have you ever been in love?"

"I know that you care for Eleira and that she cares for you. I know that you should be together, not apart. Especially at a time like this. I know—" Phillip steps around me so he can look into my eyes, "—that you are a better man when she is near."

The knot of anger threatens to explode. I fight it with all I have.

But the constant pain in my leg augments the perpetual agony. It makes my thinking murky and unclear.

Still. Still! Who is Phillip to lecture me now?

"You haven't seen us *together*," I say, with no small amount of venom in my voice. "If you had, you'd realize that same thing I do. That right now, we need to be apart."

"Why?" Phillip asks. "What are you afraid of?"

What does he think I'm afraid of? I want to scream at him. It's glaringly obvious to me, and yet Phillip does not seem to see it.

I grunt. "Nothing."

He takes my shoulders. "Tell me," he insists.

With a grotesque snarl, I rip away. It's all I can do to stop from punching him in the face.

"I've granted you too much leeway," I hiss, "because you are my brother. No more. You will respect the boundaries set by the vampire hierarchy. You are *beneath me*, Phillip, and you will not question what I do!"

But if I expect my brother to back down, I have greatly underestimated him.

"That's not you speaking," he fires back. "Listen to yourself!"

"Leave," I command. "Leave me now."

With my mind, I push out using the vampiric influence I possess.

Phillip looks at me in disgust. He feels the force, but resists it. "So it comes to that," he mutters. He shakes his head. "Maybe you are right. Perhaps you and Eleira *do* need to be apart."

He turns and exits the room. The door closes with a bang.

I wait for a count of twenty. And then, in a blind rage, I hurl my globe into the wall.

It shatters into a hundred tiny fragments. It's not enough. My muscles tense, my claws threaten to come out. My breathing deepens. I feel the need to destroy, to *kill*, with all my being. My fangs protract, and I catch the very, very faint scent of human blood in the air, coming from the cavern where the villagers are kept.

I am so tempted. So very tempted, to race down there and feast on their blood. Forget this agony! I could satiate in the reprieve, in the bloodlust, in the rage and violence inherent in me.

I could kill them all, and who would stop me? Their blood might not stave off the corruption taking hold of my body forever, but it would revitalize me, it would reenergize me, it would make me more into the vampire that I truly am. It would open up the floodgates. I would welcome the beast. I would feast on them all with absolute conviction, the blood would be mine, *their* blood, theirs, theirs, theirs, so sweet and rich and hot and full of life!

But then the depravities of my thoughts come to me. I stagger back from shock. My shoulder hits the wall.

I'm breathing hard—nearly gasping. The wound in my leg pulses with sickening intensity.

That's the cause of this, I know it. It's why I had to send Eleira away. The wound is robbing me of who I am.

I've been given chance after chance after chance. But there is no denying the inevitable. Maybe *that* is the root of my behavior. Maybe *that* is the root of all my discontent.

Because the fear Phillip asked me of? It preys on my mind. Eleira cannot be with me now. She cannot be allowed in my company.

Because if she is, and she falls even a little bit deeper for me—well, I cannot sentence her to such a fate.

I cannot doom the woman I love to a broken heart when I die.

Chapter Twenty-Seven

ELEIRA

DEEP BENEATH THE HAVEN

I'm pissed. I'm pissed, and I think that I have every right to be.

The moment Raul announced his intention to go see his Father he made it clear that he would do it alone. His explanation—something about my safety, something about my being needed here, in case Morgan wakes—was lame and feeble and devoid of conviction. It was tepid and weak.

Before I could get a say in, he simply left.

So I went with Phillip to find the appropriate guards to stand at Morgan's door. I stayed with the Queen for a bit, but could not help the feeling of utter uselessness that took me every time I glimpsed her still and quiet form.

So, eventually, I left and started wandering the halls of the underground stronghold.

That's where I am now. Walking around, by myself. So far, nobody's given me any trouble. My new senses alert me to the presence of other vampires.

They've been doing a great job avoiding me, too.

Maybe they can sense my growing anger. Or maybe they're all planning, plotting, conjuring up some scheme to—

I catch myself thinking that. Some scheme to do what, exactly? My suspicions have never flared as much as they are now.

Why is that? Is it the uncertainty that is playing with my mind? Is it Raul's strange iciness?

Or is it the turmoil, this upheaval, the absolute lack of safety that has me feeling like a rat caught in a trap?

My bloodlust is growing, too. Without the steady stream of drink from the banks, the hunger pangs are a constant. My body needs nourishment—needs it to grow, to prosper. To help become who I am meant to be.

I don't shy away from that reality anymore. I am meant to be a *vampire*.

No use in fighting the inevitable.

So I'm not entirely surprised when my path leads me to the entrance of the cavern where the humans are kept.

The two guards at the door try to stand in my way. "We've been given orders not to let anyone through."

But I'm not having it. Not in my current mood. I exert my vampire influence over them and say, darkly, "Do you know who I am?"

"Of course." One of them bows his head. "You are the Queen's chosen successor. But we answer to the Royal Court. Our instructions are clear. We… cannot…"

He struggles with the words as I force onto him more and more of my strength.

"…cannot… let you through!" He finishes with a gasp. He snarls at me and looks at his companion. "Bitch tried to influence me," he gripes.

"Excuse me?" I demand. "What did you call me?"

The second guard steps closer. "You better run along now, little girl," he says, hiding none of his disdain. "You don't want the Royal Court to hear of what you tried to do."

Then I realize where I'm standing... and it occurs to me that all I'm really doing is trying to pick a fight.

That's so unlike me.

I huff and turn away—and step right into that grey-haired vampire, Carter.

"Ah, Eleira," he says, taking my elbow. "Just the woman I wanted to see." He looks over my shoulder. "Are either of these guards giving you trouble?"

"No," I stay stiffly. There's something greasy about Carter. He'd obviously sensed me and followed me here—and that rubs me the wrong way.

"Will you come with me?" he asks, while tightening his grip on my arm. "You would do me a great honor if you gave me but a minute of your time."

Somehow, I get the feeling that his "request" is not a request at all.

"Fine," I say. I jerk my arm free of his grip. "But I can walk myself there."

"But of course." Carter gives an obsequious smile. "Follow me."

He takes me along a twisted route through many hallways and doors. We don't pass another vampire once.

Finally, we arrive before a set of grand double doors. They tower over us, stretching all the way to the ceiling. They are made of heavy oak, lined with iron bars, and inlaid with all sorts of precious stones and rubies.

"What is this?" I ask. "Where did you bring me?"

"I wanted to show you something I thought would help with your... decision," he says.

"Decision? What decision?"

But instead of answering, he reaches into his pocket and takes out a long, silver key.

He pushes it into the hole and twists. The heavy mechanism inside the doors rattles as it's activated.

Then the door pops open, ever-so-slightly, looming ajar. Carter smiles at me and motions me through. "After you."

I don't like this—but I won't have him see me intimidated. I push open the door the rest of the way and step inside.

The sight that greets me is unlike anything I could have imagined.

There are paintings on the walls. Huge, enormous paintings, framed with elaborate finishes of intricately worked gold.

Each one of the paintings contains a vampire soul inside.

"Quite a collection," Carter notes. The door closes with a jarring thud. "Don't you think?"

I do a quick count. There are at least thirty paintings on the walls. The chamber contains nothing else.

Carter senses my wonder. "What? Did you truly think the Queen kept *all* of her prisoners on display in her home?" He chuckles. "No, no. Those were only the ones who were publically convicted of their crimes. *These* men and women—" he sweeps a hand around us, "—were vampires who had simply... disappeared."

Carter begins a slow walk around the circular room. "They were cast as runaways. That had always been the explanation for a vampire who'd gone missing. *He wanted to get away,* they would say. *He wanted the freedom afforded by the Outside.*"

Carter shakes his head. "In truth? The Haven's vampires know they will not find anything better out there. Moreover... they know our Queen would *never* let them escape."

He looks at me and waits for the words to sink in.

"So maybe some of these *were* runaways, you see. They did not get far. They would be caught, and the spell would be cast that severed their souls from their bodies."

"Why are you telling me this?" I dart an anxious look at all the portraits. The vampires inside seem to be watching me with shifting eyes.

"I want to further your education," Carter replies. "It helps to elucidate you on matters that will be of import to you soon, don't you think? I simply want you to understand the type of ruler you are dealing with as you cozy up to our Queen."

He stops in front of a portrait of a stunning male. "Ah, Lucien," he says. He traces the outer edge of the portrait. "He was my brother and amongst the very first damned to this fate."

I suck in a ragged breath. The temperature of the room has noticeably dropped with those words.

"It's why you have not been Outside," I whisper. "It's why none of you have."

He smiles. "So you understand why I took to the accusation aimed at me so poorly."

"So all those things you said—about hunting humans, about going Outside—were those a farce?"

"No. I want all those things. The Queen has forbidden them for so long. Most of our vampires are not even aware of the prohibition. They simply go on living as they do, with no thought of escape." He chuckles. "What a strange word. 'Escape.' And yet, that is exactly what getting out of The Haven would be.

"The Queen did not act alone in this." Carter turns to look at me. "Every single spell cast to condemn a vampire into these prisons was sanctioned by the Royal Court. And I hope *that* helps you understand, Eleira, the sort of vampires who can stand beside you... or be rallied as your foes."

He walks to the door and pulls it open. "That's enough of a history lesson for now. If I may give one last piece of advice?" He doesn't wait for my response. "Think very, *very* carefully on who you make friends with... and who you pick as your enemies."

I swallow.

"Oh, and before I forget." Carter pulls out a thin, square envelope from his breast pocket. "This was left for you. By an... acquaintance of mine."

He starts to hand it to me but stops with it an inch away from my hand. "Take care not to read it where others are around, hmm? Certain associations would be smart to avoid for one in a position as precarious as yours." He gives one last, empty smile. "Thank you for granting me your time. I appreciate it. I truly do."

Chapter Twenty-Eight

ELEIRA

DEEP BENEATH THE HAVEN

I recognize the flowery, flowing script on the envelope's front instantly. There are only two words—*To Eleira*—but there is only one person in the entire world who writes the first 'E' of my name with such an elaborate swirl.

My mother.

My heart is racing when I get to my room. Quickly, I lock the door. I take the letter out and try to steady my shaking hands.

A million questions storm through my mind. How did Carter get this? If he hasn't been Outside in hundreds of years—does that mean my Mother is *here?* But no, of course not. I would have seen her amongst the humans if she was.

Another terrifying possibility flashes: what if she's a vampire? What if she's *always been* a vampire?

I shake my head. I'm being ridiculous. I've seen her out in the sun. She can't *be* one of us—

A chill takes me.

"One of us."

Does it make me a horrible daughter, knowing how little thought I've given to my family ever since my abduction? Or how much easier it is for me to associate with The Haven vampires than it is with my own mother?

I try to steady my frantic thoughts. But they won't be calmed until I see the contents of the letter.

Perhaps, not even then.

On shaking legs I make my way to the bed. I perch on the edge. My entire body feels tight, stressed, as if a plastic sheet has been shrink-wrapped around me.

I open it and start to read:

To my darling daughter:

I knew that a time would come when you would be taken from us. I'd known it all along, since the moment you were brought into my life. This message is... difficult to write. How do I express in mere words how much I love you, how much you mean to me? The first time I saw your face seventeen years ago, a flood of love came over me. I was mired, lost, in a deep depression then. You were the light that came from the sky and parted all the clouds.

I pause. My mother had never been anything but happy and energetic for as long as I've known her. Depression? It seems nothing like her.

A bit of worry gnaws at my insides: now that I'm gone, might she fall into that awful state again? I pray not.

I read on:

You were such a gift, Eleira. A beautiful, wondrous, flourishing gift. As your father and I watched you grow, you amazed us with your curiosity, you inquisitiveness, your innate, inherent intelligence.

We knew right away that you were special. You're finding out just how special you are now. But that is not what I mean. You were always so full of joy, so full of life. You were so eager to explore the world, and to make everything you came in contact with better. Your enthusiasm was contagious, and, even as a child, it helped change your father and me.

We both became better people. More content, more at ease. Freer. Happier. All because of you.

So we both owe you everything, precious child. For seventeen amazing, golden, wonderful years you were the central focus in our lives. We knew we would not have you forever. Believe me when I say that we both cherished every single moment you were with us.

As I said: I knew from the start that our time together was limited. It was a secret endowed onto me first. I did not share it with your father. But once I saw how much his love shone for you, I had to tell him. Otherwise, he would be crushed when it came time for you to leave. He does not reveal his vulnerabilities often. He did, with you. For you.

And both of us now understand that you are gone. Maybe not where, maybe not even exactly why... but we've accepted it as an inevitability. Do not cry for us. This is not the end, but the beginning. For you, for your new life, and for all the adventure that will come your way.

I feel some tears building up exactly at that moment. My mother knew she would have to give me up? How?

I notice a dried drop on the page that nearly makes me lose it. Still I read on...

I know it's hackneyed for a mother to give her daughter advice. I know you're way too smart for your own good, and that all these things will be obvious to you. After all, most of them I learned because of you, because of that amazing gift of life that you have given me.

Still, indulge a loving parent. Don't dismiss these out-of-hand.

The first is to always remember who you are. Your life circumstances have changed. I cannot imagine the turmoil you might be going through. But if there's one thing you've proven time and time again, it's your resilience, your adaptability, your ability to find the good in any situation. So take the good with the bad (and I pray there will be significantly more good than bad for you) and don't lose sight of what makes you you.

The second is to always take a moment to appreciate the wonders of life. The trees outside, the flowers blooming in the sun, the amazing planet on which we make our home—it is a miracle. It is a miracle to be witnessed and adored. The possibilities out there, for you, are boundless.

Third is to always leave room in your heart for love. At times that might seem impossible. You are not naïve, but you are not yet experienced—not in the full aches and pains of the heart. Fall in love, make mistakes, value those moments. Fall out of love. Allow your heart to be broken. No life is complete without that tragedy.

But you will emerge from it stronger on the other side, and the experience will ground you, it will help you, it will make you appreciate all you have so much more.

The last is to never forget your roots. I do not know if you and I will ever see each other again. I hope, of course, that one day, a few years in the future...

But I'm getting sappy. Eleira, I am so excited for you. There is sadness in my heart, yes, but it is overwhelmed with joy for the simple fact that now, you are coming into your own. You are becoming who you really are and what you were always meant to be.

I stop reading again. My eyes are moist. My heart beat has slowed down a tad, but it's still pounding with enough force for me to feel each contraction.

My mother *knew*? She knew I would be taken away, and that I wouldn't be able to come back. But how? Who told her, and what—

I stop that line of thought and turn back to the letter. There might be answers there.

Even if I don't see you again, know that you have gifted me the best seventeen years of my life. Nothing can compare to the joy I had watching you grow. Nothing can compare to the all-consuming love I felt for you. You gave me all those things, but a hundred, a thousand times greater than I could have ever imagined them to be.

I've dawdled long enough. There are things that I need to tell you, things you need to know. They may be difficult truths, but my hope in revealing them is that they will help you, in some small way, to find your true path through the world.

The first, and biggest, is this: while your father and I are your parents, and we will forever remain so, we are not linked to you by blood.

My breath catches.

I had a horrible premonition from the start of the letter. The way everything was framed, I was expecting something, *something* like this…

But to actually see the words written out, to read them in my own mother's handwriting on the page…?

It brings a new gravity to it all.

But that lessens nothing. *It does not diminish the love I feel for you. It does not make me any less your mother. You grew up with me, you were my child, and you will forever be my truest daughter. Biologically, we may be unrelated—but what does biology know of love?*

And now, you have every right to hate me. It takes a special sort of coward to tell her daughter something so important only through a written letter. But trust me when I say that this decision was not made lightly. Your father and I debated many times telling you the truth when you were still with us. But we had something so, so good, the three of us did, and a revelation like that, when we knew that our time together had a deadline, could have ruined it all.

Ultimately, he and I, together, decided to wait.

It was like your decision to leave our little hometown and go discover your place at Stanford. We were so thrilled for you when you got in. Of course we didn't want you to leave us, we wanted you close to home. We wanted to extract every moment of joy that we could from you until the time came for you to be taken away.

But we promised each other, also, that we would never disrupt your happiness. And that was the justification for keeping your birth a secret. We only wanted to return to you the exact same gift you bestowed upon us.

Now tears are really flowing. I snuffle and wipe them away with my sleeve. How could she think I would hate her? The fact that she's not my biological mother means next-to-nothing to me. She—and my dad—have all my love. They have all my love, all my appreciation, and whenever I think of my *parents*, theirs are the only faces that will ever come to mind.

But that does not hamper this new, growing sense of curiosity within me about who my real mother and father were.

Let me say one more time how much I love you, how much you mean to me. Your father has stood over my shoulder the entire time I spent writing this. His love is here, too.

I wish I could glimpse a small way into the future and promise you that we will meet again. But such is not in my capacities. I hope this letter finds you well, Eleira, and though I do not know if it will reach you, the man who came assured us that it will.

One last thing. Only the beings you are with now can elucidate you on the true circumstance of your birth. Look to them for that final truth.

With boundless, eternal, forever love...

Marie.

Wow. I take a deep breath. Wow, wow, wow.

"Beings." She didn't use the term "vampires." How much does she know of them?

What else do I say to that? I can't imagine how difficult it must have been for my mother to write. She *knew* that I would be taken away? She *knew* that our time together would be short?

I flip back to the first page and read the letter again, hoping to find some hidden clue, some extra meaning. But no, all is as it appears on first impression. My mother definitely laid her heart on the line.

As carefully as I can, I fold the letter up and place it back in the envelope. I clutch it to my chest for a moment as I let the tears fall. I don't feel overly sad, or sappy, just... emotional. This is a lot to take in.

I look around the room.

This is my life now, I think. *There's no denying it.*

The next question is... how did Carter get the letter... and how would I pass a return one to my mother?

Chapter Twenty-Nine

RIYU

THE CRYPTS

"The staff was not it!" the King rages before me. He hurls a crystal vase into the wall. It shatters with an ear-splintering crash. "You—and you—" he flings a finger out toward me, then Beatrice, "—both assured me that the *staff* was key to her power!"

I remain absolutely still and try to make myself as small as possible. I dare not speak against the King, given all that he has against me.

But the woman in the room is a capable ally.

"The staff was a torrial of great power, my Lord," Beatrice says. She's wearing nothing but a sheer white night robe. I can see her womanly shape underneath. It appeals to me not at all. "It was stronger than any we have in our possession."

"That *you* know of," Logan snarls.

Beatrice makes a sound of impatience in her throat. "Yes. That I know of. If you allowed me unfettered access to the storerooms beneath the earth—"

The King cuts her off with a harsh laugh. "And expose even more of myself to your whims? Never."

"Then, yes, the staff is stronger than anything in our possession," she says, the annoyance clear on her face.

I'd been summoned into the King's private bed chamber an hour ago. I came as fast as I could. When the King calls, you answer.

But so far, all that I've witnessed is this ongoing argument between him and his... lover.

"And what do you think of all this, boy?" Logan demands, glaring at me. "You're the one who showed James the book. *You're* the one who always used the damn thing!"

He does nothing to hide his distaste for a male wielding magic.

I take the barest, most intricate step forward. "The staff served its purpose," I say, picking my words carefully. "We successfully destroyed The Haven's wards with it."

Of course, *I* was the one to do that...through the link between James, The Ancient, and me ...

But I would never presume to make such bold claims before the King. So I use the plural, "we."

"And you *successfully*," the King mocks, "destroyed the very same torrial that was so important to us!"

"Easy. Be easy, my King," Beatrice says, flowing up behind him and taking him by the shoulders. "It is not Riyu's fault."

She starts to massage his muscles. Her touch seems to help ease some of his sour mood.

He takes a deep breath, visibly trying to calm some of his rage. "Explain yourself," he says, though whether to me or Beatrice is not exactly clear.

She and I share a look. She gives the most miniscule nod, a sign for me to go ahead. I steel myself and start to speak.

"A single torrial can only handle so much magic flowing through it at once. What was done with the staff—" I want to say, '*what I did with the staff*', but drawing attention to my abilities in front of the King is a poor idea, "—pushed it past its limits. Then it shattered, it broke—it burnt out. Such is always the risk."

"Imagine if it had not," Beatrice coos in his ear. "Imagine if James had returned wielding it and handed it to you. We would have assumed that the staff *was* it, that the staff *was* the great torrial that maintained The Haven's wards. We would—you would—have taken it to battle. And it would have failed you then. Failed, because it was not the right object.

"Better we learn of it now than in the middle of a war. We've suffered nothing like this. There have been no casualties."

"Oh?" Logan demands. "Then what of my son? What of James? Where is he, then?"

A muscle in my cheek twitches at the mention of my half-brother.

Logan catches it. "You!" he exclaims. "You know something. Speak!"

I curse myself in my head. I give a tight, narrow shake of the head. "Nothing."

"Don't lie to me." The King flips away from Beatrice and strides straight for me. Faced with a vampire so strong, it's all I can do not to cower and back away.

But Dagan has instilled in me no shortage of discipline. He's helped give me a backbone, even in situations where the vampire hierarchy would have me on my knees.

So, wrapping all the discomfort swirling around inside into a tight bow, I regard the King evenly.

"What do you know of my eldest son?" he whispers.

I do not look into Logan's eyes, instead fixing my gaze on a spot just above his ear. "Very little," I answer honestly.

The King strikes me. The blow hits me across the face, and I tumble down.

"Do not lie," he growls in warning. He unsheathes the dagger at his belt. "I will give you only one more warning."

A speck of pride rises up inside me. Without thinking, I push myself back up and stand. I still do not look my father in the eye—but if he cares so much about *James*, whom he's shown nothing but utter disdain for previously, then my own predicament might be more salvageable than I first thought.

"I know nothing of James except that I cloaked him and then used him to channel magic through the staff." Maybe the realization that magic flowed through *James* will make the King reconsider his opinion of me. "After it was done, the link between us broke. I've felt nothing since."

"There was a battle," the King glowers. "Could he have been killed?" He turns around and screams at Beatrice, "*Why isn't he here?*"

A flush of relief washes over me now that his attention is on someone else. I allow myself a soft but calming breath.

"There were many casualties in the fight," Beatrice offers. "But I do not suspect James would have taken arms against The Convicted army."

177

"Then where... is... he?" Logan hisses. "I did not think him cowardly enough to run!"

"He has a unique advantage now," Beatrice says. "In that he cannot be detected by other vampires. Perhaps your treatment of him was too harsh. Perhaps he decided that striking out on his own would give him the best chance for survival."

"That is," the King begins, "a pile of horseshi—"

The remainder of the curse is cut off when the door to the bed chamber creaks open.

Logan spins around, eyes bulging, a thick vein pulsing in his neck. "Who DARES disturb me now?"

On the doorstep stands the only vampire in the entire coven who can remain unperturbed at facing the King's wrath.

The Ancient.

He ignores the King, and looks right at me, his eyes going to the new mark on my face. A flicker of concern shows then—so fast that if I didn't know any better, I'd say it was imagined.

But ever since collaborating with me on the attack against The Haven, the Ancient has shown a certain protectiveness over me. It's been very subtle, of course, and probably indistinguishable to most—but I feel it.

Without answering, he steps inside and closes the door. Putting his hand behind his back, he stops and waits beside one of the many pillars dotting the room.

Logan grunts. He knows he's not going to get anything out of The Ancient unless the most-revered vampire decides to volunteer it himself.

"Turn your attention away from James," Beatrice suggests. "You did not call Riyu here for that."

"No," the King agrees. "I did not. You are right."

What did he call me for? I wonder.

He looks again at me. Hesitation, a trait I have *never* seen from the King— crosses his features.

Then it's gone, and he speaks.

"You were near this girl, Eleira. Eleira. Is that right?"

I nod.

"And you were also somewhere in the vicinity of their Queen?"

Once more, I nod.

"So tell me. Is what James said true? Is Eleira the one? Does she rival the Queen in strength?"

"Yes," I say immediately.

"As both a vampire... *and* a witch?"

Again, I nod. "She does."

"Then *she* is the one we need with us!" Logan exclaims. "A witch of her power, on our side, wielding the most powerful torrial in existence... we will cloak the world in eternal night, our race will rise above the scourge of humanity that currently possesses the world, and *we* will become the dominant species...! Yes, yes, yes, yes!" The King's sudden zeal shows no signs of stopping. "Yes, *she* is the one we need!"

"She must come willingly, my Lord," Beatrice volunteers. "She cannot be forced to it. It is a process—"

"That will take time, yes, yes, yes," he finishes hastily. "First, we need her here."

He turns to me. "Relay a message to The Haven. Tell them Eleira must come. Tell them, she must come... or our offer of peace is void."

Chapter Thirty

The doors to my holding cell come open. Phillip steps inside.

He walks in without any reinforcements.

On his own, just like this... I could crush him. The cloaking spell cast on me by the Order's witches still remains. None, except for James, know the truth of my strength.

It's a pity, really, that I must be patient and temper my hate. I know my vengeance will come. I know I will get my revenge.

But I know that if I do anything stupid now, my entire position—with Carter, with the Queen, with everybody in The Haven—will be completely ruined.

So I bite down my anger at this... this *boy*... who stripped me of my rank and stole my post. Instead, I assume the most subdued attitude I can.

I look at him, and ask, "How can I help?"

Phillip stops and looks me over. There's judgment in his eyes and a new sort of curiosity... or maybe interest.

"I want to know what you told Victoria," he says, "When she came to free you."

"Certainly," I incline my head. "I told her she was a fool for trying to help me. I told her that my place was here, and that despite recent… circumstances, my loyalty to The Haven remains unshifting."

The boy eyes me. "Why," he wonders, "do you claim such loyalty?"

He pulls a stepstool closer to where I'm bound and sits on it. "Your betrayal has already been discovered. The thirteen vampires you brought with you have all abandoned you. Yet here you remain."

"There was no betrayal," I reply.

"No? Then why did you bring them in? Why did they all run when you fell?"

"Can you truly not see the bigger picture?" I shake my head. "The Queen appointed me Captain Commander of The Haven's guards. When I first came, I knew none of your men. How could *I* guarantee their loyalty, their discipline, their *trust* in me?" I sit down on the cot. "I could not. Trust had to be earned. Discipline, that could be taught. But loyalty? That was essential, and it would take the longest to develop."

I give a shrug. "I needed men I could trust, especially after the attack, so I brought in my own. Simple as that."

"So, why did they run," Phillip asks, "if it really is as simple as you claim?"

"Everyone fears uncertainty," I respond. "When they saw what fate had befallen me, they rightfully became concerned with what might happen to them. After all," I give a grim smile. "They know about your Mother's *paintings*."

Before, the mere hint of those things would have made Phillip wince. Yet now, he remains stoic.

Is that a sign of his maturity, perhaps? I reach out with my mind to gauge his strength. He *is* stronger than before… but at the expected, regular rate. His progress has not been expedited by external factors that I can tell.

"They wouldn't have run if they didn't have secrets," Phillip says. "You're going to tell me what those secrets are… and why they might give enough motivation for your vampires to leave their place of safety in the most coveted coven in the world."

I can't control the reflux of disdain that comes from his words. "Safety?" I snort. "They heard what happened to two of their own. You think with the demon on the loose, any of them would feel *safe*?"

"The Narwhark is an equal threat to all of us," he says. "It picks its victims without distinction."

"So you assume."

"So I *know*."

"Maybe, then, the vampires who left, who concern you so, do not share that opinion," I suggest. "Maybe they are more cautious when it comes to risking their lives. Or maybe, just maybe, they realized The Haven is not so valuable as it once was. The wards are gone. Their commander has been reduced to *this*." I look down at my stained shirt and cotton pants. "Look me in the eye and tell me honestly that you would stick around in a hostile, unfamiliar place in a time of turmoil. They had no security, Phillip. They just valued their lives."

He shakes his head. "You and I both know that isn't true."

"You're going in circles."

"*You're* leading me there."

"I admit," I say loftily, "that I don't precisely mind. It gets lonely in this cell without visitors."

"You've seen Carter," Phillip says.

I blink in a moment of surprise. Has the fool vampire already reneged on our agreement?

"You didn't think I'd know," Phillip observes. "That tells me something."

"All it would do is fuel your baseless suspicions against me," I snarl. Inwardly, I curse and reprimand myself for once again losing control.

What is it about the youngest Soren brother that so easily incites my rage?

"You consider him an ally, do you not?" Phillip questions. He moves closer to me. "He has always been one to try gouging out any advantage he could. He saw you rise. He saw you fall. But you do not know Carter the same way I do. You do not know what he is capable of."

Phillip stands. "A suggestion, if I may? Next time Carter comes to speak to you... refuse him. I would hate to prosecute another member of the Royal Court for going behind my back."

On that note, Phillip turns around and makes as if to leave. But, right on the door's threshold, he stops.

"I came to inform you that there's been another Narwhark attack. It happened in plain sight, before all the members of the Royal Court and gallery. The creature moves fast—we did not see it come or go."

"You're telling me that your guard is failing?"

"No," he says. "I'm telling you how *easy* it would be for the demon to find, and kill, a lone prisoner. Much like it found, and killed, Patricia."

"You're threatening me," I say, my voice cold and hard.

"An objective observation of fact differs very much from a *threat*, Smithson." Phillip opens the door. "Have a good rest tonight. You'll need it for when you're called before the Royal Court tomorrow.

"You will stand trial for treason."

Chapter Thirty-One

PHILLIP

OUTSIDE THE HOLDING CELLS

As soon as I round the corner and am out of view of the vampire standing guard outside Smithson's cell, I stop, lean against the wall, and run a tired hand over my eyes.

I went in there to try and extract answers... and all I got was a big, fat nothing.

In truth, seeing Smithson was just a diversion. A stupid one, at that. After the argument with Raul, I felt the need, deep inside, to exert my dominance. To feel some small semblance of the power that my post as Captain Commander should bring.

I satisfied that urge challenging the man.

Yet everything else is in disarray. We are helpless to stop the Narwhark. I've ordered The Haven's vampires to take as many precautions as possible, but I know that can only be a sham, little more than mere theatrics.

After all, if the demon can strike at the Queen, out in the open, what chance do the rest of us have?

I did not realize how exhausting being responsible for the safety of so many others could be.

But it's all about appearance. I have to maintain the *illusion* of safety... even if I know how flimsy it really is.

Realistically? The Haven vampires aren't stupid. Both the Elite and the Incolam—those vampires not of the Elite—know what happened. They know who it happened *to*. They know their own strengths. They know their weaknesses.

If the most experienced vampire in our company can be brought down by a creature from the underworld, odds are not so good for the rest of us.

And yet they need a leader. They need somebody to look up to. With Mother in her coma, and Raul about to leave... the responsibility falls onto me.

Strange, how the tables have turned.

I decide to go see Eleira. Maybe she has some insight about the Narwhark.

But when I open the door to her room, I find her scribbling furiously on a lined piece of paper. Her neat, precise handwriting fills more than three-quarters of the page.

She looks up with a start. "Oh, Phillip," she says. "It's you. You frightened me."

"Sorry to interrupt," I begin. Then I notice the red around her eyes, the faint flush in her cheeks.

"Have you been *crying*?" I ask, going straight to her side.

She looks away. "Is it that obvious?" she asks softly.

"It's about Raul, isn't it? Look, I know my brother has been a real jerk—"

"It's not Raul," she whispers.

"Oh." I feel like an idiot. "I shouldn't have assumed. Then what?"

She hesitates for a moment and looks at me. "I can trust you," she asks, her eyes full of earnest pleading, "can't I?"

I place my hand over hers. "Of course," I say.

"I don't know if I would share this with Raul. But you've become almost like a brother to me. Some things require... a certain degree of understanding between two people, to be revealed."

"I understand," I say. "That is very wise."

She nods and pulls out a small envelope addressed to her. She hands it to me. "Read that," she says.

She waits in silence until I finish the letter. When I'm done, I look at her through my glasses. "Wow," I say. "That's... heavy."

As carefully as I can, I fold her mother's letter up and give it back to her. I know how important this is to her, so I add, "I will never betray your trust with this, Eleira."

She gives a small nod of appreciation. "Do you know what she means? About the true circumstances of my birth?"

I exhale. "Unfortunately, no. The Queen told us where to find you. And Raul is the one who studied the stars. Yet even he consulted with her about your... whereabouts." I give an uncomfortable shrug. "Before your arrival, I mostly avoided participating in... anything to do with you." I give a sour chuckle. "Look at me now."

"So you *don't* know anything?" she asks.

"The Queen is the only one who would," I say grimly. I hate drawing attention to her when she's in her current state. "How did you get that letter, anyway?"

"Carter gave it to me," she says.

"Carter?" I frown. "He hasn't left The Haven personally for hundreds of years."

"Someone else must have given it to him, then. Right?"

"I'd assume so."

"What about the man the letter mentioned. Do you know who that could be?"

"No. But Carter and my Mother never exactly saw eye-to-eye. For him to get this letter... well, I'd bet anything that at least one other of the Elite knows something."

For a moment, hope gleams in Eleira's eyes.

"...but we have no way of discovering who," I finish. "I don't think you'd want to bring extra attention to yourself now."

"No," Eleira shivers. "I definitely do not." She looks down at the desk. "I'm writing her a response now. Do you think... would you help me get it to her?"

"I'll certainly do all that I can," I promise. "That I guarantee."

"Thank you."

"You could..." I hesitate. I don't know if I should say this or not.

In the end, I decide to speak my mind.

"You could go see her yourself, you know." I gesture around us. "Once all this is over."

She smiles at me sadly. "No, Phillip. I don't think I can."

"Why not?"

"It would be too painful. The way she said goodbye last time I saw her, when my parents dropped me off to the airport to go to university—she knew. I didn't realize it at the time. I didn't sense that there was anything off. But she *knew,* she knew that it could be the last time she ever saw me.

"I don't want her to deal with that twice. The grief it would cause, her sorrow?" Eleira shakes her head. "It would be like opening an old wound. Her letter gives me reassurance and peace of mind."

"How so?" I ask gently.

"Because I know my parents aren't worried. I mean they're probably *concerned*, as anyone would be, but not *worried*-worried. Like they're not scared, you know?" She huffs. "I'm doing a terrible job at explaining myself."

"No, no. I totally get it."

"They knew to expect this," she finishes. "So it's almost a blessing, not a curse. And..." she looks up and meets my eye, "...And, I mean, honestly... do you think this will *ever* be over? I mean, *truly* over?"

I turn my head away from her.

"We are eternal creatures," I say after a moment. "Everything about us continues. We linger on. They say change is the only constant in the world. They're wrong. *We* are."

At that, Eleira gives a small smile.

We sit in silence for a bit, appreciating the comfort of each other's company.

Then Eleira asks, "How is the Queen doing?"

I grunt. "The same as a few hours ago. Her condition hasn't changed. I have our doctor watching over her. He's to inform me the moment there's a change."

"How would he do that?" she asks. "Would he send a messenger?"

I give a humorless smile and take out my cell phone.

Eleira gasps. "But I thought—"

"That vampires are antique, that we eschew technology?" I give a sly smile. "It's The Haven's humans who have no conception of the outside world. You'll find most vampires prefer the tried-and-true methods of communication, yes... but we are not averse to modern luxuries.

"There's no cellular reception this far underground, but I set up a secure Wi-Fi network down here to communicate on. The cell phone is like a walkie-talkie. Mother's wards used to block electronic signals from penetrating The Haven. That's why you didn't see more of these devices in the hands of our vampires before we had to retreat underground."

"Looks like there's lots I still don't know," Eleira says. Suddenly, her head whips around, toward the door. "What was that?"

There's real alarm in her voice. I'm on my feet in an instant. "What was what?"

"You don't hear that?" She runs to the door. "Somebody is calling for help!"

I strain my ears. I don't pick up anything but silence. "Are you sure?"

"Yes, I'm sure." She grabs my hand and pulls me out the room. "Come on!"

Together we run through the dark halls. Everything is so quiet and still. But Eleira's sudden concern has me watching the shadows for any hint of movement.

I don't pick up anything. Eleira's senses are stronger than mine, to be sure, but I've been a vampire much, much longer. She and I should be on equal footing in this scenario because of that.

Yet we're not. She runs down the hall with a single-minded purpose. It doesn't take long for me to recognize where we're going.

The holding cells. The place I had just left.

She skids to a halt as she rounds the corner to Smithson's door. Alarm rips through me when I see the two guards who had been posted there earlier.

Their throats have been savagely ripped out.

"The Narwhark," I breathe.

Eleira, showing a flair of fearlessness, does not hesitate in the slightest as she starts for the door. She throws her shoulder into it, and it crashes open.

On the other side, I find a scene straight out of hell.

The Narwhark, blood staining its front, has Smithson backed into a corner. The former Captain Commander has claw marks all over his shoulders and his arms. There are bite marks on his legs, and his vampiric blood streams from a long cut across his forehead.

The Narwhark is taking its time with him.

Smithson's eyes flicker to us. For the first time, I see genuine fear in them.

But as soon as Eleira enters the room, the Narwhark stops. It turns its head. Then, slowly, the rest of its body follows.

It has no concern about leaving its back exposed to the vampire it'd been toying with.

My body tenses. My claws come out. I steel myself, readying for a desperate fight...

The Narwhark flips its pointed tail and jumps on the bed. The beady eyes, dark as night, are focused solely on Eleira.

I glance at her and realize with a start that her lips are moving. She's muttering something, maybe a spell, maybe an incantation, but the treble of it is too low for me to hear. She seems to be transfixed by the Narwhark.

It, in turn, pays attention only to her.

The tension builds. It's like a Mexican standoff.

Suddenly, Eleira exclaims, *"Voltarum Incas!"* A blue ball of light explodes from her hands. The Narwhark leaps aside to avoid it.

But it's not fast enough. The ball singes its side as it's in mid-air. The foul smell of demon flesh burning immediately fills the room.

The Narwhark crashes down hard. With a hissing snarl it rights itself. Its eyes dart from me, to Eleira, and back to Smithson.

It brings its head back like a roaring lion and emits a piercing screech. Shadows that weren't there before suddenly fill the room. They stream into the demon, clouding it in darkness.

The darkness swirls, and the Narwhark is enveloped by it, until its shape is no longer distinguishable from the rest. It happens faster than the time it takes to blink.

And then, in a black blur, it streams right between me and Eleira and flees the room.

Once it's gone Eleira visibly sags. I start to go after it, but she stops me.

"No," she says. "You'll never catch it. Nobody can."

193

"How do you know?"

"Because I…" she licks her lip, and looks at Smithson. "Because I can *feel* it."

I step toward her. "What do you mean? Is it like we can feel other vampires?"

She gives a hesitant nod. "Almost. But not quite. It's… different." Again her eyes go to the third vampire in the room. "I'll tell you later."

I nod grimly, then turn my attention to him.

"This is what you wanted, boy?" Smithson growls. He looks down at his body, at the wounds inflicted unto it by the demon. "You wanted to see me suffer, to see me weak?"

He ignores Eleira completely. His hatred for me is a palpable thing.

He takes a step toward us. But his knee buckles. He falls cursing to the ground.

Eleira gasps. She has softness in her heart after all. But Smithson only laughs.

"Now I know what fate my two dead men faced," he snarls. "I pin their deaths on you. You will always be responsible for that. And, one day… revenge will be mine."

"He's delirious," Eleira says. "The bites are affecting his brain."

"I'm not delirious!" he cackles. "That's a steaming pile of bull—"

A tremor rocks the earth, cutting him off.

It's over in a second. But Eleira's eyes are wide.

"They've come," she says in a hushed breath. "I felt it."

Chapter Thirty-Two

ELEIRA

SMITHSON'S CELL

When the earth shook, a tremendous influx of magical power burst into being, like a star being born.

It frightened me… but not as much as facing the Narwhark again frightened me.

Because, in the confrontation with it just now… I *felt* its growing sentience in my head.

The spell I used to attack it bubbled up from deep in my subconscious. It's nothing I'd ever been taught. Saying the words and channeling the magical energy that way was completely instinctual.

It reminded me… it reminded me, in a way, of the time I'd been possessed by that unknown force.

There was a difference, of course. The spell Morgan put on my mind as a protective barrier broke the moment she fell. But because of it, I'd been able to learn how to shield my mind—in my own, rudimentary way—and to be able to tell if or when some external force was trying to probe it.

That's how I recognized the connection with the demon. A link exists between it and me. I cannot deny that any longer. What it means, how it came to be, or how it'll affect me in the future, I cannot say.

But it's on a level deeper than what I can protect myself against. It's a part of me, of my psyche, almost like the connection between Victoria and me had been.

"Who?" Phillip exclaims, breaking me from my reverie. "Who's come?"

I look at him. "The other coven," I say.

He swears. Smithson laughs.

"Where?" Phillip demands. He grabs my shoulders. "Eleira, where are they?"

I raise a hand and point vaguely in the right direction. After casting the spell and attacking the demon, I'm strangely light-headed. A daze has come over me, and the words that come from my lips carry none of the urgency they require.

"They've come…" I mumble, "for Raul."

Smithson's laughter increases. Phillip stares at me in disbelief. "How do you know?"

"The burst of magic," I respond. Are these words mine? Is this body mine? "It came from his room."

Again Phillip curses. He looks at the bleeding prisoner. I smell the blood from Smithson's wounds, smell their rife corruption as his body tries to fight the demon saliva infecting them.

"We have to go help," Phillip says. "Eleira—" then he notices, *really* notices, my vacant daze. "Eleira, what's wrong?"

I shake my head. "It's nothing," I lie. "I just feel a bit… numb."

Did casting that spell take so much out of me?

"You're not like yourself." I can tell Phillip is itching to go. I should be, too. But for whatever reason, I cannot muster up the requisite determination. "Eleira? Eleira!"

Phillip's voice grows increasingly distant. I can see him, but it's like he's yelling at me from across an enormous canyon. There's a gulf, a dissociation from reality that seems to be coming over me.

It feels like hours pass. And yet, as I look from Phillip's concerned face, down to Smithson's laughing form, I know that no time has lapsed at all.

What is happening to me? Why do I feel so... out of it?

"Eleira. Eleira!" Phillip keeps calling my name. "Eleira, we *have* to go!"

"Raul..." I say. The last tendrils of magic are fading from the air. As they wither away, so does the discombobulation that fills my head.

In a flash, all of it is gone. I'm jerked right back to myself.

"Raul's in trouble!" I exclaim. "We have to go to him!"

Phillip immediately agrees. I start out the doors in the direction I felt the rip in reality, that gaping hole...

But on seeing the two slaughtered guards outside, I come to a complete halt. "What about Smithson?" I ask. "We can't leave him behind. Why aren't there more guards? Phillip, where *are* all the other vampires?"

"In their rooms," Phillip says grimly. "Where they are supposed to be safe. But if the demon could do *this* and get to a prisoner..."

He doesn't finish the thought. Instead, he turns back and heaves Smithson up. "We're taking him with us."

I don't have time to argue or disagree. I just run back and put my arms under Smithson's other shoulder to help Phillip carry him.

Just like that, the three of us race in the direction of Raul's rooms. Smithson is a dead weight, but between Phillip and me, he does not slow us much.

The entire underground is eerily quiet. Quiet, still, and silent.

It's spooky.

We arrive. Raul's door is closed. Within is exactly the spot I felt the flare of magic from.

"Put me down, put me down," Smithson coughs. "I won't be any use to you in there, even if I am on your side."

"That," Phillip grumbles, "remains to be seen."

We lower Smithson. Phillip looks at me. "Ready?"

I nod.

"If my brother's in there," Phillip says. "Then I cannot feel him. Can you?"

"No. But it makes sense that a masking spell would be put up."

Phillip steps to the door. "Whatever happens," he says, "your safety comes first."

And then, before I have a chance to reply, he pushes open the heavy door.

Chapter Thirty-Three

PHILLIP

RAUL'S ROOM

For the second time in the span of minutes, I enter a room and see a grisly scene before me.

This one, however, affects me completely unlike the last.

A massive, hulking behemoth of a vampire is inside. The top of his head brushes against the ceiling. He has thick cords of muscle all over his back and arms and shoulders and neck.

He has my brother pinned to one wall, holding a sickly-looking dagger to his neck.

He does not turn around as he speaks. "One wrong move," he warns me, in a deep, crude voice, "and your Prince dies."

A snicker comes from the corner. My head jerks that way.

There's a smaller vampire hiding in the shadows. He's slender, almost feminine, and at the same time so weak that I can barely sense his strength.

The contrast between the two intruders could not be more glaring.

"Who are you?" I say. I bring an arm out to hold Eleira back. I feel her tension, feel the potential for violence roiling about like a building thunderstorm inside her body.

"I am Dagan," the big vampire says. "Over there is Riyu. We have come as delegates from The Crypts."

"You have a blade at my brother's throat," I say flatly. "That is not what delegates do."

"Oh, but you have the wrong impression," Dagan says. "Your *brother* was the one who attacked us when we arrived. He forced me to act in self-defense."

"This is the bastard who cut my leg," Raul grunts.

Dagan forces his head up by pressing the blade tighter against his throat. "Now, now," he says. "Play nice." He turns his head back and looks at me. His eyes widen in momentary surprise when he sees Eleira.

Then they fill with such greed that I take a protective step toward her.

"You brought the girl," he says. "Good. She is exactly who we need."

"You are trespassing on The Haven's territory," I say. "That is an act of war. Let my brother go, and it will be forgiven."

The huge vampire laughs. "Do I give the impression this is a negotiation? I'm sorry. It is not. We came to take the witch."

"You will *never* have her," Raul growls. Inwardly, I curse my brother's bravado.

"Says the vampire with the knife at his throat," Dagan laughs.

Raul's eyes turn to me. "There's three of us," he gasps. "Two of them. Fight! You can defeat them."

Dagan makes a sound of displeasure. "*That*," he emphasizes, "would be a spectacularly bad idea. How long do you think it would take me to slit your

200

throat? A flick of the wrist is all it'd take if either your brother or the girl moves against me. And what then?"

"You can take them," Raul tells me. "While his back is turned, he's vulnerable. Go!"

"Shut up!" Dagan takes Raul's head and slams it into the wall. I grimace at the sudden display of violence. It's all I can do not to fly to my brother's defense.

But the huge vampire is right. He would kill Raul before I even take a step.

Eleira speaks and takes the decision out of my hands.

"Why do you want me?" she asks.

"Our King requests your presence," Dagan says. He turns his head to her and gives a sleazy smile. "You will be treated very, very well as our guest, my dear."

"If I come, you'll let Raul go?"

"No!" Raul and I exclaim at the same time.

Dagan shrugs. "If you come, I will do one better. The wound in the Prince's leg is killing him. It is eating away at his life force. Sooner or later, he will succumb to its effects. Only in The Crypts can he be healed. You come... and we will remove the taint."

"Then I'll come," she says, without a second's hesitation.

I stare at her. "Eleira," I hiss.

"It's the only way, Phillip," she tells me. She sounds... fatalistic... in a way. But also determined.

"You really do love him," I whisper.

"Yes," she says. "I really do."

"How sweet," Dagan sneers. He takes the blade away from Raul's throat. "It's too bad, I was looking forward to shedding a little Soren blood." He shrugs. "Ah, well. Riyu?"

At that, the smaller vampire mumbles something under his breath and moves his finger around as if he's playing cat's cradle. The door behind us slams shut on the wind. There's a brief but powerful expansion of power, followed by a flash of blue.

Next thing I know, a portal is rotating halfway off the floor.

"You're a witch," Eleira breathes. "*You* were the one I felt!"

Riyu snickers and inclines his head briefly. He doesn't say a word, but there's a certain joy in his eyes at being acknowledged for his magic.

"How did you... " Eleira begins. The awe in her voice is evident. "How did you do that so fast?" She sounds genuinely impressed.

"Don't patronize him," Dagan barks. He pushes Raul forward with the tip of the blade. "You first, Prince."

"Eleira..." Raul begins.

"It's the only way," she tells him softly.

I feel the most frustrating inability to affect things.

Dagan pushes my brother to the edge of the portal. "The journey down," he says, "has been known to be *unpleasant*."

And then he shoves him through. Raul disappears into it the moment he makes contact.

I gasp. Just like that, all sense of my brother is gone. Just like that, he's been

202

taken away from here.

"You next, witch," Dagan says, beckoning Eleira with his knife. "You come with me. We don't want any... funny business."

With a sort of steely resignation, Eleira walks around the portal and stands next to Dagan. He grabs her by the waist and pulls her close, then takes a long, thorough inhale of her hair.

"Ahh," he says. "Smells like woman."

And with that, the two of them jump in, him holding her tight.

Then it's just the smaller vampire and me in the room. On a sudden impulse I realize that I cannot just let Eleira and Raul go. I make a leap for the portal—

But just as I do, an invisible force slams into me and pushes me back. I'm pinned tight against the wall. Riyu gives a soft laugh and waggles his finger in a "*no-no-no*" motion.

He used magic!

Then he hops into the portal. A moment later, it winks out of existence, and the spell holding me dissipates.

I stagger forward, disoriented. The room is empty. All the other vampires are gone.

Just as I try to get my bearings, a scream sounds from deep underground. I jerk toward it.

It sounded distinctly human.

Chapter Thirty-Four

JAMES

THE WOODS AROUND THE HAVEN

I rip away from my last victim, his blood streaming down my chin in thick, red rivulets.

The man falls back, dazed, confused—and deliriously happy.

The stupidest grin I've ever witnessed comes upon his face as he stares up at the night sky. His eyes are vacant, wide with dilated pupils. He has just enough blood left in him to live.

Next comes the woman's turn. She is the leader, insofar as I can gather, of this insane cult. She'd insisted on letting all the others go first as a demonstration of her generosity.

Her body shakes with ecstasy as I step to her. My hand wraps around the small of her back. Her eyes are closed, her head angled back to expose the ever-precious carotid artery to me.

Even though I'm bursting at the seams with human blood, I rip into her savagely. My hunger is long gone. Right now, all I'm doing is giving in to hedonistic pleasure.

Her hot blood pours into my mouth, vital and pure. I draw on it quickly and deep. I cannot remember the last time I've had such a feast.

Certainly it was not in this century.

When it's done—when I've drawn enough blood to slow the beating of her heart, when I've drawn to the point that just another sip might kill her—I let go.

She falls to her knees, clutching at my legs. Her eyes are glossed over, much like the man's.

But there is more *appreciation* there.

"Thank you," she breathes. "Thank you, for..." a shudder of ecstasy breaks off her speech.

"Yes?" I whisper, intrigued and fascinated—yet also repulsed—by this human woman.

"For finding me worthy," she finishes. Then she falls back and stares open-mouthed into the sky.

I make a sound of displeasure and step away from her. All around me, the members of the Fang Chasers lie in a circle formation, in the exact spots I'd dropped them when I fed. There are twenty of them—twenty humans who have willingly given me their blood.

I feel reenergized. I feel rejuvenated. I feel whole. I feel like a *god*. With so much blood pulsing through me, my body finally has the substance to heal all of its afflictions.

I am, in short, the vampire James Soren again.

I glance up at the sky. There are hours left before dawn. But none of these humans will recover by then.

Hell, a few of them might not recover at all. The first few who offered themselves to me, for example…

Well, you can't blame a vampire for drawing too deep after he's been deprived of blood for so long.

I debate simply leaving them. I have no loyalty to these men. Or the woman. I owe them nothing. But if I leave them as is, vulnerable and exposed on the ground, I am certain the smell of blood will attract the animal predators who hunt these woods.

And I am curious. Curious as to whom they are, about what they represent, curious about their connection to April, curious about their knowledge of me and my kind in general.

It takes a certain type of lunatic to seek out a vampire sanctuary of his or her own free will. Yet these people did exactly that. And they did it not because they welcome death. They welcome us, the children of the night, but they do not wish to die.

If only they understood that vampires are the only true harbingers of death in this world.

I sit back on my haunches in the midst of the stinking bodies and think. My presence now is the only thing keeping the predators away. If I abandon this group…

I make up my mind. I'll give them until daybreak. When the sun rises, I'll have no choice but to go underground. By then, if enough of them have awakened, they'll survive on their own. If not…?

Well, if not, then the fault lies squarely with them—and I will bear no guilt over their deaths.

Chapter Thirty-Five

The scream that sounds in the distance sounds vaguely familiar. But with the amount of blood I've lost, I don't have the capacities needed to make the connection.

The door to Raul's room bursts open. Phillip—gods, how I loathe him, him above all the rest—runs out.

His eyes flicker to me.

"Is that surprise?" I chuckle. "You thought I'd be gone, didn't you? But as I've said all along, *boy*—my loyalties are here."

He goes to his knees immediately at my side and presses a hand over my biggest, still-bleeding wound. "You're not healing," he says, a touch of concern present in his voice.

"A demon will do that to you," I say. My fingers itch to wrap around the knife hidden at my waist and sink it into Phillip's heart.

Is he truly so naïve as to expose himself to me like this?

He grimaces and pulls back. "Will you heal?"

"I suppose so," I say. "I'm not dead yet. I've got more fight in me than you

208

know."

He nods. "Then you're coming with me."

He hauls me to my feet. Pain shoots through my body with every sharp movement. But I do not show it—just like I do nothing to hide the utter disdain I have for needing help like this.

Especially from *him*.

"Where are we going?" I ask.

"You heard the scream."

"Where's Eleira? Where's your brother, Raul?"

"Gone," he tells me.

"What?" Alarm takes me. "What do you mean, gone? Gone where?"

"Vampires from The Crypts…" Phillip begins. Then he stops. "I shouldn't be telling you."

"From *The Crypts*?" A mix of rage and incredulity takes me. "You let the coven's most prized possession be taken by vampires from The Crypts?"

"I don't need to justify anything to you," he grunts.

An insane sort of laughter bursts up from inside me. I cannot stop it. "It's not me you should be worried about, you fool!" I exclaim. "It's the Queen. It's the Royal Court. If you think they will take news of this sort lightly—"

"I don't need *your* advice," he snaps. "Besides," he adds under his breath. "I doubt the Queen is in any position to protest."

"What do you mean?"

"Damn you, what do you think I mean? The Queen is unconscious. She was attacked—" his eyes widen in realization. "You didn't know."

"Of course I didn't know. I was held prisoner on your orders."

"The Narwhark struck her down," Philip says. "What I don't understand is how it attacked you and left you standing."

"I'm tougher than I look. Even in prisoner's garbs."

"You're not as strong as the Queen," he says. "There's something else." And then he exclaims, half to himself, "Of course! The tail."

"What?" I grunt.

"It did not touch you with its tail. Did it?"

"No. Only its claws and fangs." I shake my head. "Idiot."

"Watch it," Phillip warns.

I shut my mouth. I'm pushing my luck. And if I continue to interact so negatively with him, well, I wouldn't put it past myself to actually *use* that hidden blade of mine.

"Can you run?" Phillip asks.

"Does it look like I can run?" I snarl.

"Then hold on to me," he says. He hoists me onto his back. My arms go around his neck. He runs…

We arrive at the entrance of my former cell, with the two guards' bodies lying mutilated on the floor.

Cowering against the opposite wall, with both hands over her mouth, is that wretched human girl, April.

Phillip gasps the moment he sees her. He lets me go and runs to her.

He whispers something in her ear as he wraps both hands around her shoulders. She starts shaking her head and then begins muttering, muttering, muttering something I have no interest in listening to.

My attention, instead, is drawn to the two bodies.

This is the first time I've ever had the chance to examine the Narwhark's handiwork. The first time I've had the chance to do so dispassionately.

The damn Soren brothers robbed me of the opportunity when they buried Patricia before.

While Phillip is dealing with the human, I crouch down by the guards. Their throats are ripped out. Neither of them looks like he had any chance to defend himself.

Why, then, did the Narwhark not kill me the same way? Why did it strike at me only as a chew-toy?

Was it savoring the moment before the kill? Did it take a certain pervasive pleasure in acting as the most fearsome predator in The Haven?

All my knowledge of demons from my time with the Order tells me that they are intelligent creatures. But all of that is drawn from second-hand accounts. The Vorcellian Order has never actually had a demon in its grasp...

Few know, I suspect, how valuable that would be.

None, other than I, of those in the Order, have such knowledge.

Some knowledge is better left unshared.

I lift one of the guard's shoulders to turn him over. I make a face when I see

211

the hole in his chest. His heart is gone—the demon obviously fed on it.

It's a measure of my fascination, or perhaps more of my weakened state, when I feel Phillip's hand on my shoulder.

I did not sense him walking over.

"Get away from them," he commands.

I let go of the dead vampire. The limp body falls to the ground.

I turn and look up.

Phillip is standing directly between April and me. The girl is doing all she can to not meet my eyes.

"She was sent here to deliver a message to you," Phillip says. His voice has gone ice cold. "A message from *Carter*. Do you have any idea why that might be?"

"None," I lie.

"Then you won't mind if it doesn't get delivered." Phillip holds a folded piece of paper up. "Or, I suppose, if it got intercepted along the way."

I force my facial features into a mask of indifference. "I hold no secrets from the Captain Commander."

Phillip scoffs. "Right." He stuffs the letter in his pocket. "This is where we part, Smithson. The cell—" he nods toward it, "—is waiting for you."

"Oh, that's cruel," I say with a sneer. "You're going to leave me here, right where the demon can find me again, is that it? As payback for your pathetic friend, Patricia, if I don't miss my mark."

"I'm not leaving you as bait," Phillip says. "I am not so sadistic as that. But I do need you somewhere I know you won't be a nuisance."

212

"Let me help, then," I say. "You let Eleira and Raul go. You think the Royal Court will look favorably upon that? You've neglected proper relations with those vampires your whole life. But *I* know them. They trust *me*. Especially if what you said about Morgan—"

"The *Queen*," Phillip corrects.

"Especially if what you said about the Queen is true," I finish. "You need me. You need me on your side."

"No," Phillip says. "I don't."

"You don't trust me. I understand. But look at my condition now." I glance at my wounds. "What can I do to threaten you? How much of a risk would letting me help *really* be?"

"Enough of one." Phillip shoves me by the shoulders. "You will remain here."

"Fool," I spit. On a whim, I pull out my hidden knife. I flash it before his eyes. "I've had this weapon on me the entire time. How many opportunities have there been for me to stick it through you? If I wanted you dead, Phillip, trust me... you would not be standing now."

Conflict shows on his face. I know I'm getting to him. I press on.

"We've had our battles in the past. I understand that. But my loyalty is *here*. It truly is here, in The Haven, with my Queen, no matter what's been done." I flip the knife around in my hand and offer him the hilt. "So here. My final trump card. I offer it to you as a truce."

Phillip hesitates. The tension builds.

He looks down at the bodies. He looks back at April. He looks once more at me.

Finally he takes a step forward. His fingers wrap around the hilt.

"But," he warns, just as I'm about to let go, "if you prove false, Smithson, you will not be given another chance."

"Then I will have to prove myself true."

Chapter Thirty-Six

Dagan lands, holding Eleira, a second after I do. He has the horrendous blade pressed against the small of her back.

He grins at me. "Not so eager to risk your girlfriend, are you?"

My eyes meet Eleira's. I cannot believe I managed to get her wrapped up in this.

Over and over, I fail her, over and over again.

But the fact that she would offer to come, for *me*... it sweeps aside just a little bit of the darkness crowding my heart. If she truly cares that much...

Well. I *know* she cares that much. The difficulty lies in making her forget those feelings, because if I allow them to prosper and grow, I am only betraying her heart.

She cannot be in love with a man sentenced to death. And despite Dagan's promise about my leg wound, I'm under no illusions.

I know there is no cure. I know I'm going to die.

And somehow, knowing that, I screwed up enough to entangle Eleira with me. *Again.*

Dagan steps forward. A few moments later, Riyu drops through. The portal closes.

For the first time I actually look around to take in where we are.

It's an enormous, blue-tinged crystal cave. Light shines from everywhere all at once—and yet there is no source. It seems to come from within the rock itself.

Eleira is immediately entranced by the surroundings. She does not even seem to notice the blade at her back.

"What is this place?" she asks, her voice full of awe and wonder. "It's beautiful."

Riyu looks to Dagan for permission. The bigger vampire nods.

"These are called the Paths, my Lady," he says. The title he chose for her is not mocking. If anything, it is absolutely sincere. "They are the domain of warlocks and witches."

"Is that what you are?" she asks. "A warlock?"

He inclines his head in acknowledgement.

"Some, though," he adds, after a second, "refuse to see it that way."

Dagan blinks in surprise at the addition. I take in as much as I can to try to understand their relationship with each other... and to discover how I might spring Eleira free from this trap I've led her into.

"Hold your arms out." Dagan nods to me. "Riyu will bind them. Do it, and don't argue."

I do as I'm told. Riyu comes forth and clamps a pair of silver manacles on. I don't know how he managed to handle them without feeling their effects—I guess it has something to do with his magic.

Once they're secure, Dagan lets Eleira go. He offers her a warning, however.

"Try anything we don't like, and I'll prove to you just how powerful the link between my weapon and your Prince really is."

"I understand," Eleira tells him. She avoids looking at me. "I made the decision to come. I'm not going to compromise it now."

Her explanation appeases Dagan. "Good," he grunts. "Riyu—lead the way."

The small vampire takes a moment to orient himself, and then starts to trot in the proper direction.

We follow him in silence. I keep trying to catch Eleira's eye, without being too obvious about it.

But she is either oblivious to my attempts or purposefully ignoring them.

We walk for what seems like an inordinately long time. The caves become darker. There are places where Riyu turns, seemingly at random, to take us through a narrow gap or crevice.

The whole time Eleira looks around her with obvious fascination.

"There's so much magic here," she says under her breath. "I've never felt it so pure."

Riyu gives her a knowing smile and a secret wink.

Finally, we emerge into a clearing indistinguishable from the one we arrived in. Riyu starts to mutter a spell—but Eleira stops him.

"Wait," she says. Her eyes dart to Dagan, still completely avoiding mine. "Do you think I could try?"

"No," Dagan says immediately. "Absolutely not. It—"

But Riyu stands to Eleira's defense. "A portal created here can only open in one destination," he says. "There is no risk."

"What about to *her*?" I growl.

I find myself ignored by all three of them.

"Fine," Dagan says after a moment. "As yet another showing of good will. But even *try* to deceive us, girl..." he pulls out the blade. "Well, you know what this can do."

She swallows and nods.

As Riyu takes her forward and starts to teach her the spell, Dagan lumbers over to me.

"She cares enormously about you," he says.

I meet the proclamation with stony silence.

"Just saying," he adds. "She would never recover were something... *unfortunate*... to befall you."

My gut tightens, because I know just how right Dagan is.

"But fear not," he continues. "I am a vampire of my word. When we get to The Crypts, the link between you and the weapon will be cleanly removed. That is, of course... dependent on your Father's *mercy*."

He walks away, chuckling to himself.

So already he's lied.

I turn my attention to Eleira and Riyu. She has her eyes closed and her hands held out in front of her as if warming them against a fire. Riyu watches, adjusting their position, muttering his own words of magic under his breath—which Eleira repeats back to him verbatim.

Finally, the small vampire seems satisfied. He steps away and gives a quick nod. Eleira smiles—she actually *smiles*, despite us being prisoners, and closes her eyes to concentrate.

Half a second later a burst of light comes from her palms. A portal at least two times larger than Riyu's has been formed before her.

One of her eyes cracks open. She gives a tentative, cautious smile. "Did I do it right?"

Riyu stares as if he's never seen her before. His shock is only temporary, but it carries with it a great deal of new respect and reverence.

He quickly makes his features go blank. He gives a little nod.

"He goes first," Dagan motions to me. "If something goes wrong, the rest of us will be safe. Heed my warning, girl."

Eleira holds her shoulders back, defiant. "I'm no fool."

"Get on with it, then."

I come up to the portal. For a brief second, I manage to catch Eleira's eyes.

There is so much caring, so much angst in her gaze that it staggers me.

That flash is all I need to confirm the extent of her feelings for me.

She covers it up a second later, breaking eye contact.

At that moment, I realize what she's been doing. She hasn't looked at me because she didn't want to give Dagan or Riyu any ammunition against us. She's trying to protect me—which is highly ironic, given that I should be protecting her.

"Go ahead," she says, her voice stiff. "It's safe."

I give a solemn nod. I peer into the portal, but it's impossible to see through to the other side. "This will take me to The Crypts?"

"Yes," Riyu says.

"If the magic is right," Dagan adds.

"It *is* right," Eleira stresses.

"Even if it's not…" Dagan shrugs. "Your boyfriend is the one to be our guinea pig. Let's hope nothing unfortunate befalls him." He grins. "Off you go. The King is waiting."

I step right to the portal's edge. The swirling energy inside is so strong that even I can feel it. Or maybe—more likely—I am just imagining it.

I don't have The Spark.

I'm about to step through when Eleira calls out, "Wait!"

I stop and turn back. She runs to me, before Dagan can react, and throws her arms over my shoulders. She kisses my cheek and whispers in my ear, "Be safe."

By then, Dagan's recovered enough to grab her arm and yank her back. He growls in annoyance. I try once more to look into Eleira's eyes, but they are glued to the floor.

"No more wasting time," Dagan says. "Go."

On his command, I jump into the portal… and the world turns black.

Chapter Thirty-Seven

RAUL

THE CRYPTS

I tumble through a never-ending darkness tinged with red. Red from blood, red from fire, red from death and destruction and red—above all—from rage.

The feeling consumes me like a never-ending inferno. I feel like I've been plunged into the heart of a volcano. The darkness is nothing my sight can pierce. Likewise, the red is nothing I directly *see*. It's more of a feeling, a sense of impending doom and destruction and decay. It's like the wound corrupting my body has taken on its own strength and expanded, doubling, tripling, even quadrupling in size.

A vile, pulsing strip opens up before me. I hurtle through it... and find myself standing upright, on the marble floor of a vast, golden chamber.

Immediately, the feeling of the place is familiar to me. I am in The Crypts.

Half a second later, Riyu appears at my side. Then come Dagan and Eleira.

I look back. There's no portal they came through. They simply appeared out of thin air.

Riyu looks around him, wide-eyed. Eleira is trying to hide it, but she has a smug sort of smirk on her face.

Dagan, on the other hand, looks angry.

He seizes Eleira's arm. But before he has a chance to do anything else, I throw myself at him. I don't know when, or how, it happened, but my injury is no longer holding me back. In fact, I don't even feel the wound.

Dagan and I crash to the ground. My wrists are bound, but I use the chain between them as a weapon. I press it against Dagan's neck, pinning him in place. My strength, astonishingly, is coming back to me. No longer am I weakened by the wound. No longer is my body fighting against the corruption.

It's like... it's almost like... *I've been cleansed.*

Dagan throws a punch, but it merely glazes off the side of my body. I press the chain harder into his neck, cutting off his air supply, pressing down, down, hard enough to crush his windpipe and break his neck. He coughs and sputters, struggling against me. He tries reaching for the knife, but my knees, pinned to either side of his body, prevent him from pulling it out.

He realizes he won't get it. So instead, he grabs my arms and tries to pry me off. But I am consumed by rage, by rage and anger and by an all-encompassing fury. *Yes, fight me,* I think. *Yes, let me satiate in my strength. Yes, let me feel the power I have over you! Yes, yes, yes!*

"ENOUGH!" an angry, brooding, male voice booms through the room.

A force sweeps into me from the side, knocking me right off Dagan. The blow throws me against a huge pillar. I grunt and fall.

A second later, I'm on my feet—but I see that the whole situation has changed.

Dagan is slowly picking himself up, blinking in a half-daze and rubbing his throat. The silver burned him there. I can see the mark on his skin.

That sight fills me with no small amount of pride.

Across from him stands Eleira, chin up and defiant. Beside her, kneeling with one fist on the floor, is Riyu.

I feel the presence of two great vampires behind me.

I turn around... and see my Father for the first time.

I know it's him right away. There's no doubt about it. He has the Soren features.

He is not quite as tall as James, but he has a presence about him. He's wearing a dark, hooded cloak. Gold thread makes up the stitching, and there are small jewels encrusted along all the edges. His complexion is darker than any vampire I've seen—other than Victoria. An assortment of rings decorate his fingers, and gleaming chains hang from his neck.

All in all, his dress would be a gaudy showing for any vampire. But that is not what draws my attention.

His *strength* is.

Never in my life have I encountered a vampire so strong. His strength flows from him in waves, in great huge currents. He is many times stronger than Eleira—and that, in and of itself, absolutely astounds me.

He has the menacing power of a great white swimming in a pool of fishes.

Father's companion is no less fascinating.

He is not quite so strong as the King, but he is not far off. He is dressed simply compared to my Father's gaudy robes. Yet I immediately feel in awe of him, in an altogether different way than I've ever felt in awe of another vampire before.

His manner seems subdued. He has no need to flaunt any of his power. He is firm in who and what he is. There is a feeling of great wisdom that radiates from around him.

It's in his eyes, I realize after a moment. *His presence is contained entirely in his gaze.*

"Impressed?" A voice sounds in my head. I take a step back in surprise.

I've heard that voice before—it is the voice of The Ancient!

"Kneel before your King, boy!"

And, suddenly, an invisible force pushes me down by the shoulders. I'm forced to my knees.

It's the same force that threw me off Dagan.

The Ancient is using the Mind Gift against me!

The room has gone eerily quiet. The Ancient keeps me locked in place. I'm unable to move any part of my body.

Father approaches. My eyes are locked on him. He keeps his eyes narrowed as he watches me.

He stops right in front of me. The Ancient forces me to crane my neck up. A quiet moment passes. I search for any feelings inside, but I feel absolutely nothing for this man.

That frightens me. I feel no anger or rage. I know he is the one to cause the ruin of The Haven. And, even so, I cannot muster up even the smallest bit of resentment toward him.

Why not?

Father finally speaks. "I saw you attack Dagan." A long pause. "...Well done."

I blink. "What?"

The Ancient releases his grip, and The King offers me his hand.

Cautiously, I take it.

"I like my sons to show a bit of courage," he says. "I like them to have a little bit of spunk. To fight for what's theirs, to go for what they want. To protect—" he pulls me closer, "—the ones they love."

His gaze darts behind me. I turn around—and find Eleira standing on her tip-toes, Dagan's poisonous blade held at her throat.

A white-hot pillar of rage erupts inside me. The bastard distracted me, drew my attention away so Dagan could get to Eleira!

"What will you do now, son?" Father asks. He does not release my hand. "If I gave you a choice—your life, or the life of the woman you love—which would you spare?"

"I'd save Eleira." I say immediately. "Without hesitation. Every single time."

"Good," Father says. "Passion for your woman is an admirable thing. Unfortunately, this time... I am not giving you a choice."

He nods. The moment he does, Dagan's knife slashes across Eleira's throat.

"No!" I gasp. I rip out of Father's grip and run for her.

Dagan lets her go. She falls—but I'm there before she can hit the ground.

"No, Eleira, no, no, no!"

Her head hangs forward as the life bleeds out of her. Her eyes are glazed over.

"No, Eleira, no!"

She tries to reach for my cheek. Her hand falls halfway through. Her body goes limp against mine.

"WHAT DID YOU DO?" I scream at the King. "WHAT DID YOU DO?" I hold Eleira to me, I feel her blood, hot and sticky and wet, running over my fingers and soaking into my clothes.

"Her strength was stolen," Father says as he strolls toward us. "Now, we demand it back."

He stops between Dagan and me. With one hand, he motions The Ancient forward.

Eleira's blood continues to pool on the floor. Her life force is draining out of her. Just a few more moments and she'll be dead...

"As her blood stains the palace floors, a guiding star will rise," Father quotes. *"And the Worthy One shall lead all our kind to salvation."*

I look at him. He sounds like a madman. My head is spinning. I can't comprehend what's going on. I can't think. I don't know what to do. A terrible anguish comes over me, one from which there is no escape. Darkness surrounds me. Eleira's heart beat comes slower and slower and slower. The blood pouring out of her neck slows to a trickle.

Father kneels down. He dips his fingers into the pool of blood. He brings them in front of his face, holding the red-stained fingertips between the two of us.

"Such a precious thing, her blood is," he murmurs. "Who would have thought it would be *I* to grant it such power?" He leans across to me. "Do you want her to live?"

"Yes!" I exclaim.

"Good," Father says. "Then stand aside, and let her go."

I stare at him in disbelief.

"Quickly, now," he murmurs. "Time is running out."

With a grunt, I do as I'm told. I lower Eleira to the floor, and glare at my Father, chock-full of hatred.

The Ancient sweeps in from behind and cradles Eleira in his arms. He looks down at her, and, for a moment, I think I see genuine compassion cross his features.

I blink and shake my head and the vision is gone. It must have been my imagination.

"And now," Father says, "there will be a permanence to what we give."

Shock ripples through me as The Ancient bites two small holes in his wrist and presses it to Eleira's lips.

A direct transfusion.

Somewhere in the background, Dagan or Riyu makes a coughed sound of surprise.

I pay them no attention. Time slows to a halt as The Ancient holds his bleeding wrist to Eleira's mouth. Her lips remain sealed. The seconds span into eternity as we wait for her to drink.

My eyes dart to the King. His confidence is not quite so solid as before. The corners of his eyes tighten. His hands shape into fists.

The Ancient is the only one unaffected. He sweeps Eleira's hair back, gentle as a doting father. He brings his lips close to her ear and whispers, "Drink, child."

On his words, Eleira's mouth opens. A drop of The Ancient's blood drips inside.

Then Eleira's eyes pop open, and she clutches the wrist held to her mouth. Extraordinary relief, such as I've never felt before, overwhelms me.

Eleira drinks and drinks, taking huge, savage swallows of The Ancient's blood. The wound on her neck closes. The grisly scene still looks like something from out a horror movie, but at least, at least, Eleira is alive.

Finally, she stops drinking. Her eyes move in wonder to The Ancient. Then she looks at me.

"I feel no hunger," she breathes. "At all."

Beyond us, Father starts to laugh.

Chapter Thirty-Eight

ELEIRA

THE CRYPTS

I look around the lavishly decorated room. Rich Persian carpets dot the floor. Exquisite silks of every color are draped over the furniture pieces. There are cut-outs in the wall, shaped like windows, curtained with fabrics of a deep, delicious red.

Bulbs on the other side give the impression of sunlight. It's fake, of course, but it makes being so far underground feel a lot less oppressive.

I look down at my gown. It's a light, baby blue. There are lace trimmings on the ends of the sleeves and the hem of the dress. It is a bit antique, a tad old fashioned, but nonetheless beautiful.

Is this how a prisoner would dress?

But, of course, I'm no prisoner. Not in the traditional sense. No, after waking to find The Ancient's wrist pressed to my lips, his life-giving blood flowing down my throat... I knew that something very dramatic had taken place.

His blood had reenergized my body like a torrent of red-hot fire. The pervasive hunger that had defined my vampiric existence was simply *gone*. That astonished me. I had thought the feeling would forever be there.

But, no. The Ancient helped me to my feet, and I was led out of the chamber in a satiated daze.

In the hall outside, I was introduced to one of the most beguiling women I have ever encountered.

She said her name was Beatrice and that she was there to assure my comfort. She made herself sound like a servant, but I knew she was anything but.

No servant would make eye contact the way she did with the King.

She told me I was a distinguished guest. And as such, I would be given all the luxuries that were afforded to a vampire of my strength.

"Raul will be taken care of, don't you worry," Beatrice said as she took my arm. "You will see him soon."

It was a measure of how out of it I was that I hadn't given him any thought.

Then she led me to this room, presented me the dress, told me to change, then informed me that I would be received by the King once more, "formally," soon.

I did all that and have been waiting ever since.

I float over to the grand piano and sit on the bench. I run my fingers over the keys. I've never played, but I always admired those who could.

My pinky presses down. A high, vibrant note sounds. I close my eyes and do it again, listening to the pure perfection of the crystal sound.

I feel... different. For the first time since my transformation, I feel at ease. There's no storm of boiling emotions or trouble in the background. My mind feels cleansed and my body purified.

Is this what all vampires feel like?

That internal struggle to contain the beast inside me is gone. I don't even feel the duality anymore. I am who I am, as a single cohesive whole. I'm not Eleira-the-vampire. I am just Eleira.

I am simply *myself.*

The freedom that grants is absolutely astounding.

My hand moves over the keys, and I press down on another note. Its crisp sound fills the air. I breathe in deeply and let it wash over my body and my soul.

Then comes silence. The room is still. My *mind* is still. I feel a peace like I have never known before.

My entire life I was always striving for something more. Chasing the next secret door, looking for the next hidden passage. For all of high school, I thought Stanford would be it.

But now, with a tiny bit of perspective, I can look back and say that it *wasn't.* Sure, I was only there a few months—and sure, The Haven vampires ripped me straight out of my life—but back then I could only think about the next day, the next week, *maybe* the next month.

Now that I am an immortal? The four years I would have spent at school will pass in a flash. If I were in school, I'd have graduated, and then what?

I'd still be *chasing.*

And now, finally, with The Ancient's blood, there is tranquility. I am who I am, and there is no changing that. My body is mine, my spirit is mine, my mind—of course—is fully mine.

Whatever comes could not possibly be more exciting.

A distant door comes open. I turn around.

Raul is standing there in a crisp, white dress shirt. His hair is combed back, his green eyes shine, and there's a vibrancy to his complexion that had been missing for so very long.

I allow myself a tiny smile. His leg is better.

I made sure of that.

The portal I created leeched the corruption out of the wound. Dagan couldn't have known, Raul certainly wasn't expecting it, but the way to do it came to me during the initial journey into the Paths. The magic in that realm was boundless, limitless, and tweaking the spell Riyu showed me was oh-so-simple at the time. It was as if the knowledge of it was buried deep inside me the whole time. Visiting the Paths simply let that knowledge rise to the surface.

"You look..." Raul steps into the room and closes the door. "...simply stunning."

My cheeks heat up in a flush. I try to force it down. I'm still *angry* with him for acting like such an ass the whole time we were in The Haven, but the relief that comes from knowing that he's better overshadows all that.

"You don't look so bad yourself," I murmur, before I can stop myself. Dammit! I'm supposed to be mad.

He gives a short, slightly awkward chuckle. "I didn't think this would be the treatment we'd receive." He bends his bad leg. "The wound is better. They kept their word."

I give a secret smile.

"What about you, though?" he asks. "How do you feel?"

"Amazing," I say. "As if all the impurities have been washed away."

Raul nods. "That's great," he says. He starts toward me, then stops and hesitates. Conflict is written clear on his face.

"Eleira," he begins. "I have to apologize. For the way I've been acting toward you. It wasn't—" he grunts. "It wasn't me. Something took over, some darkness, a sickness, a disease of the mind. I lost sight of who I was, and who you are. I lost sight of..." he runs a hand through his hair. "... how important you are to me."

I don't want it to be so easy for me to forgive him. But I cannot muster up any sort of ill-will. Just knowing that he's alive, that we don't have to worry about that ghastly injury any more... it makes anger totally impossible.

"I know," I say.

He gives a small smile. His eyes go beyond me to the piano. "Can you play?" he asks.

I shake my head. "You?"

"A long time ago... I may have tried to learn." He takes a few cautious steps toward me. He's acting as if I'm a mouse that he might frighten off at any second. "I don't know how much of it I still remember..." another step to me, "...or even if I was ever any good." He's coming closer and closer now, closing the space between us in a delicate dance, "But I could show you, I think, if you'd like."

I look at him. He sounds so genuine, and yet so very much... conflicted.

He reminds me more of a fifteen-year-old boy asking out his first crush than a powerful, six-hundred-year-old vampire.

I don't want this hesitance between us. We're both alive, aren't we? We're both here, together, bound in one room for the first time without any outside pressure...

Well. That's not exactly true. Despite the lavish surroundings, I cannot forget that we are deep in enemy territory. For whatever reason, they want to give us the illusion of comfort.

But an illusion, for the moment, is the best thing we've got. It's been nothing but turmoil and upheaval ever since the attacks on The Haven.

How ironic is it that the first reprieve we get happens to come courtesy of the vampires responsible for the attack?

"I'd love that," I say softly.

Raul smiles. He closes the final bit of space and lowers himself beside me. I take a breath and catch his scent. He smells clean and pure. That smell of corruption that had been clinging to him ever since he took the wound is gone. Only *his* essence remains now.

Raul runs his fingers over the keys in a gentle, caressing motion. I'm reminded of the way one might touch a favored lover. He takes pride in what he does, he always has. I've sensed it in him.

He takes a deep breath, closes his eyes... and starts to play.

The music fills the room. Notes fall high and low. There's a beautiful synchronicity between them. Raul's fingers dance over the keyboard. All his hesitation is gone. All the restraint, all the caution is gone. He loses himself in the music, and it's a glorious melody that he plays, full of complete notes and rising crescendos and entire sweeps of cascading sounds.

Quickly, he gains confidence. Now his whole body begins to move with the sound. He becomes absorbed in the music, totally oblivious to anything… except the wonderful music he is producing. A sort of energy pulsates from his body and ebbs into me. I'd say it was body heat, but vampires are cold, always cold, and yet I feel a sort of beautiful, blossoming resonance between us.

Like I said, I've always appreciated music. But now, as a vampire, with all my enhanced senses, and none of the turbulent unease, I find myself enjoying it so much more. The tiniest nuances, previously hidden to my human ears, are now evident in all their glory. The smallest, most subtle shifts in tone add a delicious layer of complexity to the sound Raul is producing.

It's almost hypnotizing. The piece is rich and powerful. Raul plays, and the music grows, until it envelops the whole of me and the whole of the room. I'm lifted to a higher plane as I let the music take me, wash over me, wash *through* me in an experience that could have never been possible were I still human.

Oh, how I pity the way I used to lament becoming a creature of the night. These gifts I now hold—nothing can be more precious. Nothing can be more valuable. The whole of the world is opened up to me, a feast for my senses come after a lent of starvation.

How could anyone deny the power of song, the power of sound to uplift the body and mind and let the spirit soar? It's like a link has been opened up between my soul and Raul's music. It's astounding, it's amazing, it's hypnotizing and, most of all, it's—

Suddenly Raul stops. The music cuts off. The elation dies. A silence descends upon the room, broken only by his heavy breathing.

"I… I got a little carried away," he says. "Forgive me?"

I stare at him in amazement. And then, in an impulsive flash, I throw my arms around him and hold him tight.

"That was incredible," I whisper in his ear. "Raul, I didn't know you could play."

He pulls back, gently, and cups my face with his hands. He searched my eyes for a long, lingering moment.

I feel the connection that we once had flare into being again.

"I wouldn't have shared that with any but you," he says softly. "I've never played for an audience before. It was only something I ever did for myself."

"I'm glad you let me in on your secret," I tell him, in full earnestness. "And I—"

He cuts me off by sealing his lips to mine and kissing me.

I flounder when I'm finally let go. I gasp for air, because all of it has been stolen from my lungs.

"I've waited a very, very long time to do that," he tells me.

I want to laugh. I want to cry. I don't know what I want, the music, the kiss, the situation, for all of it is making me so emotional.

But there is one thing I know for sure. I want more of Raul.

Something flares in his eyes—a sudden impulsiveness—and he kisses me again. My hands tangle in his hair. I pull him close. Our bodies press together, seated awkwardly as we are on the piano bench. His hand runs to my lower back. He tugs me closer. I give a little yelp of surprise as his hand tightens against my waist.

He continues to kiss me, exploring the contours of my lips with his tongue, tasting me, needing me, needing me as much as I do him. And I kiss him back hard, no longer afraid of the feelings he evokes in me, no longer hesitant to commit completely to who I am and what he makes me feel.

But a moment later, something starts to feel wrong. It's like there's a presence in the room with us. It breaks me out of the blissful moment and forces me to push Raul away.

"What is it?" he asks. Desire threads his voice. "Too fast?"

"No," I say. "No, it's not that. I just thought I felt—"

I don't get to finish. The door swings open and slams hard against the wall. Both Raul and I jerk back.

Dagan is standing there.

"Reunion's over," he announces harshly. "It's time for us to work."

Chapter Thirty-Nine

JAMES

THE WOODS OUTSIDE THE HAVEN

Wanda comes up to me and offers me her wrist. "Drink, my Lord," she says.

Imperiously, I swat her hand away. I have no interest in more of her blood.

Heavens know I've had enough of it in the last half-span.

I've been in the company of these humans for days. At first, I thought I would simply abandon them after taking what I needed. And for a good ninety-six hours, I led them to believe I did exactly that.

Whereas in reality, I'd stayed close and watched to see how they would react after they found me gone.

In that time, I discovered a group of humans more fascinating than I could have ever believed.

For one, they did not panic when they found me missing. Neither did they seem particularly alarmed to discover four of their company dead. They burned the bodies with a sleek efficiency, and did so in near-absolute silence. The fact that they barely had to speak to discuss what had happened tells me that they were, in some ways, prepared for this.

I followed them closer in the aftermath. I wondered where they would go, what they would do. I watched as they set traps for rabbits and small game. I waited as they roasted their meals and shared their meager provisions with each other. I listened to every drop of conversation that would reach my ears.

And as I did, I learned something that both infuriated and astounded me. Not once did they speak of the vampire who took their blood. Not once did they acknowledge what I had done or what they had gone through.

If I thought them crazy at the start, well, this sort of behavior only reinforced that notion. How could any humans not speak of something so transcendent, something so far outside the realm of the ordinary?

And yet, the irony behind all that is that coming across a vampire did *not* have the expected outcome. Most of them were still alive. The four who died did so because their bodies were too weak to recover from the amount of blood I had taken, not because I had killed during the drink—as is per usual. And as I continued trailing this odd group of humans, I found a sort of... fondness... come over me, for them. Such a ridiculous notion, that. Fondness, for *humans?*

Might as well admit to being no better than Phillip, in his misguided attempt to hold off the instincts the dark power grants us.

I waited to hear my name. But they acted as if the feast they had granted me never took place. And if there's one thing I've always craved, it's recognition.

Not to receive *any* from this group drove me mad.

But still, I waited on the sidelines. I waited to see where they would go. Would they continue on their quest toward The Haven? What could they possibly expect the vampires' reception of them would be when they found it?

But moreover, and perhaps most of all, how did they know where to look?

So a couple of days passed with me acting as their guardian angel. With all my senses restored, I could easily tell if there were any vampires from the sanctuary making an approach. I'd be warned long before any could sneak up on us.

Not that they would ever find me, given that the cloaking spell still made me essentially invisible.

When the animal predators came close to the humans, I scared them off.

Over time, I found myself becoming more and more attached to the idea of these humans as belonging to me.

Perhaps that sense of ownership was misguided. Perhaps it was a weakness pervading from the source of my feedings. I had never drunk so deeply and not killed. Now, I had all of these humans' blood mingling around inside me, and perhaps *that* was the cause of all these unfamiliar feelings of possessiveness.

It was on the fourth night that I made my return. They were camped around a fire, eating a thin sort of soup. I strolled right into their midst and, without a word, sat down.

Immediately, they dropped their bowls and fell to the dirt floor. My lip twitched in a half-smile. *Now* I was getting the respect I deserve.

That night I feasted on them once more. And, in the days that followed I learned more and more about the fascinating cult they are all a part of.

"My lord?" Wanda interrupts me from my remembrance. "It would do me great honor if you would take my blood tonight."

"Your blood has lost its appeal," I say scathingly. She flinches back. There's a growing discontent inside me, at what, I don't know—maybe at being static. I rise up. "*All* of your blood has lost its appeal," I announce.

Then, with a harsh twist of my heel, I stride into the darkened woods.

Once I'm out of earshot I start to run. It feels good to have the wind in my face, to know the power of my body. It's been returned to me, thanks to the Fang Chasers, and for that, I *am* grateful.

But the emotions are conflicted inside me. I do not want to feel like I owe anybody anything, especially not to a rag-tag group of humans. And yet…

And yet, I cannot help but think what an awful position I might be in were it not for them. Still slithering away on the forest floor, taking what little sustenance I could find from the most pathetic sources of food around me.

It's because I didn't kill them, I think. *That is the true reason for all this ridiculous angst.*

If they were dead, things would be easy. I'd have regained all of my strength. I would not be in anyone's debt. I'd be fully autonomous, and I could then consider what I had to do next to let *myself* get ahead…

And make plans for getting back at all those who had wronged me.

I know what Wanda wants. I know what all of her little group wants.

They want the Dark Gift.

They want to be made like me. They want to become creatures of the night, to stalk and hunt and kill and prey upon unsuspecting humans.

They want eternal life.

And they are trying to coax me into giving it. That's why Wanda keeps offering me her wrist. She hopes it will ingratiate her to me even more.

None of the humans have directly asked me for The Gift. But if what Wanda said was true, and April was once a part of them...

I shiver in memory. Have I been so blind as to truly believe the girl was developing feelings for me? I considered her as nothing more than a distraction, a temporary body to warm the sheets...

But she'd been aiming at something beyond that all along. The whole of our brief relationship, she'd wanted the same thing these humans now want.

That these humans demand?

Certainly they aren't as presumptuous as that. Like I said, none have explicitly asked for the Gift. And yet...

I come to a jagged stop when I suddenly recognize the spot I'm in. I've been running without thinking, letting my mind wander as my legs took me where they may.

I'm looking out at the secret lake where my younger brother once hid his true love.

A torrent of memories threatens to wash over me. The ugly jealousy, the splintering hate. Liana was supposed to be *mine*. She was supposed to be given to *me*, as collection of the debt that was owed. As payment for sparing an entire village of humans from a vampire attack.

I was the one who had struck the deal with the human manor lord. *I* was the one who was supposed to have led the hunt. But a distraction, at the very last minute, by a blonde spitfire of a vampire who invited me to her bed made me forsake the hunt...

I shake my head gruffly and dispel those thoughts. *Story of my life,* I think. Being taken in by momentary beauty, by a single shining object, only to lose out on what I really want.

I'm short-sighted. I can admit that now. Always, always, always, it was imme-diate gratification that I was after. Always, it was instant results that called to me.

And so I'd lost out on Liana. And after that, I'd lost out on Eleira. Even though *I* was the one to turn her, to inject her with the serum that was to slowly make her into a vampire who took after me...

Well. Victoria saw to negating all of that courtesy of her cryptic ritual.

But *Liana*... I had the last laugh there. I'd done the unspeakable out of greed, out of anger, out of a vile mix of lust and loathing and self-hatred. But it made me feel better, in the end... even though I knew that if Raul found out, his relation-ship with me would be irrevocably damaged.

But he never did. No one did. None but I know what I was responsible for.

It is a secret I will continue to guard to my dying breath.

Suddenly, it hits me: I am *inside* The Haven. But where is everybody else?

I open my mind and consciously scan the surroundings. I do not feel another vampire anywhere. The place is abandoned.

That concerns me. Shouldn't there be guards? Sentries? *Somebody* posted around the perimeter, now that the wards are down?

I move once in a slow circle. Nothing. The place is abandoned. Granted, this is far from the main hub of activity in the sanctuary... but still.

Something has gone wrong. Something has gone very, very wrong.

An owl calls in the distance, making me turn my head. Ah, I remember how my two brothers loved such sounds of nature. It is one thing they shared that I never had.

To me, such sounds were a distraction—an ugly smear on the smooth canvas of a silent night.

Very carefully, I pick up a loose rock. I take aim at the snow-white creature. I cock my arm back, fling it forward, and let go.

The rock sails smoothly through the air and strikes the bird in the chest. It rips through the owl as a bullet might.

I smile to myself as I watch the bird drop. It won't be bothering me anymore.

***

I walk back to the group of humans. They fall still as soon as they see me.

"Wanda," I beckon her to me. "Come here."

Their leader rises and walks to me. She bows her head in respect. "Yes, my Lord?"

Something about that title grates on my nerves. "First," I say. "I am not your *lord*. I am a vampire, and you are a human. We are two distinct species. Calling me your lord implies I have given you leave to do so. I have not."

"Yes. Of course, I'm sorry," she murmurs.

"The same goes for all of you," I continue. "When you address me, you will use my real name. James Soren. If you want," I add as an afterthought, "you may call me Prince. But only *after* we achieve what it is I desire."

"And what is that, my L—James?" Wanda asks.

"Dominion," I say softly. "Dominion over all creatures and all clans. You recognize that vampires are powerful. But you do not know the full extent of our potential. Few do. What you know of The Haven is of great interest to me. You will tell me when it comes time. But I will say this, my ambitions are much greater than the Queen's ever were. And for those ambitions to become possible... I will need an army."

Immediately Wanda's eyes glaze over, full of lust. "An army of vampires," she breathes.

"An army of vampires sworn loyal to *me*," I tell her. "An army of vampires who know they owe all that they have, all that they are, to *me*." My eyes go to each member of the Fang Chasers. "Do you know where I might find such an army?"

The implication in my question is clear enough. The group of sixteen immediately throw themselves to the ground.

"We will be yours," Wanda vows. "If you but have us."

"First," I say, "you have to tell me what you are after."

"I..." she licks her lips, looking up at me. "We all... want The Dark Gift."

"And so, it is what I will give," I announce.

A shiver of ecstasy washes over Wanda.

"Stand," I command. I point at a spot on the ground. "All of you, stand. For this to happen, we need to start a fire—one greater than anything these woods have ever known. One that will herald your creation, and one that will announce the beginning of a new coven." I purse my lips and look to the sky, where all the constellations are clearly visible. "We will be called... The Nocturna Animalia. Latin, for *Creatures of the Night*. Now hurry." My eyes blaze into theirs. "The conversion begins before sunrise."

Chapter Forty

PHILLIP

INSIDE THE HAVEN'S STRONGHOLD

Even though Raul and Eleira have only been gone for a few hours, it feels like days.

I'd had to deal with more upheaval in the last bit of time than I could ever imagine having been necessary. Every vampire, both of the Elite *and* the Incolam, believed themselves entitled to a personal explanation from me about how two more guards were slaughtered so easily, and what I'm doing to protect the rest.

Discord is growing. The vampires are getting restless. They are tired of being locked up inside with only an uncertain future to look forward to.

I wish I could give reassurance. I wish I could come up with some sort of tantalizing lie, just close enough to the truth that I don't feel like a crook spinning it.

But such is not in my nature. Control over events is slipping from my hands like fine sand through a sieve.

Thankfully, Smithson has managed to step in and make himself useful.

I did not know what to make of his offer of assistance at first. The vampire is as slippery as a snake. But so far, he's proven true to his word.

When members of the Royal Court harass me about the Queen's recovery, or the stronghold's security, Smithson steps in and offers easy assurances. When the Incolam come up and demand to know how and why the Narwhark is still allowed to roam freely, they see him and remember the gift he gave of Victoria's blood, and walk away feeling better.

The mere presence of the grizzled former commander seems to make me more worthwhile, somehow, in their eyes.

I only wish it was as easy for me to trust him.

"They need a distraction," Smithson tells me after Caroline, a vampire who I've always suspected had a thing for both my brothers, leaves the room. "Morale is low. Your vampires are frightened. They have to be soothed."

"You think I don't know that?" I snap. "But what can I do? It's not safe for them to go outside. Not with the wards down. Here, at least, in the stronghold, they are contained. The threat, the danger, comes from the demon. Every guard is on high alert, ready to call in reinforcements at the first hint of its presence"

Smithson laughs. It's not altogether a cruel laugh, but it's not entirely comforting, either. "I saw what the demon did to those guards. I *faced* it myself. Trust me when I say that even the whole of The Haven's vampires, arranged as an army, could not take it down."

Smithson walks over to my desk. His injuries have mostly healed, thanks to an offer I made him from my brother's secret store of blood. "Keeping them penned up is like putting a herd of sheep behind a rope barrier with a wolf on the prowl. The Narwhark cannot be fought, not directly, but that doesn't mean you have to make it any easier for it."

"And yet it's not rabid," I say softly.

Smithson jerks his head up. "What?"

"It's not attacking at random," I say. "It moves fast. It knows it can kill. But it's intelligent. I glimpsed something in its eyes, last time it fed. It knows what it is doing. I think it's developing... consciousness."

"That's garbage," Smithson growls. "A demon isn't capable of higher level thinking any more than a tea kettle is. The Narwhark only knows two things: kill, and feed."

"Then why didn't it kill you?" I question. "Why did it only stab the Queen with its tail? It had the entire assembly of vampires gathered in one room. It could have had its pick of any of them!"

"Eleira," Smithson says softly.

I blink. "What?"

"Eleira was there. We know that she summoned it. We know that only a witch can take it down. Maybe that's why it was cautious. Maybe Eleira's presence made it pause."

"You're grasping at straws."

"No! Listen to me, boy. I've seen more than you can imagine in my life. I've spent my whole life in the real world, fighting for survival just like any human! While you were coddled in here, protected by the wards—" he raises his hands as I start to object, "—and I mean no disrespect, Phillip, but objectively, I think it easy to say I have more life experience than you do. Simply from the situations I've been placed in."

"What's your point?" I question.

249

"My point is this. I can give you counsel. You would be wise to listen to it."

"That's what I'm doing, isn't it?" I growl. "That's why I've put up with you being by my side this whole time?"

"So then take action! You need to do something to divert the vampires' attention."

"Even if I agreed," I say. "What could I do? They all know the gravity of the situation. Until Eleira and Raul get back--"

"*If* they get back," Smithson interjects.

I walk right to him and stab a finger in his chest. "*When* they get back," I say, "we'll know more. We'll be in a better position to act. Some of the uncertainties around all of this will be dispelled."

"No. No, no, no." Smithson shakes his head. "You don't truly believe it will be that easy, do you?"

"I never said it would be *easy*," I hiss. "Only that we will have a clearer picture."

"And what do you propose we do while we wait? Sit on our thumbs, counting down the minutes to the next demon attack?" Smithson lowers his voice. "You might not fully grasp this, given your... *personal history*... but vampires are natural predators. They are not used to being frightened. They are even less used to feeling as if they are prey. The longer you wait, doing nothing, the more the discord will grow. You think members of the Royal Court aren't meeting at this very moment, discussing what to do should the Queen not awaken?"

"Mother *will* wake up!" I roar, slamming a hand against the wall.

Smithson doesn't even blink. Instead, he drops his voice an octave lower and asks, "And what if she doesn't? If your precious Queen remains in her coma, what happens then? Tell me."

I eye him without answering.

"You'll be dealing with another revolt, that's what. There are members of the Elite other than I who are eager to seek power."

"Ah!" I say. "So you admit it. You wanted power and control over The Haven, after all."

"No. All that I did, I did to serve the Queen." He grunts. "Must we go over this old, hackneyed argument again? We've made our peace, it's already happened, all of it is in the past. It cannot be changed."

"Fine," I relent. "Fine, fine. You speak of a distraction as if you have something in mind. So, tell me. What is it you propose?"

A ferocious smile spreads across his face. "The next full moon is coming," he says. "Remind the vampires of who they are. Make them remember that they are not scared, timid creatures."

"What are you saying?"

"Give them the humans," he says. His eyes glimmer with raw lust. "Announce the next Hunt."

Chapter Forty-One

RIYU

SOMEWHERE BENEATH THE CRYPTS

I pace the cold, tile floor of the secret underground chamber, not bothering to hide any of my discontent.

Beatrice summoned me here hours ago. It's the first time I've been allowed in the lower levels. This is her domain, the place the King has given to her in full, to do with as she pleases...

To do with her *victims* as she pleases.

The chamber itself is simple. It's not much more than a cut-out box. The walls are reinforced with steel rods that have been infused with iron. The entrance door is the only way in or out.

Well... the only way a regular vampire might see.

There are spells cast along the walls, hiding the secret doorways that lead deeper into Beatrice's experimentation chambers.

How did she get them there? I wonder. I was not asked to do it for her. And there are no others with The Spark residing within The Crypts anymore.

Aside from that cunning, deceptive girl, Eleira, that is.

I knew she did something different when she opened the portal out of the

Paths. It was not until I arrived on the other side that I discovered *what*.

Somehow, she managed to use the space between worlds to suck out the deadly magic lingering in Raul's body, to sever his connection to the knife, and to restore him to his full capacity.

I have to admit the maneuver was brilliant. I couldn't have foreseen it. I doubt any could have. She was supposed to be nothing but a hedge witch. I doubt she ever had much training. In fact, even if The Haven's Queen had devoted every single moment to instructing her, Eleira could not have possibly had enough time to grasp any but the most basic tenants.

And yet, obviously, she knows more. Obviously, she is capable of more.

More, I think, *than she or the Queen or even my Father dream possible.*

I start running my fingers over each hand, feeling my nails, my knuckles, the narrow, feminine bones of my body. These are the hands that can do magic. These are the hands that are capable of so much.

Or, at least, *would* be capable of so much if the invisible shackles holding my power back would be released.

I glance anxiously at the one visible door. Beatrice is known to take her sweet time—but why summon me so far in advance only to make me wait? She and I have frequently collaborated together—maybe not as friends, but at least as allies—so the delay makes little sense. We have an *understanding* with each other. She knows one or two of my secrets. I know some of hers. It is what allows the thinnest semblance of respect to show, from her to me, when we are alone.

Otherwise, the vampire hierarchy would make such a thing impossible.

My fingers keep running over each other. Across, through, down, and then back up. Across, through, down and back up. It's not exactly a nervous habit, but it is something I've found myself to take comfort in when my nerves start getting the better of me.

For one, I dislike being away from Dagan for so long. He doesn't show it, not through the tough, thick exterior, but he needs my company. I know it. Especially at a time like this, right after the link between him and Raul has been broken. He's probably reeling, trying to understand how it could have happened, dealing with the repercussions—and I'm not there to help him.

He'd never admit to needing my help. But I know he does. Oh yes, I know he does.

Finally, the door swings open. I still my hands and thrust them to my sides. Beatrice walks through.

Her cheeks are flushed, her lips swollen, and her hair has only been hastily arranged. A flash of anger takes me as I realize the reason she's late.

Quick as I can, I smother it down.

Beatrice's eyes flicker to me. "You're still here," she says. "Good."

Not a single word of gratitude, not even the hint of an apology. I shouldn't expect it from vampires so high above me in strength. But, still...

"What is it you wanted to show me?" I ask.

"I want to speak to you in private."

"You could have done that anywhere," I keep my voice deceptively meek. "You didn't need to invite me here to do it."

"No," she tells me. "You're right, I didn't. Still. I wanted assurance that we would not be interrupted."

I eye her and she walks closer. "And what would be so important as that?" I ask.

"The girl," Beatrice says instantly. "Eleira. You saw her. You brought her here."

I nod. "Yes."

"You spoke to her."

"I did."

"I want to know..." Beatrice steps even closer. "If Eleira can be *corrupted*. You're the one who taught me of the dark side of magic. Is she strong enough to ward it off? Or is she made vulnerable by who she is?"

I shake my head, "I cannot answer that. It is a judgment call of her character, not of her strength as a witch."

"Then I want your *opinion*," Beatrice tells me. "Can she be turned to our side?"

"It... might prove difficult," I hedge. I recall the ardent way she avoided looking at Raul, the vampire she clearly loves, only to try to hide that love from us. "You can force a witch to do certain things. To act in particular ways. To be tugged, this way and that, by soft, invisible strings." Again my mind drifts to the shackles holding my powers in place—the ones I am not supposed to even know of. "But you have to be very, very careful. Her Spark makes her vulnerable, in a way, but it also makes her resilient. As you might imagine."

Beatrice taps her lips. "I see."

"The best," I say, speaking out of turn but *needing* to give voice to my thoughts, "would be to convince her to come to your side of her own accord. To show her that yours is the best way."

"*Mine*," Beatrice quotes. "Surely you mean 'ours', Riyu."

I blink. That was a careless gaffe. "I did not want to presume," I say quickly.

In truth, the only side I'm on is my own.

Beatrice laughs. "Presume away. It is only you and I here, no others." She nods in the direction of the far wall. "Would you like to see what's beyond there?"

I turn my head over my shoulder. I can see past the glamour spell covering it. I can see the enormous door hidden there.

But on the other side of it? I have no idea what might be.

"Yes," I tell her curtly.

"Then come," she beckons me to her side. "I will show you."

We reach the wall. As Beatrice comes closer, the cloaking spell parts, revealing the giant door in full.

She gives no notice to my complete lack of surprise. She presses her palm against a metal plate in the middle of the wood. It dips down under the pressure, taking on the impression of her hand.

"Enchanted," she tells me, matter-of-factly, as if I would not recognize the door for a torrial.

But now my curiosity is piqued.

We wait a few moments. Then, the grand door begins to grind open.

When there's just enough space for us to slip through, Beatrice takes my hand and pulls me after her. I'm surprised by the unexpected contact. But I soon discover that it was necessary.

For the door does not just open to the other side. The door, in and of itself, is a portal... to a place miles and miles away.

The second I move over the threshold a magical chill washes over me. It's like stepping through from the back of a waterfall and letting the water cleanse you as you emerge. For a moment, that strange sensation overcomes all of my senses. Then I blink, and we're through, and it's gone.

I look around. We're in a pitch-black cavern. There's no way in or out but the way we came.

It's a hollowed out spot deep in the Earth. Immediately I dislike it. It feels wrong, somehow, to be in this place.

"Impressed yet?" Beatrice murmurs.

I turn to her—and stop short. Even though she's just inches away, I cannot see her face. My vampire sight does not pierce this darkness.

An uncanny feeling of vulnerability comes over me.

She strolls forward, full of casual indifference. "You get used to it," she says over her shoulder. "The first time I made the trip, I nearly bolted straight out."

The implication in her words is clear. *Nearly*. Meaning she did not. Meaning that even if I want to, I cannot.

I take a step forward. As soon as my foot touches the ground the world seems to tilt. I have to spin my arms like a windmill to catch my balance.

"Oh," she adds, entirely as an afterthought. "There is silver in the rock. I forgot how much it affects one like you."

She left out a key operative word in that sentence, one as *weak* as you.

I grit my teeth and call upon all the military discipline Dagan has instilled in me before continuing on.

I can only track Beatrice by the sound of her footsteps. Every time her heels strike the ground the noise echoes through the space around me.

We walk for a longer distance than I thought possible. The acoustics of the rock give the impression of a close, tight space. But it seems to be indeed expansive.

On and on we go, where we stop, nobody knows.

Suddenly her steps cut out. I go still. There is a vibration to the air. It's very subtle, and very, very hard to pinpoint exactly where it comes from.

But it does have a source. And that source is neither the silver in the rock nor the odd mix of latent magic I feel around me. It's something altogether different.

I feel a swoosh of movement in the air as Beatrice raises her arms and claps her hands, twice, high over her head.

The walls light up with hundreds upon hundreds of stars.

My jaw drops. I clamp it shut so fast my teeth click against each other. But the effect of my surprise is not lessened.

It feels like I am standing in the middle of the cosmos, looking out upon the whole of the universe. It takes me an extra moment to realize that the stars are oh-so-slowly rotating around me.

"Beautiful," Beatrice breathes. "Isn't it?"

I only nod my head in wonder.

"Do you know the stars, Riyu?" she asks.

"No," I admit. It is yet another part of my education that is lacking. "Father never saw fit for me to learn."

Right away I grimace. No matter my relationship with the woman, she should never hear me refer to the King as Father.

Nobody should. Those are dangerous enough thoughts when they're locked in my head.

She chooses to pay it no attention. "A pity. For you cannot truly appreciate the significance of this place without such learning." She sighs. "But, we will make due with what we have. Do you see that star out there, far away, to your right?" She points. "The one glowing brighter than the rest?"

I nod. "Yes."

"That is our sun. See how far we stand now? From here, we have a unique perspective on the constellations unavailable to any on Earth."

"But we're still on Earth," I say. "Aren't we?"

"Yes, of course. It is only our perspective that's changed." She motions to another group of stars. "I wish I could tell you about all of the constellations, but that would take an age. You only need to know a few select things about how the stars affect us.

"One: Eleira was not the only human girl prophesized to come into the vampire world and shake its very foundation. There was one other. Born at the opposite sign of the moon, and unknown to any but me. For I was the only one—" she smiles, "—to have access to this place."

"What does that mean for us, exactly?" I ask.

"That while Eleira is valuable..." Beatrice's smile becomes sadistic, and cruel, "she is not altogether indispensable. Not in the way others think. But this is a secret that must remain between only you and me, hmm?"

I nod in tacit agreement.

"Two. And this is perhaps the most important. There will come a time when the King, your *Father*, must unite the covens. It is written here, in the constellations." She gestures at some stars in the distance. "The time is not yet. But the signs are clear: all vampires must be bound under one rule in order for our kind's true transcendence to take place."

"Why tell me?" I ask. "I don't have the power to influence things."

"You, my dearest Riyu, are more capable than you think." She winks. "And I promise you, I will work on Logan to help him see that."

She walks closer and brings a hand to my cheek. "You deserve more than what you've been given. So much more. I can make that happen, if you let me. If you *trust* me..."

"I trust you enough," I tell her.

She gives a soft laugh. "I see the way you look at Dagan. I might be the only one. If you want, I could help make *that*, happen, too..."

Sudden horror takes me. *Have I been so transparent? Are my desires really so evident?* "No!" I gasp. "No. Please. Don't."

"Your wish." She shrugs. "But back to Eleira. It *would* be better were she to be fully on our side. Things would be so much... simpler. I also have a way of making that happen."

She claps her hands again, and the illusion of the stars disappears. But the light from them remains, and it fills the whole of the room.

Beatrice motions behind me. I turn—and once more, find my jaw on the floor.

Standing there is a large, crystal throne, shimmering in the light. It gives off a menacing sort of radiance.

That was the source of vibration I felt in the air.

"A near-perfect replica of the torrial protecting The Haven," she tells me. "It has taken years to create. But I think, finally... it's nearly complete."

"*You* made it?" I say, my voice full of awe and wonder. "How?"

"Not I," she says. "But I have found a way to fuel it, to imbue it with power. It is the lesser twin of the other, but, given the right situation, very, very powerful." She beams at me, proud as a mother showing off her child. "And Riyu? If I can be made certain that our visions for the future of the world align... I will offer it to *you*."

Chapter Forty-Two

BEATRICE

THE CRYPTS

"So? How did he take it?"

I glance over my shoulder at the King. He is lounging half-naked in bed, his powerful chest exposed by the throw that comes up just to his midriff.

"It was too easy," I say with a casual shrug, and return to studying my reflection in the mirror. My, but how fascinating it is that so many years have passed, so many things have changed, and yet my face has always—and will, forevermore—remained exactly the same. "He did not suspect anything was wrong."

"You give Riyu too little credit. He's sly, always has been. Can you be sure he took the lie?"

I give an exasperated sigh and turn around. "I am one of the few vampires he *trusts*," I emphasize. "Riyu fashions himself remarkably clever, but it is a form of arrogance. He thinks his desires are hidden from the world, but you know as well as I do what they really are."

Logan makes a disgusted sound. "That is why he is not fit to be acknowledged as my blood."

"But he will have to be, at the proper time. You know that."

"I know only because you insist on it," the King growls.

I slowly rise and make my way seductively to the bed. "Do you know *why* I insist on it?" I ask, swaying my hips as I walk. Logan's eyes go immediately to my curves; he's never been one to hide his appreciation for me. "Because Riyu..." I sit down and trail a finger up his strong leg, "...is but a pawn. A pawn for you to use to get what you want."

His breathing deepens as my hand finds its way under the cover. "He is a pawn in the great cosmic game. We all are, my King—except for you."

A smile of languid pleasure comes over Logan's face. My hand starts to move in a rhythmic motion beneath the sheet. "You have ruled here long enough. The time has almost come for the rest of the world to know your power. The time has come for you to rise and to take command of all those vampires rightfully below you. You are a King--," I grip him tighter, "--but with me at your side, I will turn you into a *God*."

Logan's eyes glaze over as a rush of ecstasy takes him. I can see him imagining what that will taste like—what it will be to rule, to truly *rule*, and be feared and respected by vampires and humans alike.

"The transfer of magic," he says. "It will work? You are sure of it?"

"The elemental forces are tricky things," I hedge. "They can be unpredictable. I am not a true witch, so I could not tell you. To claim otherwise would be a lie. But I can guarantee you this—if anyone can survive, it is you."

He sits up, pulling away from me. "You gave me your assurance before. If I let you lead Riyu on this merry little game, the end result--"

"Will be worth it, still, I swear, my King. A little bit of patience, that's what we need."

"You taunt me," he says. I can feel him growing angry. "You promise one thing, over and over, but when it comes time to deliver you tell me it's over the next hedge."

"Such is the way of what you've tasked me with," I tell him sweetly. "Some things can be expedited by sheer will. Others cannot. Unfortunately, this is one of the latter."

I stand up. "Eleira and Raul are waiting," I say. "We need to give them a showing unlike any they've seen before. For the girl to come over to our side—we need her to be fearful, yes, but we also need to claim her respect. It will be a delicate balance between the two. She cannot be forced into anything, as you know."

Logan makes a deep, disgruntled sound of disapproval. "The things I concede for you," he grumbles.

He rises. The blanket completely falls away. He turns back and strolls for his robe. I cannot help it—my eyes go immediately to the strong muscles of his body. As he drapes his many layers of jewelry on, I allow myself a self-indulgent smile.

The most vital adornments on his body are those that no one else will ever see: the red marks, from my nails, all over his back.

Chapter Forty-Three

Perhaps I had overestimated my degree of influence with Phillip.

The moment I suggested The Hunt... something changed in his eyes. A rage the likes of which I'd never seen came over him. I expected human feedings to be a prickly subject for him, but I never thought he'd react *this* harshly.

He'd raged at me, then, and in his fury, struck out. It took all the training I've ever received to stop myself from fighting back. Only the knowledge of my greater purpose, and cognizance of how easily that could be betrayed were I to lose control now, kept me from defending myself.

As it was, things could have turned out to be worse. Phillip could have completely reneged on his word and sent me back to the dungeons.

Instead, he just commanded me to leave, and to not speak to a single member of the Elite while I was gone.

It galls me, the ease with which the boy assumes superiority. The change overcoming him is apparent even to me. The feeding his Mother forced him to take really did alter his whole persona.

But it's not like I have to be completely complicit in my exile. After wandering through the barren underground halls for a good hour, and finding no one following me, I quietly slip into Carter's rooms.

I discover them empty. That's irritating. Where could the vampire be?

But I don't have to wait long as a secret latch comes open and Carter walks out from behind a bookshelf.

His eyebrows go up when he sees me. "I thought I sensed someone," he murmurs. "Though I did not expect it to be you."

I eye the opening behind him. Carter was the one who originally informed me of this stronghold, back when I first arrived in The Haven. It would make sense that he would know more of its secrets than most.

"Hiding?" I ask. "From whom or what, I wonder."

I don't try to tone down any of the discontent in my voice.

"Mmm, more like, *taking inventory*," he says. He closes the secret passage, and it blends seamlessly into the wall. "It's always a good idea to have full control of your possessions."

"Are these possessions any you expect to be going anywhere?" I ask.

He shrugs. "Odder things have happened. How is the Queen?"

"Unfortunately, that information is beyond my current status," I say.

"Mm," Carter nods. "That *is* unfortunate. How the mighty have fallen." He looks me over. "But then again. You're not in chains. Things could be worse."

"And they could be a hell of a lot better," I say. "I made the suggestion you proposed."

"Did you? And?"

"And, what do you think?" I growl. "He did not take it well."

"So the boy is still soft," Carter nods. "Interesting."

I wouldn't exactly call him "soft", I think.

"You made sure to frame it as your idea?"

"I'm no idiot," I say. "I know I cannot link it back to you."

"Even if you talked," he chuckles. "I would deny it. And *everybody* knows I would never go against the Royal Court." A thin smile forms on his lips. "I *am* one of its most distinguished members."

"That's not what I came for," I say.

"Then why did you come, Smithson? I thought my instructions were clear."

"They were," I say. "Except for one or two small details."

"How small?"

"Oh, *miniscule,*" I deadpan. "Such as the complete lack of trust you exhibit in me."

"Have you given me reason to trust you, Smithson? *Really* given it?"

"Look," I say. "I'm risking a lot by being here. If all you want to do is mock me--"

"Need I remind you that *you* came to *me?*" Carter asks. "Your feet brought you here for a reason. What could that be?"

I fight down the surge of anger that threatens to take me. The smug, complacent fool, I could crush him! If I so wanted, I could destroy him, just as I destroyed James, just as I--

I stop that line of thinking with a harsh shudder. It seems the control I once exhibited over my thoughts has more or less abandoned me.

At least my actions are still within my hands.

"I came to ask if there's been any word—" I lower my voice, "—from Beatrice."

"From who? Carter cups a hand to his ear. "You must speak louder. I could not hear you."

"*Beatrice,*" I say again.

"Ah." He smiles at me again. Then, he shakes his head. "Unfortunately no. I presume your ex-wife is much too busy in The Crypts. A woman of her beauty, after all, must have a bevy of options available with which to occupy her time—"

"Watch it," I growl. I take a step forward. That anger continues to beat against the barriers I'd erected. "If you're not careful, I'll—"

"You'll what?" Carter scoffs. "I am your only true ally here, Smithson. The others have already exhausted their use of you. You brought us prominence in the aftermath of the attack, but the Royal Court quickly forgets its debts. It's never had to answer to them, you see. And once your rank was stripped from you, you became… dispensable."

I can rip your heart out with my bare hands, I think. *I could strike so fast that you'd be dead before the next word leaves your lips.*

But I temper the temptation. Soon I will have my revenge, not just on this pompous, blown-up fool, but on *all* vampires. All vampires, everywhere.

I've waited centuries already. What's a little bit more patience now?

So I look away and adopt a look of subservience. "You're right, of course," I mumble.

I turn around to leave.

"Smithson?" Carter calls. I stop. "Look at me."

I turn my head back over my shoulder.

"I noticed that a certain *something* was missing from your side. In the aftermath of the castle's fall. So, I took it upon myself to... well, let's just call it an extension of good faith."

"What are you talking about?" I grumble.

"If you'll come with me?"

He walks away without waiting to see if I will follow. Seeing that I have no choice, I start after him.

He takes me through a small back door in the very depths of his room. We go down a long, narrow chamber. Torches are lit at regular intervals along the walls. They seem an unnecessary addition.

As if having read my thoughts, Carter explains, "These passageways are typically reserved for human servants. The fires are ever-burning. An old spell, simple, really, cast by our Queen when this place was first constructed. It holds to this very day."

I expand my mind, testing for the presence of any others, and find that we are alone.

The earth starts to slope downward. Carter continues to lead. Eventually we come to a heavy, iron door.

It's already ajar. Carter appears to have no problem with that. He pushes it the rest of the way open and steps inside.

I follow him and discover a treasure room.

It's cluttered with arrangements of all sorts of strange sculptures, carvings, and contraptions. They line the walls, piled high upon each other on the shelves. None look particularly menacing. In fact, to my trained military eye, none seem to be anything more than toys.

Carter kneels behind a small pile of such things and picks something up.

When he stands, he's holding Witchbane.

My mind reels. *Witchbane, my old sword. How did he get it?*

It must be a replica.

He waits for my reaction. I keep my face purposefully blank and my thoughts entirely to myself.

"I hope you'll forgive me," he says after a moment. "This must seem awfully presumptuous of me. But I knew how important this weapon was to you. And I could not bear the thought of you going without it." He hefts it in his hands. "I recovered it in the aftermath and made some improvements to the steel. You'll find it stronger than before. Perhaps next time, it will fare better against a Narwhark attack."

He offers it to me. With an unsteady hand, I take it by the hilt.

It's weighted perfectly. The blade is completely repaired. Some of the more obvious marks on the hilt have been mended, but this is my sword, returned to me, through and through.

"How?" I marvel.

Carter's eyes glimmer. "Do not presume, dear friend, that all ancient knowledge is lost. Oh," he adds, entirely as an afterthought. "You asked if a message came from Beatrice. It did not. But there was one, just this morning, from The Vorcellian Order."

Chapter Forty-Four

The blazing bonfire rages high above the tops of the trees. Every vampire in the vicinity of The Haven should be able to see it.

The heat it gives off is immense. I revel in it, watching as the flames go higher and higher, swirling and twisting on themselves in an effort to reach the very stars.

My group of humans is clustered around me, equally enraptured by their creation.

"*Fire* has a very primitive power to it," I proclaim. "It has the power to destroy, to overcome, to overwhelm. Few things in this world are as dangerous as fire. Vampires have a natural aversion to flame, because it is one of the only ways to guarantee our destruction.

"But Nocturna Animalia will be a new sort of coven, a new sort of clan! All those who join must first be cleansed by the flames. Only then will they be deemed worthy! Only then will they be given the infusion of blood!"

A rabid sort of madness has come over me. I do all I can to embrace it.

"Who puts their fate in the Dark God first? Who trusts in me to rescue you, to

272

revive you, to bring you life only after you've known death?" I spin around, laughing, drunk on the blood I've already drunk. "Who amongst you will be the first to walk into the flames?"

In truth, nothing like this has ever been done before. Not that I know of. But if these humans are mad enough to follow me with this, I know they will be mad enough to follow me to the very ends of the earth.

And loyalty, unquestioning, absolute loyalty, is what I require above all else.

I half-expect **Wanda** to step forward. She is their leader, after all.

But instead, it is Norman, the tall and slender man I first spied talking to her, who breaks out of their midst.

"I'll go," he says. He locks eyes with me. "I put my faith in you, vampire."

And then, as if in a total trance, he simply walks into the flames.

A second passes. The wind howls. The world is still.

And then his clothes catch fire, and he begins the most terrible, agonizing scream.

He runs out of the blaze, a moving wicker man, yelling and yelling as the flame consumes his flesh. He falls struggling to the ground, desperately trying to swat at the fire to abate the heat. His ragged screams continue on and on for what feels like eternity...

At the last possible moment, I grab the huge bucket of water and throw it over him. The flames sizzle and die. The stench of raw, burned flesh is heavy in the air. It is a disgusting smell, paired with a revolting sight of the blackened body of this paltry man.

Silence. The group waits for me to move. Norman moans on the ground, seconds away from death...

I leap onto him. I sink my fangs right into his neck. But, instead of drinking, I bite down and inject the poison, the serum, the mystic sustenance, whatever the force is that sustains us, into his vein.

And then I drink. His blood mixes with my own in my body. It forms a link between us, and as I drink, I pump it back. His body is primed to receive it thanks only to the serum injection—without which, my blood would merely heal, but only give a small chance of a successful transformation.

We stay locked like that, together, two lovers in a heavy embrace. I take his blood, and I give him mine. I take his blood, and I give him mine. I feel his skin start to heal, feel the raw, blistering wounds start to close, and I know—I just know—that this one will survive.

I stand. Norman gives a feeble cough.

Then he closes his eyes and goes absolutely still.

His body has recovered, but the ordeal has just started for his mind. He looks like a perfect corpse. He does not breathe. His heart does not pound. There is not a shred of life left in him.

No human life, that is.

"It is done!" I pronounce grandly. The heat of the fire beats against my back as I turn to the Fang Chasers. "Let it be known that Norman was the first made! The very first of the Nocturna Animalia, he who risked fire and death to achieve eternal glory!" My eyes are wide with triumph as I take the humans in. "From henceforth *he* shall be First amongst you, the first vampire made, the one closest to me, because of his bravery, none shall surpass him. May the night cradle him and grant rebirth!"

"*May the night cradle him and grant rebirth,*" the other humans repeat in unison.

I search their faces. "Now," I ask. "Who's next?"

Chapter Forty-Five

ELEIRA

THE CRYPTS

I grip Raul's hand tight in mine as we follow Dagan through the unfamiliar halls of The Crypts.

We're in a level much lower than where James took me when he kidnapped me. I have a sense of it, a sense of all the ancient wonder of this place, of all the secret knowledge and centuries of history, through my newly-minted vampire self.

Raul is understandably on edge. He and the larger vampire obviously have long-standing issues. Both must put on a show of civility, but it is a truculent peace. I fear it can fracture at any moment.

Yet if it comes to that? So be it. Raul has me with him. I will always stand at his side.

I sneak a glance at him. I don't expect him to be looking at me—but apparently he had the exact same thought at exactly the same time I did.

Our eyes meet. He squeezes my hand. I give him a quick smile.

And then he just beams at me, so happy, so full of love, that for a moment I am swept away to a place where none of this uncertainty exists. For a moment I'm in a place where it's just the two of us, complete in our love, oblivious to the outside world, two spirits, two souls completely and irrevocably in love.

Raul breaks eye contact first.

Am I being sappy? Did I imagine the whole thing?

Or does a connection really exist between us that goes well beyond the physical plane? It's ridiculous to hope for, to even think of, to consider as a possibility… but how else can I explain the feelings he evokes in me? Those feelings that were there from the very first moment I'd laid eyes on him? The feelings I'd tried to deny and belittle as childhood fantasies, as nothing truly belonging to the harsh adult world… but the feelings that come up, time and time again, whenever I am with him?

Maybe there's something to this whole *destiny* thing, after all.

Dagan leads us to an impressive door. It's made of stone, and there are many intricate carvings around its outside frame. The symbols and hieroglyphs are unlike any I've seen before, and yet they bear a certain resemblance to the witch runes I'd glimpsed in the Book of the Dead.

He sticks a key into the lock and twists it open. "From here you go alone," he grunts. He sounds… disgruntled. He pushes the door open to perfect darkness.

Raul steps to go first, but Dagan places a firm hand on his shoulder. "Not you," he says. He turns his head to me. "Her."

Raul stiffens. "I'm not letting Eleira out of my sight!"

"Unfortunately, *Prince*, on this you have no choice." Casually Dagan brandishes his sickly weapon again. It's in his hand for a flicker of a second, and then it's gone, hidden once more in the folds of his uniform.

Raul turns on him menacingly. I feel a fight coming on. That's the last thing I want.

I tug Raul back. "It's okay," I tell him. I meet the eyes of the larger vampire. "I can take care of myself."

"Eleira—"

"I'm serious," I say. A flash of irritation simmers to the surface, but I quickly quell it back down. "If you don't think I can handle myself at this point—"

"It's not that," Raul interrupts. He glances at Dagan, who looks impatient, and then lowers his voice as he steps nearer to me. "If we separate, how do we know we'll see each other again?"

"We will," I promise him.

"What if it's a trap, in there?" he asks. "You don't know what these vampires are capable of."

"If they wanted to hurt me, they've had plenty of opportunity before," I remind him. "The Ancient fed me his blood, remember? Do you think they would do *that* and then—"

"Time's wasting," Dagan says. "Eleira goes alone. Those are the orders I've been given. I'm not letting *you*," he sneers at Raul, "—get in the way of them."

"I'll be fine," I promise. "Really."

Raul hesitates... and finally nods.

"Where are you going to take him?" I ask, looking at Dagan.

"The Prince has an audience with his father," Dagan says. "It's for a sort of... diplomatic negotiation."

I don't like the dip in his voice when he coins the term.

Dagan nods to the door. "Go, then," he tells me.

I face the endless darkness, take a deep breath, and—sensing nothing beyond the veil—step inside.

Chapter Forty-Six

ELEIRA

THE CRYPTS

A frigid cold grips me when I take my first step.

It's the cold of a hundred winters, of a thousand blistering snow storms. It's the cold a woman feels when she's lost and all alone, in the depths of the arctic night.

It's the cold no vampire should be able to feel so acutely.

In a flash, it's gone, and I find myself alone in a circular room. The walls are made of ancient stone. There are markings covering all of them—a mixture of the runes I remember from before and their variations I saw on the outside door.

In the middle of the room is a well. The sides of it reach no higher than my knees. It's an odd feature in an otherwise barren place.

I take a step forward, then turn and look behind me. There's no door, no entrance, nothing at all breaking up the solid stone wall. Nothing to give any indication that it was possible to enter the room.

I sense another vampire's presence.

I gasp and spin around. There, standing on the other side of the well—where there was nobody before—is Beatrice.

She smiles at me.

"Surprised?" she asks. "Don't be. There is magic found in all sorts of places. And there are all types of different magics. Ones that even a witch as strong as you can be blind to."

"This is a torrial," I say, looking around the room. "Isn't it?"

I'm not frightened. Beatrice could be hostile or friendly, and it would make no difference. I feel absolutely secure in my own strength.

In fact, it's the vampire within me whose instincts I now trust most.

"Yes," she says. "Of course it is. How else would you have arrived?"

"But you're no witch," I say. I can sense Beatrice's power, and all of it comes from her vampiric half.

There's a difference, a very, very subtle difference between a regular vampire and one who has The Spark. It was only because I'd spent time with Morgan…and, to a lesser extent, Victoria… that I could recognize it in Riyu.

"No," she tells me. "I am not. Yet there are things that I know—things that I've studied. Things that I've been aware of since a long, long time before you were born."

She is speaking without a shred of emotion entering her voice.

"You know who you are," she continues, stepping around the well and coming toward me. "You know that you're special. But do you know *why* it's you? Do you know *why* you were the one picked to rule?"

I blink. *Picked to rule?* She must mean over The Haven… but somehow, she made it sound much grander than that.

"No answer," she muses. "Shall I take that as a 'no?'"

"There was something about the stars," I say. "About the constellations. They predicted my birth."

She laughs. "The stars predict a great many things, child," she says. "Some of which come to pass... but most of which do not. Tell me, do you feel like you are living the life you were meant to lead?" She comes close and brings a hand up to gently touch my cheek. "Do you feel fulfilled? Do you feel secure in your purpose? Or are you floundering about in the great ocean, looking for an island where there is none to be found?"

"Neither," I say firmly. I don't know who this woman thinks she is, but I'm not about to speak to her of my deepest feelings. Despite the gift of The Ancient's blood that was given to me, I'm still on enemy territory.

Whatever Beatrice's goals are, they're undoubtedly different from my own.

"Hmm." She steps back. "I did not bring you here to confuse you, Eleira. I only wish to offer guidance. I want to give you a sense of your importance to us—so that you can benefit from a full appreciation of all the myriad things that revolve around you now and in the future."

"How can I trust you?" I say. "How do I know the things you tell me won't all be lies?"

"Unfortunately," she spreads her hands, "I can offer you no assurances there. All I can do is present you with the information I have. It is up to you what you do with it. But I think you'll find that the things you learn today will not be such heavy truths."

"So you brought me here to tell me things about myself," I say flatly.

"Yes. I wish to help you *understand*, Eleira. The Haven vampires—they want to use you. That is why you came into their grasp. I will not say that theirs is a sinister purpose. I will simply ask you this:

"Have they once, any of them, given you the words of the prophecy that heralded your coming?"

My eyes narrow oh-so-slightly. "No," I say carefully. "They have not."

"And yet, it is a prophecy known to all the creatures of the night," Beatrice says. "It's not exclusive to The Haven. Your arrival into the vampire world concerns us all. All the covens who value their place in the world know of you."

I take the smallest step back.

"You think I lie? Why did the Wyvern coven accept The Haven's offer of sanctuary? Why did the other covens of North America refuse? Oh, you're surprised that I know? Don't be. We vampires are all connected, all of us linked. We could not exist as a species if we were fully segregated. We keep ourselves separated from the human world, yes... but even that will soon come to an end."

"And what end is that?" I venture.

"Eternal night," Beatrice answers. "Cast over the whole of the earth. An uprising of our kind, where we claim our rightful spot as rulers of the earth! There will be no more cowering beneath the ground. No more hiding from the sun. Soon, it will be the humans who cower in fear of us. We will not be hidden—we will be known! We are the greater species—is it not fair that we inherit the earth? It is up to us to wrest control of it from the usurpers, from those paltry beings who cannot begin to understand or appreciate the gift they are given. To take it back from those poor stewards of the earth, and to recreate this world into what it was always meant to be!"

Beatrice's voice takes on a maniacal zeal. But there's something about the image she painted—something about the idea of an uprising, of domination over mankind—that speaks to the vampire inside me.

I feel it responding, feel it becoming excited and restless by the prospect Beatrice speaks of. The ideas appeal to it—*no more hiding! Unlimited blood!* —but they are completely at odds with my moral conscience.

"No," I say, taking another step back. "No, that is not—that is not what I want."

"Your eyes betray you," Beatrice tells me. "In them, I can see your true intentions. I can see how you fight against the instincts flaring to life inside you. I told you vampires are connected. I told you we are all linked. Do you know why, do you know how?"

She lowers her voice. "It is because a common substance animates us all. Look at your arms, look at your flesh, look at your body! You think it is still human? Humanity is but an illusion. It does not exist—not within us. A human soul enters a body at birth and is extinguished at death.

"But not with us! We are parasites, taking residence in these human shells. You will learn, Eleira, you will see, that the body you occupy is not you. The *vampire* you feel inside—that is you.

"And what a gift! It strengthens the muscles, it hardens the bones. It grants us extraordinary senses, it offers eternal life. Do not struggle against it. Give in to it fully! Only once you do, will you find peace. Only once you do, will you achieve nirvana. For some..." she frowns, "...that never comes. They spend their entire existence fighting. They want to hold on to the memories that made them human, instead of embracing their new existence as they should. They become... forsaken."

Beatrice turns away. She walks to a particular set of runes and traces her fingers over it. Her voice takes on an inflection of great sadness.

"They become lost to us. You have not come across any like that yet, have you? Of course you have not. Your existence in our world has been brief. You will not find any such vampires in the covens. They cannot stand the company of those who remind them of what they are. So, they slip away and wander to the ends of the earth. Some seek salvation. Others seek redemption. But the cruel irony?" She turns back and meets my eyes. "When a vampire turns her back on who she is, all that she finds is destruction.

"They all meet their end soon after. Some lie down and crawl into the earth, where they cease to feed, where their bodies crumble and wither away into nothingness, until all that remains is held together by the thinnest gossamer strands. The force that gives vampiric life is still there, but it is so weak as to be useless. So those poor souls linger on, forever on the edge of perpetual death, without ever being able to cross to the other side. Theirs is an eternity spent in misery. They are convicted, and they can never rise again.

"The others? Some seek the fire. Fire destroys all, you know. They walk into the flames and let their bodies turn to ash. The ash is scattered by the wind. But still, that substance animating us remains. It remains between all the infinite particles of the vampire's former body, even weaker than the strands holding together those who went underground. The vampiric essence is infinite, Eleira, and once it has hold of you, that essence can never be removed. It is like energy, or matter, never created, never lost, only changed in shape and form and substance."

She looks me up and down. "Do you see what I'm getting at? Well, I don't blame you if you don't. These are things that take a lifetime to understand. A lifetime not just of theoretical knowledge, but a lifetime of practical, physical experience. The vampire life is so far removed from that of a human's. We must all come to grips with it, in our own way. The journey leads to a single destination, for those who can endure. And that is acceptance. Acceptance of who we are and what we do and the powers granted to us by this amazing gift.

"Yet that is not the point. The point is this: All those vampires who've perished? The ones who find destruction in the end? *Their* essential energy is what fills the air, what fills the earth. And *that* energy, Eleira, is what gives rise to magic."

She lets the words sink in for a long, solemn moment.

I consider them all.

Then, she continues.

"Witchcraft and sorcery and all the extra powers you have come from the same source. They come from *us*. You are drawing on the vampire essence when you cast your spells. It is far, far removed from its origin, of course... so many steps away as to be nearly unrecognizable... but those who have studied it? We *know*.

"The whole world of the supernatural is linked, Eleira. Just as the entirety of the mundane world is linked. Very few have the perspective, the patience, to become aware of that link. But it is how I, even though I lack The Spark, have been able to make use of certain torrials in my..." she clears her throat, "...*studies*."

"And... what studies are those?" I ask. I have to admit, what she's telling me is wholly fascinating. I do not think I would have found such a treasure-trove of information anywhere else.

Does Morgan know of this? She must, and yes, I get the feeling it is knowledge she would not have easily given away.

"Studies of the Great Prophecy, of course," she tells me with a secretive glimmer in her eye. "Studies of our past and studies of the future. Reality is mutable, to an extent... but it is also predetermined. Certain things will come to pass whether we will them to or not. Great cosmic events, to which all vampires are intricately linked, hold high significance for us. As a human, you might have been granted some impression of the size of the universe. Am I correct? In school, in your learnings, you would have been given some idea of the scope of all that entails it... of the scope of the whole of living existence. And yet how can someone with such a short perspective on life *truly* begin to understand? Humans are the lesser species, and they are crippled by their mortality. No, to truly understand, to truly appreciate, all that our universe offers, one must possess the perspective of the gods. And we are, Eleira, every one of us, truly God-like."

"No," I step away. This is the same type of zeal that Morgan frightened me with when she spoke of the power our collaboration would grant her.

"It is not I who gives us that title," Beatrice tells me. She comes closer. "Who do you think the earliest humans worshipped when civilization came to prominence on this earth? It was *us*, and our ancestors, who first opened their minds to the possibilities afforded by this world. They gave it up, we made it real. There is nothing more. We are their vision of the perfect being, the perfect human, the absolute paragon of beauty and creation and life. While they suffer their human diseases and afflictions, while they grow old and sickly, we remain, locked into these perfect vessels of being for all eternity. Now tell me, if that is not the image of a god, what is?"

I shake my head roughly. This is getting too intense, too much.

"Think, child!" Beatrice stresses. "Who else is afforded such opportunity? Who else is given such a chance? We have remained hidden for eons. The existence of our kind should be celebrated. We should be known! *We* should be the ones to hold power on this earth. Why are we satisfied with hiding in the dark, with stalking the places humans dare not go? Seeking something greater is not outside our realm of rights. We have the ability to dominate, the potential to rule. Why deny ourselves such gifts? Why not go up, above ground, and claim all that which is rightfully ours?"

"If it's so easy," I ask. "why haven't vampires done so before?"

"Ah." Beatrice smiles. "Now you are asking the right questions. It has been tried, once before. It ended in… failure."

"You wish to try again."

"Yes. The mistakes of the past will not be repeated now. We have a better perspective. We have…" she runs the back of her hand through my hair, " …a better witch."

Chapter Forty-Seven

ELEIRA

THE CRYPTS

I stare at Beatrice. The warning I was given back in The Haven flashes in my mind:

All will want to use you.

"Don't look at me like that," she snaps. "I'm well aware of where your loyalties lie, Eleira. The Haven vampires are the ones who brought you into our world. Naturally you would align yourself with them. But what I am trying to show you is that you are meant for things much greater than that. You will not lead one coven. You will lead them all."

She holds out her hand. "I'm here to make you an offer. Forget whatever has been promised to you in The Haven. They would make you Queen, would they not? But what type of Queen would you be? You would act as a surrogate for Morgan. She is not one to let go of power so easily. Commit to The Haven and you commit to an existence that is not your own. You will forever be her puppet. Certain things she will teach you, I'm sure. But many she will also hold back. You will be fed the knowledge you so deeply crave in but a tiny trickle. Secrets will always remain. You would never realize, grasp, or understand your true potential.

"But... if you were to join us? We would offer the entire world to you. Not just that of vampires. But the world of humans and all other beasts as well! The entirety of the planet will become your playground. Do with it as you will!"

I'm not exactly certain what she's playing at. *What's the catch*?

"If I join you," I begin slowly, "what does that entail? What will that look like, practically?"

"You would turn your back on The Haven and commit fully to The Crypts. Only three alive will be your superiors. The Ancient. Logan. And—" she smiles, "—myself."

"How is that any different from going back to The Haven?" I demand, feeling a sudden spike of anger. "At least there, the way you described it, only one will be above me! In the picture you framed, that is Morgan, and Morgan alone. At least I *know* what she wants. I cannot say the same about any of you."

"You know what we want," Beatrice replies. "I told you the vision we share for a vampire future. The world will be covered in night. Our kind will rise. You will be at the very helm. Perhaps 'superiors' was the wrong word. The Ancient, Logan, and I would act as your... advisors. Together, we would form a council of four. Four equals, united by a common purpose, and unrivaled by any in the world."

"Why should I trust you?" I say. "You want me to believe that you would just let me in on your little coterie and give me equal say? I know nothing about The Crypts."

"But that is why we have a lifetime to learn," she counters. "You need our guidance to fulfill the prophecy. Likewise, we need you to be an ally, not a foe. You have our respect, Eleira. We can offer you so much more than what you would find in The Haven. We offer you *fulfillment.* Your life will be empty without us. You will end up like the lost vampires, doomed to wander until you perish in the dust, were you to go back to Morgan. Your potential would be wasted. The opportunity that we—all of us—have been given would be lost! Do not deny yourself the position that is yours by birth. Others would divert your eyes from it. Others would be glad to keep you blind to your true potential. We would not. We will expose you to it and make you unstoppable. You will rise above all, as was predicted in the stars!"

My eyes quickly scan the walls for an escape. Beatrice is falling victim to the increasing hysteria. I'm still not frightened—I'm stronger than her—but I need to get away. I need to clear my head.

"Whether you will it or not, the choice has already been made," Beatrice says softly. "The prophecy speaks of you. You will fulfill it. That, at least, is out of your hands."

I need to stall, to buy more time.

"What does the prophecy say?" I ask. "When was it given? By whom?"

"Eons ago, long ages back, in the time before that of even The Ancient. A great witch was born. She was the first of a clan dedicated to predicting the future. She was the only one to have any measure of success. None since have possessed the ability."

"What ability?"

"The ability that cast her net back and forward in time. The ability to float on the river of time itself and look both ways. Her claim was that she could see all things, both future and past, that they came to her in visions."

"But she wasn't a vampire?"

"No. She remained mortal. Yet she assumed these trances that would take her away for days. She would retreat into her mind and remain still as a statue, unmoving, oblivious. Attempts to rouse her were never met with success, though of course, after the first few times, it was made known that she was not to be disturbed. She was travelling on a cosmic journey, and her purpose served the highest human longing.

"Every time she went on one of her trips she returned with bustles of information. Scribes were hired to write down all that she had to say. The words would erupt out of her like lava from a volcano, spewed with vigor and unrelenting passion, unfathomable heat. This was the way of her existence. Days of meditation would be followed by days of uninterruptable speech. The things she said, some of them concerned the past, others had to do with the future, but most were cryptic, and all had one thing in common, when the speaking spell was done, she claimed to be unable to remember a thing.

"So both the journey there and the journey back were part of the same trance. None know how she achieved this state that gave her these abilities, though many have tried to replicate it… to utter failure. Her descendants, the latter members of the clan, hoarded her prophecies, as was their right. But some of them leaked the prophecies, and, as the years passed, and her predictions were proven accurate, more and more became aware of her life.

"Vampires, naturally, had an utmost interest in all that she had come to say. Even the earliest of our kind knew that their lives were not measured in years but in decades. Perhaps later, they would understand that even that was too short a time.

"But the witch clan guarded the secrets closely. They passed them down from generation to generation, thinking that, armed with them, they would be better positioned to increase their influence over the world.

"For what greater need is there in the human psyche than the need for influence, for acknowledgement and recognition? None want to wither away in the dark, committing their lives to a cause that is never to be known. The secret, of course, the great lie, is the false beliefs that there *is* a witness to what we do, that there *is* someone who cares and looks upon us, that those we influence actually *are* being influenced by us and are not merely pawns in a cosmic game of creation, in which they have no true say."

I shake my head slightly. This is fascinating, but yet...

"You're losing me," I tell her.

"Am I? I think not. You understand where this is going. One of the witch's prophecies, dear girl, had to do with you."

"What did it say?"

Beatrice quotes: *"She comes, she comes! Chi*ld of the Stars, *born of the sun, she, the breaker of bonds, shall extinguish the darkness that rules her kind and unite them all, casting them into a world made new by night eternal!"*

I blink. "And you think that's me?"

"I *know* it's you, Eleira," Beatrice smiles. "There is more to the prophecy, of course, but that is the central bit. The witch who made it, she described the precise alignment of the constellations that would herald your coming. The unfortunately part... is that portions of the prophecy were lost. And there was a time, once before, as I've said, where another vampire witch tried to rise..."

293

"The one who failed."

"Yes. Logan and I knew she was false. We did not interfere. We watched as she was built up into something she was not, watched as she was promised prominence and then floundered. The vampires who brought her in used her, sapping her of her strength, and then, when it was discovered that she had not the capability they assumed, they destroyed her, so that their secrets would not be spread."

"Is that a threat?" I ask. "Is that what you say will happen to me?" I feel the strength in my body, feel the vampiric essence that gives me complete confidence in my ability to fend for myself.

"Not a threat, dear girl, but a warning. There is a precedent here. What is happening now, around us, has been attempted before. The consequences of that time linger to this day. The mistakes that were made then define us now. But we, as a kind, will break free from the shackles. Shackles of our own creation!"

"And if I refuse?" I ask softly. "If I say no to your offer, and instead go back to The Haven?"

"Whether you will it or not, the covens *will* be united," she says. She holds her left hand out to one side. "One is the path of peace." She holds her right to the other. "The other, of war. They both lead to the same destination."

She puts her hands together, angled out in front of her, and points them at me.

"You will fulfill the prophecy, Eleira. But if you do it willingly or not... if the way to that conclusion brings you pleasure or pain... has yet to be decided.

"If destruction must be wrought, so be it. Refuse the offer, and you will be allowed to return. But the second you place foot on your coven's lands, the extension of peace will be broken. You've seen what we are capable of." She smiles. "You saw how easy it was for us to cripple your precious Haven. And if that is the second most powerful coven in the world? Well, you must admit that the others would sooner side with us than risk their own destruction."

"You speak of war."

"But war is not an inevitability! Come to our side, and the other covens will follow. We do not need to fight as a species. Because the true enemy," she points a finger upward, "resides up there. Those creatures who live in the sun. The despicable humans."

"No," I say. I shake my head. "You're wrong. Humans are not our enemies."

She laughs. "Then what? Our food? Our prey? Face it, they do not deserve the prosperity they have inherited. They know not what to do with it, or how advantageous their position is. The true key to life, to existence, is the ethereal vampiric essence. And it is denied to them! They are nothing but vessels of blood, ripe for our taking."

"No," I repeat. "No, you're wrong. I will not help you."

"Then you will be used," she says flatly "if that is your final decision."

"It is," I tell her firmly.

"Then I pity you, Eleira. Truly, I do."

She steps back, and her form melts into darkness.

Chapter Forty-Eight

RAUL

THE ROYAL CHAMBERS OF THE CRYPTS

I follow Dagan through the long, empty corridors without saying a word. The silence that surrounds us seems fitting to this place.

Despite the very precarious ground I'm standing on, I can't help but think of Eleira. I hate the way I just left her. Sure, my hand was forced, and, yes, she might have consented… but still.

And yet, I know that if I had tried to remain, she would have seen it as an affront to her capabilities. She is a strong, strong woman. Much stronger than she knows, I suspect. Hers is internal strength, a strength of character, and it is part of the reason I admire her so.

As we walk I feel the presence of hundreds, perhaps thousands, of vampires beyond the walls. Their strength is astounding. Even through the barrier I can feel them all.

We reach a far-off doorway. Dagan opens it and beckons me through. I step inside.

I'm presented with a vast, cavernous expanse. The ceiling rises many stories above my head. The walls are a mix of concrete and rock. In places there are marble pillars showing, giving evidence to the supporting structure beyond the walls. Television screens line sections of the walls, each set on a different channel, each showing its own telecast of world news.

Overall, it's an uncanny mix of the old and the new.

One of them even has a movie playing. I recognize the actors from the trailers I've seen before. It's *Batman vs. Superman.*

A figure emerges from out of the far corner.

Father.

He's dressed only in loose fitting pants, though they are of excellent quality and cut. There are markings all over his body. From a distance, they look like tattoos, but I know that no ink can penetrate vampire skin like that.

That means they are brand marks. Made by silver implements, unless I miss my mark.

Dagan immediately goes to one knee. "My King," he says quickly, "I've brought the one you asked for."

Logan does not even bother to look at him. All of his attention is on me. He waves Dagan away. "Leave us," he says.

"But, my liege—"

"I said, *now*!" He doesn't yell, but the quick crack of his voice serves better than any exclamation.

Dagan gives a curt salute, and leaves the way we came.

I'm alone with my Father for the first time in my life.

The King of The Crypts looks at me. He doesn't say a word. I feel his power, and his strength, but I refuse to be cowed by it.

I stand taller and bring my shoulders back. I look him in the eyes. If he takes it as a sign of defiance, so be it. The truth is that I would rather stand for what I believe in than be made an unwitting victim in someone else's life.

"Why does it take great calamity to bring us together?" he wonders all of a sudden. "We are family, are we not? And yet... and yet, you are so distant from me."

"We are strangers," I tell him firmly. "Our relationship ended the moment you chose to step out of my life."

A brief smile flickers on his lips. "How do you know it was my choice?" he asks. "You were so young when it happened. What do you remember of those days?"

"I remember enough," I lie.

In truth, that entire period of my life, before I was made into a vampire, is clouded in a perpetual haze. Mother refused to speak of it. James would not offer anything, either. All that I know of my humanity I know in an ineffectual haze of drab colors and shapes. There are no concrete memories to latch onto. Nothing, really, helps me to recall from before I was made.

I've always wondered if it was like that with all vampires, or only me. But speaking of your life before being given the Dark Gift is a subject filed with taboo. Few would discuss it, even with their Prince.

Besides, prior to this point, I had no great interest in the past. The reality I know is the present, and it is the reality that I inherited when I was given eternal life.

But... faced with the prospect of my destruction, as I so recently was, made me rethink some of the things I had taken for granted for so long. Now, I have a vested interest in my origin—only if it is for Eleira's sake.

"So then you know the fight that caused the split between your mother and me? You know the reasons for our separation?" He scoffs. "Of course you don't. You were but a child when it happened. And she turned you, when you were still so very young…"

Logan lifts his hand as if to touch my face. I brace myself for contact, refusing to flinch away…

But he drops his arm before it reaches me.

My gaze goes back to the marks covering his body. They are similar in style and yet completely different in form from the runes that I've seen decorating magical objects.

Logan's eyes flash to me. "Do you know anything of James?" he demands suddenly.

A wave of surprise sweeps through me. Through a determined effort, I manage to hide it. "What is your interest in him?"

Father grunts. "I'm unused to being questioned," he says. "Seeing how we're alone, I'll let it slide. My interest is this, I have heard nothing of his whereabouts since the attack."

"The attack *you* orchestrated against my people," I remind him. "You do that, then invite me here, and expect any sort of forthcomingness?"

"You are here as a guest, protected by parley," he says. "It matters not what happened in the past. The circumstances that brought us together are what they are. We are here now. That is what counts."

"I did not expect you to be a philosopher," I quip.

Father scowls. "You're testing my patience, boy. Answer the question about James."

"James? I know nothing."

"You haven't heard from him? Haven't seen him?" A hint of desperation creeps into his voice. "You do not know if he's alive?"

"I would not think you would care," I say.

"He is my blood. As are you. Of course I care."

The admission shocks me. I had come to imagine the King of The Crypts as a cold-blooded ruler who kept his coven bound by strict military order. Such sentiment... it is surprising.

Father's eyes scan my body. He goes silent for a minute. Then, he says, "No. You truly do not know. You would not lie to me in this."

"James has handled himself fine for as long as I've known him," I say. Despite my eldest brother's wavering loyalties, I also do care about what happens to him. "I very much doubt that has changed now."

"He was sent back to you in a weakened state," Logan admits. "It troubles me that he... never mind." He gives himself a gruff shake. "That is not what I called you here for."

"What is?"

"I want to extend an opportunity to you," he says. "One I think you might appreciate."

"You want me to commit my coven to yours," I say directly. "That much I've already gathered. Your message made those intentions clear."

"It is not as simple as that," he says. "But in essence, you are right. That is what I want."

"If you know anything about The Haven's vampires, you'd know they would never yield."

"Oh?" Logan's eyes sparkle. For a moment I see a fleck of black stream beyond the iris.

I blink, and it's gone.

What was that? Could I have imagined it?

"*Never*," I repeat. "Each one would fight to his dying breath before surrendering to you."

"And yet how many were lost in the attack?" he asks. "You've seen our numbers. You know our strength. If I could inflict so much harm to you, without leaving the safety of our home, imagine how quickly you would be wiped out if I were to unleash my entire force."

"So why haven't you?" I asked. "If you wanted to take over, you've had ample opportunity to strike. But you haven't. Why not?"

"War is not a simple game, son. The loss of vampire life is always a great tragedy. I do not make such decisions lightly."

"And yet you turned The Convicted on us."

"The Convicted were aberrations, wrought out of you r mother's depravity. There is no place for such things in this world. They had to be destroyed."

"You expect me to believe that? That you directed them against *my coven* so that we would win?" I scoff. "That's a roundabout way of doing things."

"I also had to demonstrate my strength."

"To whom? Us, or your followers?"

"The vampires of The Crypts know who they are. They know our standing in the world. It was for your benefit. And now, it is time to take the next step." He gestures at the television screens. "It's time to retake the earth so it is ours."

"The earth does not belong to us."

"No? Then who? Not those pathetic humans, surely not. Those weak and supplicating creatures? They are destroying the beauty of the world. They do not appreciate what they have or what they are given. It is high time we take it from them."

The way he's speaking reminds me eerily of James.

"*We* are the aberrations," I tell him. "All vampires are creatures of darkness. There is a reason we are barred from seeing the sun. The sun gives life. We are death."

"No, you're wrong. We are not death, we are existence. We are the epitome of life! Who else has the chance to learn all its secrets? Who else has the time needed to discover all of its wonderful mysteries? *Human* knowledge is built upon generations of progress, on a base that is added to with every new wave of births.

"But imagine what vampires would be capable of, were we not locked away. Imagine the riches we could discover, the mysteries we could solve! The progress humanity has made in the last century is astounding, but how many thousands of years did it take mankind to get there? What if all the great artists and scientists and writers and thinkers had the freedom that we do—the gift of unlimited time? What creations would Da Vinci be capable of were his life extended indefinitely? Faust? What would he write? Rembrandt? What would he paint?"

"Don't tell me you care about such things," I say drily.

"I do. Why would you not believe me?"

I gesture around us. "Look at your kingdom. Nothing here speaks of your interest in the arts. The only thing that is visible here is your greed for power, dominion, and might."

The king shakes his head. "We all have roles to play in front of the ones who surround us," he replies. "I am giving you a glimpse into my soul. This is who I truly am." He taps his chest. "This is what the others do not see."

"And why do I get the privilege?" I ask. "Don't tell me it's because I'm your son. I doubt you ever offered James such an elaborate confession."

"You differ from James."

"How? How would you know? We are both strangers to you."

"Don't think I don't have eyes in The Haven," he tells me. "Would you be so naive as to believe the King of the most powerful coven in the world would be blind to the goings-on of other covens? No. I watch them all. I see them all. I have—"

"All you have is a fistful of lies," I cut in. I am growing tired of his rhetoric. "Nobody from the Outside has ever penetrated The Haven. That I know for a fact. The wards were impenetrable."

Logan chuckles. "'*Were*,'" he quotes. "What about now?"

"They will be resurrected," I say. "When they are, your threats will cease to hold meaning."

He shakes his head. "Do you truly believe that? You've seen our might. You truly think that the wards can protect your coven when confronted by the strength of thousands of Crypt vampires?"

"Would you do that?" I ask. "Would you pit our covens against each other in open warfare?"

"If you stand against me? Yes. There is no question." Logan smiles. "But I've invited you here to give you an opportunity to prevent all that. Kneel to me. Acknowledge me as your rightful ruler, and no more vampire lives shall be lost. Submit The Haven to my rule, and in return, I promise you prosperity... prosperity of a kind you have never imagined!"

"The Haven vampires won't yield," I say. "They will fight to defend their home, each of them, to their last breath."

"So that is what you would sentence them to?" Logan asks. "Certain death? There is no need for more vampire blood to be spilled."

"Even if I were to agree," I say. "How could I trust you? How do I know you would not renege on your word?"

"My word as King is absolute. None have questioned it, because all know that I stand by what I say. A leader who cannot be trusted is a leader who is opening himself up for a coup. But there has not been rebellion or dissent amongst my vampires as long as I have ruled."

"You're talking about members of your clan," I say. "Nothing about those from Outside. A track record here means little to me."

Logan's eyes narrow. A spasm of anger crosses his face.

He suppresses it immediately. "You are young," he says softly. "You still have time. You will learn."

I feel a shift in the air between us. "Learn what?"

"Learn where prosperity lies. And learn which paths lead to destruction. Deny me now, refuse my offer, and you write your own death sentence.

"But join me... and we will rise together, my son. You are used to life beneath a woman. It is men who should lead! It is men who make up the powerful sex. Join me, and you will see, in your ascent, that there is no comparison. You and I together can stand above all. Me, as King, and you, as my rightful heir. You will become Prince in the true sense of the word! I offer you a gift—the gift of power, of dominion, of might! I extend my hand to you and offer all that I have built. Everything I have spent a lifetime creating can be yours, if only you reach out and take it!"

Another speck of black floats across his right eye.

"And in return...?" I ask him. "No offer comes without strings. What are your conditions? What do you want from me?"

Father smiles. "I want you to give me Eleira," he says.

Chapter Forty-Nine

RAUL

THE KING'S ROYAL CHAMBERS

My gut clenches in a mixture of hatred and fear, and I step away.

"Never," I breathe.

"A powerful witch is needed for what I intend," he says. "She is the most powerful of all. But she was brought into our world by your coven. The proper way to join us, if peace is meant to take precedence, is a union between the vampire King and her."

"You would *wed* her?" I cannot keep the incredulity from my voice. "That is what you're proposing? No. That's laughable."

"It is the only way our covens will ever be linked," he says, "without further bloodshed."

"I will *never* give Eleira to you," I hiss. "I would die first."

"My, my," Logan mutters. "So very possessive. The girl has sunk her claws into your heart, hasn't she? That matters not. Marriage is but a political proposition. I would bed her, of course," his eyes shine with desire, "but you could have her on the days I am occupied."

Revulsion builds in me with every word that comes from his mouth. "You speak of Eleira as some common whore," I growl. Every single instinct in my body demands me to fly at him, to fight, to defend the honor of the woman I love.

But if I do, it would be my end. Father's strength is enormous compared to mine. He would crush me like an empty aluminum can.

"You care for her." The side of his lip twitches up in a semblance of a smile. "That will be your weakness for as long as she lives. You must learn that there is nothing and no one more important in life than yourself. Your instincts, your wants, your needs and goals and desires are the only things that matter.

"You will be vulnerable as long as you are linked to her, son. The sooner you recognize that, the sooner you break free of the bonds holding you back, the sooner you will realize your true potential. The sooner you will become worthy of being named my heir."

"Worthy in whose eyes?" I scoff. "Yours? You assume I even *want* that title. I do not. I want nothing to do with you or your dirty promises."

"Spoken like a true non-believer," Logan says. "What is it holding you back, son? Is it a weakness in your character, some type of fatal flaw I am unaware of? Why do you say *no* when the world is offered to you on a golden platter?"

"A golden platter?" I almost laugh. "You bring me here, after executing an attack that killed many of my people. You frame an offer and make it sound like the most generous gift, when in reality all it serves is to further your sick purpose. You ask for me to give Eleira to you—as if she is mine to give, and not a conscious, sentient woman with a free will and free volition! And somehow, you expect *gratitude?* Must I remind you that it was one of your vampires who gave me a wound that nearly killed me? We might be family, you are right. But we will

307

never be allies. *You will forever be my enemy.*"

Father stares at me for a long time. "Such an impassioned speech," he says finally. "Said with such conviction! I could almost believe you meant every word."

"I do," I tell him darkly.

"No, no." He shakes his head. "You are speaking with your intellect, with your reason, with your mind. But not a single word that passed your lips came with the conviction of the heart."

"You flatter yourself," I tell him. "Thinking you can see into my heart."

"I don't need to possess such abilities to know the true nature of every vampire. The essence that sustains you, that sustains each one of us, it does not differ from one to the other. It wants the same thing. It craves the same purpose. It leads us, naturally, to the same final goal.

"So speak as you do. It does not matter. I know you will come around. But ask yourself this, when your desires change, will I still have you?"

Logan trails off. "I think," he says in a whisper, "not."

"So you claim to be all benevolent? To want to bring our kind into some sort of idealized future that only you see? You want to tell me there are no underlying motives for what you propose?" I scoff. "I may not know you very well, *Father*, but I do know a thing or two about our vampiric nature, as well. I know we are cunning. I know we are deceitful. We lie and cheat and steal with nary a thought for the consequences when it suits us most."

"You present me this offer. You say I would be a fool to reject it. Well, so be it! Label me a fool, call me a child, but never say that I abandoned my coven. Never will it be said that Raul Soren stood with the enemy and agreed to terms of surrender."

I take a step toward him. "I came here with Eleira, as we were asked. You presented your offer. I refused it. Now, let us return to The Haven where we belong. You would not be so cowardly as to attack without us there, would you?"

"Cowardice is one thing you cannot accuse me of," he says. "If that is your final choice..." he lets the last word hang in the air. "Then I pity you. Perhaps it was my mistake bringing you here. It is your mother the Queen who rules. Maybe she will be more receptive to what I propose.

"I'll let you return, son. In fact, I'll be generous and give you an extra day. A day to fortify your defenses, to prepare yourself for the slaughter that is to come. But... then again..."

He pauses for a long moment. His eyes lose focus as he retreats into himself in thought.

"...then again," he repeats, "...if it is Morgan who holds ultimate rule, perhaps it is time I speak with her. Extend an invitation to my former wife. Centuries have passed since—"

With a start he comes back to himself and seems to realize I am still there. He addresses me directly.

"Go back to The Haven with your girl. Tell your Queen that I have given you a day's grace. But tell her, also, that if she were to come here, to sit down and *negotiate* with me... I would not turn her down. And the ceasefire that exists between our covens would be extended for the duration of her stay."

I look at him in disbelief. *Does he not know?*

My doubt must have shown on my face, because Logan pounces forward.

"What?" he demands. "What is it? Something is wrong."

I shake my head. "The Queen wouldn't come," I tell him firmly.

"You think the thing that caused the rift between us stands in the way? What do you know of it?"

"Nothing," I say. "But that is not the reason she won't take you up on your offer."

"Oh? Then what is?"

"She won't come," I say, "because she can't. She was attacked by—"

Suddenly, I realize what I'm saying, how much information I'm giving away.

I would never do it in my right mind.

The bastard exerted his vampiric influence over me to loosen my tongue! He did it so deftly, I didn't even notice!

With a flash of fiery anger I seal off my mind. I hate how careless I have been recently. Not at all fitting behavior for the Prince.

"She was attacked?" Logan asks. "By whom?"

"No," I growl. "You're not getting another word out of me."

I turn to leave—and a great force of energy slams into my back.

I go sprawling on the floor. Before I can pick myself up, Logan is on me, pinning me to the ground, his face a mask of uncontrollable rage.

"Morgan," he demands, spittle flying from his lips. "Tell me what happened to her!"

I struggle against his grip on my wrists. But I can barely make him budge. His

310

strength is absolutely phenomenal.

I clench my jaw together to stop from speaking. I feel him trying to claw his way into my mind. I double down on the mental defense I've erected against him. Physically, I may be no match, but at least in my own mind, mentally, I have enough of an advantage to avoid succumbing to his strength.

"No," I say.

"Tell me!" he screams. He grabs my shoulders and slams them against the floor. "Tell me what happened to my wife!"

Logan's hand closes on my throat. He starts to squeeze. He's going to crush my windpipe. No matter how I struggle and fight back, I am no match.

"Tell me," Father demands. His eyes are blazing with madness. "Tell me now… or die."

In that moment, I know this is no bluff. I cough, and a single word escapes my lips.

"*Narwhark.*"

Logan blinks. He relents on his grip and sits back.

"What did you say?"

"Narwhark," I tell him again, rubbing my throat. Humiliation and wounded pride combine to fill me with a vile mix of self-loathing. But so be it—what can I do?

"I've heard that term before," he says. "A demon."

"Yes," I agree. Something shifts in Logan's expression. Is that greed shining in his eyes?

He steps off me and offers a hand immediately to help me up. I swat it away and stand on my own.

"Your Mother was attacked by a demon?" he asks. Then, before I can speak, he says "No, don't answer. I can see it's true. But that is… interesting. It adds a new wrinkle to things."

"What are you talking about?" I demand. In the back of my mind, I had always assumed that The Crypts were somehow behind the Narwhark attack. But Father's surprise is genuine, as is his reaction to finding out Morgan was harmed.

He ignores my question. "I assume your mother is still alive? Of course she is. I would have sensed it if she'd died."

How? I wonder.

"But the demon harmed her." Logan walks to a distant column covered with runes. "Yet it did not kill. She will not come, as you say, not because she is unwilling, but because she is incapable. She is unconscious, is she not?"

He turns his head back. His eyes seal into me. "Is she not?"

"Yes," I admit grudgingly.

He taps the stone he is looking at. "Come closer, son," he tells me. "There is something that I wish to show you."

It takes an enormous effort of will to cover up my absolute disgust, but I manage it. I walk to where Father is standing and look at the strange marked column.

"You're the scholar of the stars, aren't you?" he asks. "Yes, well, Beatrice says you are. I believe her."

"Who *is* she to you?" I wonder.

He chuckles. "Do you think I would give away all my secrets at our first reunion?" He shakes his head. "No, no. I am not you."

I grit my teeth together in irritation.

"A demon has not been sighted in this world for generations," he continues. "But the prophecy that informed you of Eleira's coming mentions one." He turns to me, making a fist, and holds it between our faces. "It is no coincidence. And now, there can be no doubt. Eleira *is* the one we have been waiting for. She *is* the one we need."

"You speak as if we're allies," I say.

"We are blood. And I *am* your father. At some point you will recognize that. And then you *will* do as I say."

I scoff. "Hardly."

"I was too rash before. You must forgive me. It is a flaw I have. I can be patient, and yet, sometimes, I tend to rush things.

"My coven will not attack yours. Not yet. Your mother must be given enough time to recover. When she awakens, *I* will come to her." He looks at me in full seriousness. "Such a concession would have been unimaginable even five minutes ago."

I say nothing.

"Is she being protected?" he asks. "There are those, even right around her, who would do her great harm."

"And you profess to care?" I almost laugh. "The most casualties The Haven has ever suffered were done at your command. Now, you want me to think you care about the Queen's well-being?"

"You are too harsh a judge," he says. "Yes, son, I do care. In the attack, specific orders were given to ensure that no harm befall the Queen or any of my sons."

I gesture at my leg while keeping my expression blank. "Small good that did."

"You are healed now, are you not? You are better? I take care of my family, Raul. Even the members reluctant to be anointed as such."

I keep my mouth shut.

A silence grows between us.

"The way forward is to forsake the past," he tells me. "Our differences are not so great as you might think. We want similar things."

"We do not," I tell him. "I don't have any clue of what you want, but I know that our interests do not align."

"We both need the girl."

"You won't have her."

"It is not in your hands to choose. She is the one spoken of in the prophecy. She will fulfill her role."

"You think the prophecy touches all vampires, don't you? And you'll take it upon yourself to exploit that. You want to take advantage of the discord you sow in order to advance your own position."

"There is no higher calling."

Logan turns and faces me. "Listen, Raul. Our covens should be united. Let us look to the future. Infighting such as has been the norm for centuries needs to be abolished. We need to look above—" he points at the ceiling, "—and take the world back from them."

"You make the mistake of assuming all vampires share your greed," I say. "Most are happy, content, with what they have. With what they've been given." I think of Phillip, of the relative prosperity The Haven vampires have enjoyed under our Mother's rule. "They do not want to be exposed to the world in the way you propose."

"No," Logan says. "In that, you are right. But the fatal flaw in your thinking is that the world above will remain static. It will not. When I lead our kind forward, everything above ground will change. Vampires who fear the sun will never have to worry again."

My eyes narrow. A dark suspicion forms in the back of my mind. "What are you saying?"

"I'm saying, son, that with Eleira on our side, we will coat the earth in eternal night!" His eyes blaze as he grips me by the shoulders. "Do you understand what that means? Can you even grasp the significance of such a thing? I will remake this planet to be our rightful home.

"I will tell you a secret now, one I think you should know. It has to do with your mother and me.

"The Haven is bathed in night, is it not? I wanted to extend that darkness to envelop the entire world.

"She refused. She was frightened. Of course, in hindsight, it is obvious she was not the witch to do it. Eleira is. And now that the stars have aligned and Eleira has come, she has a chance to fulfill that ancient prophecy that has been my guiding light for all these years."

I can't believe what I'm hearing. All this time, I had this impression of my Father as a crude, harsh, uncompromising ruler. I thought he maintained his rule through intimidation and sheer strength.

But now, I'm starting to understand that it was his *intellect* that let him prosper.

That makes him more fearsome an opponent than I'd ever given him credit for.

"It will happen. Whether you will it or not. You can choose to stand in my way, or you can submit and join us. All the covens will be given that choice. Those who resist will be crushed. But all vampires must stand united, must be led by a single ruler before we can inherit the earth."

"And you think Eleira will just go along with it?" I ask softly. "You don't know her. She has had every chance to succumb to darkness. No vampire alive has been given more opportunity. And yet, she has resisted the call every single time."

"She is but a fledgling," Logan says dismissively. "The darkness will make her cave. Give it time, and it will happen."

"And if not? Her humanity is a more vital part of her than your greed for power is of you."

He scoffs. "Again you speak as if you understand who I am. You know little about me, son. But I will still take you under my wing. Let me show you what it means to truly rule. Let me give you a glimpse into my life. Let me teach you to see through the eyes of a King—not through the eyes of a boy following his

Mother."

"A tempting offer," I say dryly, "but still I refuse."

"You will think on it," Father promises. "Once you do, you will see that this is the only way."

"Eleira will not be used. I won't allow her to."

He laughs. "You still think you have a say? Every freedom I've granted you here as my guest can be taken away with a snap of the fingers. You feel the power of my vampires flowing around you. There are thousands of them, thousands, loyal only to me. Thousands, all of whom are many times stronger than any in The Haven.

"How many do you have in your force? Two hundred? Three? Four? Even if The Haven hosts one thousand vampires—it would be swept away by the power of The Crypts. And yours is the second largest coven in existence?" Again he laughs. "Face it, son. Submission is the only prospect you have of survival."

He turns and walks to the door. "I've given you enough of my time. You know what I propose. I do not seek the destruction of The Haven in any way. But if you decide to oppose me..." his hand closes into a fist and he squeezes hard, "...your coven must be crushed."

He's bluffing, I think, to myself. *If it were truly so easy, he would have done it before.*

"Riyu and Dagan will escort you to your home. When your Mother awakens, you can tell her all I've said. You will not be under threat from us until then."

I walk stiffly to the doorway. I feel almost like a leaf caught in an enormous current—incapable of affecting where it takes me or how fast it goes.

And I am entirely unused to feeling that way.

As I pass my Father, he reaches into his pocket and hands me a small vial of blood.

There is less than two drops inside.

"Give this to her," he tells me softly, but with grave seriousness. His eyes search mine. I see something new and different in his. Concern? Worry? Actual *caring*, perhaps?

"It is the only chance she has to live," he finishes.

And then he turns away and walks to the midpoint of the room, where he resumes his study of that erected pillar.

I slip the vial up my sleeve and leave the chamber.

Chapter Fifty

JAMES

THE WOODS OUTSIDE THE HAVEN

The final flames of the great fire flicker and die, and I stand before it, reveling in my creation.

I am at the heart of a perfect circle of sixteen bodies. Each one of the Fang Chasers now has my blood.

None are conscious. Of course not. I held back not in the slightest when infusing them with the serum. Each was given the maximum amount.

Will all of them survive the transformation, when it comes next nightfall? No. Some might even be harmed as they lie under the rays of the sun, as their cells begin the series of mutations, the hardening of the ectoplasm and cell walls that convert ordinary flesh into immortal marble.

But that is something I cannot prevent. All of my offspring have been touched by fire. The greatest fear of the vampire had been confronted by each of them on their creation.

That is how I know they will be strong. When they rise, they will be unlike any vampires who came before. Their loyalty shall be mine, and mine alone.

I will be their god.

The first rays of the sun show over the horizon. I shield my eyes as I look up. Almost time for me to go beneath ground, and back into hiding.

But there is something about the tranquility of this scene that speaks to my heart. Here is a site of great violence. All of these former humans were burned, each of them willingly stepped into the fire to follow *me*. And then they were given my blood, given the gift they had spent their entire lives searching for.

And now look at them. Each one lies still as an angel. The perfect beauty of their faces strikes me. They have been made in my image.

One thing rankles me, however, that makes it impossible to turn away.

The bonfire was not only meant as a rite of passage. It was also meant to herald my new coven's coming, to be a shout of announcement of their creation to the world.

None witnessed it.

I had been certain the fire would have drawn attention of The Haven's vampires. In fact, that was the whole point. I had almost *wanted* them to interfere, to come after me either as enemy or friend.

I wanted to see what they would do, what they would think, how they would react.

I wanted to see whom Mother would send.

In truth? I had wanted it to be Smithson. The Captain Commander of her guard caught me unaware last time. *I* wanted to be the one to return the favor today. I could have taken him by surprise, as he had me, only this time, with the blood of my followers flowing through my veins, I would have been victorious. I would have destroyed him.

The satisfaction gained from that would have been the culmination of every-thing I was after.

But Smithson didn't come. Nobody did. The fire was large enough to be seen from miles away.

Why had none cared to investigate?

The rays of the sun start to get a little stronger. Time is running out for me to find a suitable burrow.

But did I even want to hide, on this of all days? I survived Father's torture cell. I survived the desert sun at its very peak.

And I am stronger now than I was then.

If one of the newly made Nocturna Animalia were to wake and see me... I would become an even greater legend.

Of course, staying in the sun it is going to be painful. But sometimes, even in the most hedonistic pursuits, sacrifices must be made.

A flash of a shadow darts through the undergrowth, catching my eye.

I spin on my heels.

The shadow moves again. It's too fast to make out.

Then it comes to a sudden stop. And there, standing across from me, outside the ring of bodies... is the Narwhark.

My muscles tense. The hairs on the back of my neck go up. I've seen what this creature is capable of. It is *not* the one I wanted to attract.

Time slows to a standstill as the Narwhark and I regard each other. I see a certain intelligence reflected in its eyes that had never been there before. Its grotesquely shaped head is black as night, but those eyes… they're even darker. But now it's not mere instinctual force guiding it forward.

There is something more.

The Narwhark's tail swishes behind it. Left, right, left, right, like the ticking pendulum of a clock.

It *knows* that I cannot stay out here in the sun.

"What do you want, you goddamned bastard?" I growl. If it attacks… well, I've seen what it can do.

But it has never faced *me* at full strength before.

The Narwhark's lips curl back. Two double rows of tiny, pointed teeth show on either of its jaws. It snaps at me and digs at the ground, but it does not move.

My claws come out. I feel the adrenaline coming over my body. It's been too long since I've had a decent fight. And with all the new blood coursing through me, the vampire inside me craves an outlet.

Suddenly, and without warning, it leaps forward. I brace myself for impact.

But the demon lands beside the closest human to it. In a quick jab it sinks its pointed tail into the man's shoulder.

He convulses as soon as the point pierces his skin, then goes still. By then the Narwhark's already moved off, running at astonishing speed. It goes around to every single body laying on the ground and pierces its tail into their flesh.

It completes the circle before I can react. The speed it is blessed with is astonishing. The convulsions take my humans in a dynamo effect.

The worst kind of anger settles on me. "What have you done?" I mutter.

Without thinking, I launch myself at the Narwhark.

It simply skips away.

It lands between two trees. I'm in that spot in an instant, but the demon is too fast; it's another hundred yards away before I get there.

It looks at me from a distance. Once more I get that unnerving perception of its intellect—and of its unabashed evil.

By then the sun's rays have started to pierce the canopy. The Narwhark blinks and tilts its head, almost as if mocking me... and runs off.

I dash forward in the same direction as fast as I can. But by the time I arrive, the demon is long gone. I cannot track it even with my preternatural senses at their full capacity.

A moan comes from behind me. I spin back. Norman, the first man I converted, is up. He's awake, and he's clutching the spot on his shoulder where the Narwhark struck.

I stagger toward him through the increasing sunlight. I drop to my knee at his side. I cup his head in my hands and peel away the burnt remains of his clothes that are covering the new wound.

There is only the tiniest mark there. "It hurts," he groans. "The pain... the sun... it *burns*..."

Quickly I check his pulse. His heart is beating twice as fast as it should, many times faster than a vampire's does. That means he is still in the midst of the conversion.

I glance up at the sky. There are only seconds remaining, now. I lie him back down.

"It'll pass," I promise. "I cannot help you yet. You must endure until night."

He clutches at his arm. "That thing," he says. "What *was* that? It—*argh!*"

He screams and grabs at the wound again.

"Rest," I say, laying him down. "Close your eyes. Sleep, heal. Your body must recover."

I stand. The sun's rays beat against my exposed skin. They are still weak, only the thinnest tendrils of the morning, but they will grow stronger soon.

And if the Narwhark is around, I cannot risk being weakened by the rays.

I race over to the spot I'd designated for myself and quickly dig into the ground. As the fresh soil covers my skin and eases my discomfort, I only hope the cloaking spell makes me invisible to the demon as well.

Chapter Fifty-One

ELEIRA

SOMEWHERE IN THE CRYPTS

I'm reunited with Raul in the same room where I was left the first time.

He's already there when I arrive, pacing the empty floor. His face is a mask of consternation.

I wonder what happened to him while I was away.

As soon as he sees me, he stops and runs over. He takes me by the shoulders and rubs his thumbs over my bare skin. He says nothing; he doesn't need to. His eyes betray the truth of every emotion running through his head.

Suddenly, he clasps me to him. I give a little squeak—maybe of surprise, maybe of astonishment—as I'm pressed tight against his body.

After a moment he lets go and touches his forehead to mine. "You're safe," he says, finally. "You're safe, you're here. That's all that matters."

What happened while I was gone? I wonder.

He sweeps my hand up in his. "We're going back," he says.

"Already?" I ask. "Have we accomplished anything here?"

"I spoke to Father. He made a proposition…" Raul shakes his head. "I refused."

My breath catches. "What does that mean for us? For the coven?"

"The ceasefire still exists," Raul growls. He looks troubled for a second. "I may have revealed more than I intended to."

"What did you say?"

"I told him about Morgan," he says. "How she was stabbed by the demon."

"No!" I gasp. "That means they know we are vulnerable! They can strike The Haven at any time."

"They won't," Raul says. "Father gave his word. Not until the Queen awakes. He... Eleira, I think he still cares for her."

"After all these years?" I wonder. It's astounding that love can carry through the centuries like that.

"I don't think my Father is the callous man we all assumed him to be," Raul continues. "He couldn't have extended so much influence if he didn't have any brains. No. He's ruthless, but he's also highly intelligent." He looks down at me. "What about you? What happened on the other side of the veil?"

I shudder just thinking about it. "The woman—Beatrice—made me an offer as well. She wants me on her side. But the things she was talking about, Raul, they're just dreadful! World domination, a culling of all humans, covering the globe with eternal night..."

"She said those things to you?" Raul considers. "That's exactly what Father proposed to me."

"But you refused." It's not a question.

"Of course."

"Are they really going to allow us to return?" I ask. "Just like that? After all they went through to get us here?"

Raul reaches into a pocket and takes out a small vial of blood. "Logan gave this to me to administer to Mother." He pops the top and lets the scent drift out. "It's blood of The Ancient, isn't it?"

I recognize the smell as soon as it hits. My body thrums in resonance with the blood. "Yes," I tell him. "Yes, it is."

Raul closes the top. "Father says we'll be let back. He told me to use this to save the Queen. But I wonder..." He trails off.

"What?" I take his hand. "What is it? What do you wonder?"

"I wonder if it's a trap," he says softly. "A Trojan horse. When he spoke to me, he implied some sort of link exists between him and her. I've never heard of its kind. But what if this blood is infused with, I don't know, some sort of magic? What if it strengthens the link between them, and puts her under his influence? Or, even worse—" he swallows, "—what if it kills her?"

"Let me see the vial." I hold out my hand.

Raul hesitates... then grunts, and drops it into my open palm.

I turn away from him and bring it close to my face. I close my eyes and focus on the ever-present, but ever-faint, tendrils of magic flowing through the air. They are weakened here, for some reason, but their energy is still there. It's subtle, but it's present.

I exhale sharply and push all of them away. A void opens up around me—a void cleared of magic, a space that is completely isolated.

And then, I turn my attention back to the vial. If it were tainted... I would feel something thrumming inside.

But it's clear. It's pure, it's clean, it's unadulterated.

I look over my shoulder at Raul. "There is no taint," I tell him. "It is exactly what he says it is."

Raul marvels. "The value of it is... it's unimaginable."

"Maybe the King did mean it as a gesture of good faith," I say.

Raul scoffs. "Don't let any of the Elite hear you say that. This is the same man who commanded the forces that took down The Haven's wards."

"About that," I say. "I was thinking. Something doesn't jibe. If The Convicted were made only of The Haven's vampires—how were there so many of them? They outnumbered us badly in the fight. Surely there couldn't have been that many vampires sentenced to eternal damnation when Morgan ruled."

"No," Raul says. "There were not. That is something I've been thinking about myself. I have no answer for you. Only one person does." He drops his gaze to the vial. "And you hold the key to her revival in your hand."

Chapter Fifty-Two

SMITHSON

INSIDE THE HAVEN

I clutch the letter closer to me, hidden beneath the flap of my cloak, as I rush through the underground hallways back to a place where I can safely read it.

I burst into the privacy of my room and do a cursory scan of the surroundings. I am alone. Still, I am not one to take risks—not when my entire position can be exposed.

So I do a more thorough sweep of the room, using both the telepathic vampire senses that would alert me to another's presence and all of my normal, 'human' skills learned during my initiation to the Order.

Only when I'm satisfied that I'm truly alone do I open the envelope holding the letter.

There are three words written on the page. Three short words... that immediately change everything:

She has awakened.

Chapter Fifty-Three

RAUL

THE CRYPTS

We prepare quickly for our departure. There isn't much to do. All we have are the clothes on our backs—given as gifts by these other vampires—and the new ideas that were implanted in our heads.

I would have liked an opportunity to explore more of The Crypts. Of course, there are secrets in these myriad of passageways. Father has spent his whole life building his coven into what it is. Even if you don't consider their strength, the sheer *number* of vampires housed here is staggering.

Each has his story. Each has her tale. What understandings could they grant me were they allowed to speak to me?

But Eleira and I are both barred from exploring. Obviously. It would not do for a hostile to snoop around in enemy territory unfettered.

Soon, the time to leave comes. The doors to our guest chambers boom open. That massive vampire, Dagan, steps inside.

He is accompanied by his ever-present shadow. The smaller, more meddle-some vampire. Riyu.

He is the one I have to keep an eye on. Dagan's strength is obvious—but so is his MOA. He is a brute, and there isn't much going on behind his cruel eyes.

But Riyu... Riyu looks like a trickster. For one so very weak, he has somehow implanted himself next to a vampire extremely close to my Father. He doesn't have the brawn, so it must have been his brains that brought him to where he is now.

And I don't believe in coincidences. Not one bit. Riyu has been near us from the start. He has a role to play yet.

I don't voice my suspicions to Eleira. For one, she has enough on her mind. Two, they are my own, and meant only for me.

A man should be able to care of such troubles himself.

"Let's go," Dagan grunts. Eleira starts and looks over her shoulder. She'd taken to studying the grand piano's lacquered surface while we waited.

I hold an arm out to her. She comes to me. I put it around her lower back. It's more of a protective gesture than an intimate one—and from the small flash of a smile I receive, I know it's appreciated.

Dagan looks at us, the disgust clear on his face. I think it's mostly resentment for me.

Riyu, however, keeps his eyes hidden by looking at the floor.

Dagan gestures roughly with his head and we start out of the room. Again, I feel the strength of all the other coven's vampires on the other side of the walls. It's a pervasive awareness of their presence. It's not like they are literally lined up to make a path for Eleira and me. But here, there is no doubt that I am in the midst of some very powerful vampires indeed.

Just as we're about to enter the place where the portal had opened last, a lone figure appears from around a corner. My eyes instantly fixate on her.

Beatrice.

"Not so fast," she calls when she sees us. Dagan goes still, his eyes full of suspicion. Riyu says nothing, but for a moment, I think a secretive look passes between him and the woman.

My hackles rise.

Beatrice approaches. She looks absolutely sensuous in a satin black gown and tall heels. The outfit does nothing to hide her feminine curves. The way she walks, too—sashaying her hips, elongating her leg with each step, holding her neck high—it is a walk meant to attract the attention of men... and evoke the envy of women.

It is a walk, I am sure, that she has perfected over many years. And now she makes it look effortless.

"Logan said you're leaving," she admits when she comes close. "I thought it was a rather hasty departure for two so valued."

"Don't interfere, bitch," Dagan growls. "I've been given orders."

"You dare call me that?" There's no venom in her voice, just... amusement.

"The King is not here to protect you now," Dagan says. He stretches to full height. He is stronger than she is—she should be deferring naturally to him.

But Beatrice only laughs and touches his arm. "I'd be careful with this one," she tells Eleira and me. "He's fiercely loyal."

"You're interfering with the King's direct orders," Dagan repeats. "I was to bring the prisoners to—"

"*Prisoners?* No, no. They are our guests. Unless, something has changed without my knowledge…?"

Beatrice trails off and steps away from Dagan. She addresses me. "Logan told me of the conversation he had with you," she says. "I don't doubt our King's judgment… but I do consider him sometimes too rash. He gives too freely. Such as the gift for his ex-wife."

Dagan blinks but says nothing. Clearly this is the first he's heard of the secret vial.

"The King is a man of iron will, but he also has a soft heart, especially to those who have been important to him in the past. I believe he is letting you go too early."

Eleira tenses beside me. I tighten my grip on her as a way of reassurance.

"You will not stand in our way," Dagan reiterates.

Beatrice laughs. "Certainly not. But I think a little detour wouldn't hurt."

Dagan opens his mouth, but before he can speak, Riyu butts in. "I agree with Beatrice," he says.

Dagan looks at him in surprise. And in that moment, I feel a distinct shift in the dynamic of our group.

Beatrice smiles. "Thank you. This won't take a second." She turns and starts to walk away. "Eleira, Raul, if you would follow me?"

She frames it as a question, but it's an obvious command.

Eleira glances my way. I give her a miniscule nod. Beatrice, however much I hate to admit it, intrigues me.

We go after her. When Dagan and Riyu make to follow, she stops them with a simple, "Just our guests. I'll return them whole and well, I promise."

What is she playing at? I wonder as we leave our escorts behind.

We go along a series of paths that progressively lead deeper and deeper into the earth. The tension has not left Eleira's body. She is still on high alert.

"I don't trust this woman," she whispers to me. Her voice is so soft that even from a foot away I can scarcely pick out the words. "She is not a friend."

"None are friends here," I say.

Beatrice turns around. "Conversing without me? You know it's rude to neglect a member of your company." She pouts. "It makes me feel like a third wheel."

"Perhaps that is what you are," I say quickly.

She holds a hand to her heart. "You wound me."

"Where are we going?"

"Ah. That. Of course, that is the most important question of all, is it not? Where are we, any of us, where are we going? Where are our lives leading us? What will tomorrow look like? How will it differ from today?"

"That's not what I asked," I tell her. My patience is growing thin.

"I know, I know." She is toying with us, exploiting her advantage while she's fully in her element. "But that is mostly because you haven't the slightest inclination of what the right questions *are*."

"We're guests, not prisoners," I remind her, "as you told Dagan. We don't have to be here. Eleira and I can turn away at any time."

"But would you?" she asks. "Doesn't the thrill of this, the mystery—doesn't it entice you? You want to know the things I know. You want to know who I am."

"Enough," I cut her off. "You're dawdling. Take us to where it is you want us to see and be done with it."

"Very well," she nods. "I understand that your Father made you an offer. Of a similar kind I made Eleira. Perhaps it was our mistake to do it separately. But I am here to correct that."

She turns down a side passage and leads us into a very narrow hall. The temperature around us drops.

"Some think of me as little more than your Father's mistress," she continues. "But both of you are far too intelligent to make such a mistake. Those who underestimate me do so at their peril."

I share a look with Eleira. So far, this little speech has been filled with nothing but empty words.

"No fault of theirs, of course. I purposefully hide what I do."

We pass a series of cell doors on either wall. The iron bars are rusted. They don't look like they've been opened in centuries.

"Very few have been given entrance to my chambers. These levels… are where I conduct my experiments."

"What experiments?" I ask, suspicion rising in me.

"Oh, little things. Certainly nothing as cruel as what your Queen has managed with The Convicted. Of course—" she gives a little smile, "—none of those crude creatures exist anymore, do they?"

Something clicks in my brain. "*You* wanted them destroyed," I say.

She flutters a hand over her mouth and gives a small, mocking gasp. "You caught me! How did you guess?"

I growl and say nothing.

Beatrice laughs. "And now you truly show your ignorance." She addresses Eleira. "He is the one you'd follow? Him, over Logan, who has demonstrated his prowess, his influence, his *power*, time and time again?"

Eleira does not reply either.

Beatrice shrugs. "Fine. Keep quiet. You make for a more receptive audience that way."

We come up to a shadowed entrance with stairs leading down. Beatrice starts down the steps. I stop and hold Eleira back.

"No farther," I say. Something feels very wrong about this place. There's a dark energy here, altogether different from what vampires represent.

Beatrice's eyes crinkle in delight as she turns back on us. "No? Many others of the Crypts would give an arm and a leg to see what lies beyond this point."

"We are not *of* The Crypts," I remind her. The room feels dank, rotting. There is a pervading sense of death and decay in the air. It is not death that the vampire brings. It is a more rotten sort, a festering, vile, repulsive thing that soils the atmosphere and fills you with dread. It makes you feel dirty. It makes you feel unwhole.

"Not yet," she answers. "I hope to remedy that. Come."

"No," I stand firm. "Not until I know where you're leading us."

She sighs. "Very well. What I want to show you is a vision of the future. A vision of the way the world might be. What things might devolve into... should your refusal to cooperate continue."

Eleira looks at me. I don't see fear in her eyes, only determination. "I think we should go with her," she says.

Beatrice smiles. "Smart girl. Never look a gift horse in the mouth."

I wonder at the wisdom of following through. But Eleira's consent, coupled with my own curiosity, makes it impossible to resist.

I give a curt nod. Beatrice leads us down.

As soon we reach the bottom floor the whole atmosphere shifts. I cannot feel the vampires of The Crypts anymore. We're all alone here, isolated in a spot none else can reach.

I cannot judge how far down we are anymore, either.

The cut-off from the typical vampire sensations comes as a shock. I look at Eleira, expecting her to show some measure of discomfort... but she is nearly completely at ease.

"You have a ward up," she says. "Maintained by yet another torrial. How many do you have?"

Beatrice smiles. "Who knows?"

Eleira doesn't answer.

"Welcome," Beatrice spreads her hands, "to my little laboratory. It is here that I conduct the majority of my research. It is here where things are done... that not even the King dare acknowledge."

I look around the empty, cavernous room. Is the woman mad?

But then she walks over to a switch on the wall. She presses her hand into the stone. There's a hissing sound, and then, all around us, six equidistant openings appear in the stone.

As soon as they do, horrible cries fill the room. Great wails of pain, many times worse than the screams of The Convicted had ever been, blast into us from within each of those openings.

They sweep into the room with the cataclysmic force of a tidal wave. My hands reflexively cover my ears as I behold the horror of the cells.

Inside each one is a wretched, naked, pale-white creature being burned by a bright, blinding light that shines on from high above.

"Oh, that won't do at all," Beatrice mutters. She shifts her hand on the stone slab, and all the cries are cut off.

An empty silence fills the air. She exhales. "That's better."

Neither Eleira nor I can look away from the tortured creatures behind the bars.

They look like they may have been vampires, once. But their skin has all burnt away, so that only the thinnest layer of translucent hide remains. Their expressions, their faces, are twisted in absolute agony as they scream and scream and scream. The light from that interminable source shines down on them without abatement. Their eyes are huge, wide, and unseeing. Each one of the wretched beasts is so consumed by his own suffering that not one knows that we are here.

"What is this?" Eleira breathes. Her voice is filled with horror.

Beatrice does a single spin, the skirts flowing around her ankles. "These are my children," she says proudly, and with a giddy little smirk. "It's taken many, many attempts to get them here. Still, the process is not perfect. But perfection is an unachievable goal. Those who chase it are fools. For now... this is good enough."

She waves over to the closest cell. On her approach, the creature inside actually manages to shrink back.

"Devon was the first," Beatrice says fondly. "And he has proved the most enduring. Many times I thought this would be too much. But he has proven me wrong, over and over again. He lingers on."

She moves to the next cell over. "This beauty is called Phoebe. She was one of the last to join the cause. But she has survived many trials and now remains."

"What are they?" I ask, not hiding my disgust.

"Hybrids," Beatrice says proudly. "A new breed of vampire, designed to endure the sun. The lights shining on them are pure UV rays. They would fry any regular vampire to a crisp. But these six wonderful individuals... they remain."

Beatrice returns to the panel and activates it to seal the cells. The creatures are blocked from sight as the openings close. The room descends into darkness once more.

"You're torturing them," Eleira says. "Killing them! Why?"

"I wouldn't go so far as to say I'm *killing* them, my dear. As you heard, each is quite determined to live. The light hurts them, yes, but it does not kill. They all persist."

"How long?" I ask. I take an angry step toward her. "How long have they been here?"

"Is that concern lacing your voice?" Beatrice laughs again. "How sweet. The length of their imprisonment is none of your business. In their current state, who knows if they can distinguish how much time has passed, anyway? That is unimportant."

"Why show us this?"

"Ah." She raises a finger. "Now we hit the key point. I want this vision to serve as a warning. I want both of you to take this memory back with you to The Haven, and to think on it long and hard when you deliberate whether to join us or resist."

"This has nothing to do with anything!" I snarl. "So what if you torture your own? How does that affect us?"

"It is not torture, Raul, but sacrifice. These six have given their bodies to me so that our kind may prosper. They will continue to be burned, but eventually, they will be released. Their strength shall be phenomenal. Their hunger will be great. If you thought the bloodlust of The Convicted was something to be feared...? Just wait until you see how hungry my children are. And—if there is no sun to stop them? Watch as they ravage the earth and give rise to a new, twisted, stronger, all-powerful type of vampire.

"The type that cannot be stopped by any force known to man or God."

She gestures around her. "These six are just the start. When the process is perfected, I can create legions of them. Hundreds, then thousands, then millions of bloodthirsty vampires who will answer only to me... and whose thirst can never be quenched.

"So think long and hard before you refuse the offer you've been given. With your help," she looks at Eleira, "we might cloak the world in eternal night. It will be just like your Haven. Some humans will be lost, of course—those who resist—but many will be spared. They will learn to live in harmony beneath us.

"But if you refuse? Well, even if you refuse, the earth will be overcome by vampiric rule. Yet it will be a world ruled by fear. We may not get eternal darkness, but, trust me, the vampire will rise. My hybrids will strike fear into the hearts of all those who dare stand in the way."

"You're mad," I say.

Beatrice laughs. "Am I? I promise you this, return with Eleira, and bring us the torrial used by your Queen to create the wards. In exchange, I will destroy these vampires. The knowledge of their creation is bound up here—" she taps the side of her head, "—and I vow that such monstrosities will never be made again. The world will not devolve into chaos. It will instead welcome a new and everlasting age of prosperity. The choice?" She spreads her hands, "Is entirely up to you."

Chapter Fifty-Four

VICTORIA

SOMEWHERE IN THE VICINITY OF THE HAVEN

I force my way through the blistering sun. Part of me satiates in the pain that every step brings. Every moment spent in the golden rays is agony. My skin burns. In my weakened state—after having been coerced by Smithson into sharing my blood with the Haven's Elite—the sun seems so powerful. The effects it exerts on me are significantly more than they were before.

But I live for this pain. It is my form of defiance against the foul creatures that made me. Even if none know my suffering but I, forcing myself to be out here, to withstand the awful rays, to purposefully put myself in a position that other vampires would do anything to avoid... it makes me feel superior.

What's more, it makes me feel in control.

And it's been one hell of a time since I've actually had control.

I thought that when I'd shared Smithson's bed, in the aftermath of the great battle, it would help me rise.

But I had misjudged the man. When he demanded that I let the others of the Elite drink my blood... when he *insisted* that it was the only way I could prove I was loyal... I had no choice. I had to comply.

The bastard trapped me. He knew what he was doing the whole time, knew the position I was in. He'd exploited my weakness when it was most obvious. And then I found out he intended my blood to be given not just to the Elite but to *all* of The Haven...

That was when I made the decision to escape. I had to find a safe house, a sort of shelter where I could gather my thoughts and decide on what to do next. It had to be somewhere I could remain indefinitely, with absolutely no concern for my safety.

The only reason I'd offered Smithson the chance to come with me was to strike at him when his back was turned. It was rash and impulsive—but I'd been burning with hatred for the man. The plan was to get him out of reach of The Haven's Royal Court, and then, quite literally, put a silver dagger through his back.

But he refused my offer, and so I here I am, wandering alone through the outskirts of The Haven, near the former boundaries of the coven, biding for time.

A fire burned in the forest late last night. The conflagration was huge and all-destructive. I watched it from a safe distance, hidden in a makeshift nest in the treetops.

I waited to see if others would come to investigate. Of course, that had been my expectation. After the attack and subsequent breakdown of The Haven, anything of the *unusual* sort should have been cause for alarm.

But as I watched and waited... I neither felt nor saw any vampires approaching. That alone was interesting. But what intrigued even more was that the fire did not spread. It should have engulfed the whole forest. Yet it had not.

That meant it was a controlled flame.

That piqued my curiosity. Who was responsible? Why?

Maybe it was not the most intelligent decision I'd ever made, but when the sun rose, I decided I would sacrifice my hiding spot and go investigate.

That's where I am now, less than a hundred yards away, picking my path carefully through the trees. I avoid the shafts of sunlight that dot the ground. In my current state, just the ambience of light is enough to grant the pain I so crave.

The smell of burnt wood is heavy in the air. It is mingled with another scent, one that I find utterly repulsive:

That of burned flesh.

I stop in a shaded alcove between two great evergreens. A trickle of fear crawls down my spine. Why do I smell *flesh?*

I look around the woods. There's nobody here that I can sense. The wild creatures that inhabit this place are nowhere to be found.

Looks like they are the intelligent ones. I am the fool walking straight into danger.

I do a thorough scan of the treetops. They are empty. There is always the chance that this is a trap. For whom, I wouldn't pretend to know, but it would be utterly ridiculous for me to stumble into it blindly.

I see nothing up there that is particularly alarming. Only that awful, lingering scent gives the impression that something is wrong.

I remind myself that I won't bump into any vampires out during the day and force my legs to take me past the last row of trees and into the clearing that housed a bonfire.

When I cross the threshold, an involuntary gasp escapes my lips.

There are sixteen bodies on the ground, arranged in a perfect circle. They are all human—or rather, they recently *were* human.

Now they are in the midst of being transformed into vampires.

That explains why I couldn't sense them earlier. They are all stuck in that rare position where they are not fully human, but neither are they true vampires.

But who would do this?

I look around. Charred bits of clothing cover some of the bodies. The remains of the fire make a great black pit in the earth.

I approach the circle cautiously. None are yet conscious. The sun falls on some of them—and the ones who are further along in their transformation show the ill effects. Where the rays hit their skin is red, raw, and peeling. Nasty blisters ooze corruption from those spots.

I snort. These fledglings are weak. The sun has never done that to me.

But then I notice an odd dark mark on each of their bodies.

I kneel beside the man closest to me. I reach out and touch his skin.

Immediately, I pull my hand back. He's scorching! Vampires are never hot. Our body temperatures drop permanently when the Dark Gift sets in.

Yet this man is feverish.

I move to the next one. He is the same. Although he is protected by the shade of the trees, there are still blotches of corruption showing on his skin. They are faint compared to the ones on those exposed to the sun... but they are still there.

Never in all my years have I heard of vampires reacting to sunlight like this.

The light burns and hurts and yes, even kills, but these deformities look like they are caused by some festering disease.

And vampires cannot get sick.

I shudder suddenly. Only one explanation comes to mind, and I cannot bear to think of the implications.

These poor souls have been touched by dark magic.

I examine that little mark on the shoulder again. It's almost like the spot a human victim would have after being bitten by one of my kind. Yet it is also wholly different. It goes deeper into the skin. Instead of being red, it is a gruesome black.

Could the demon have done this?

I rise as fast as I can. The Narwhark is the only explanation for the mark that I can come up with. Does that mean that whoever initiated the conversion of these humans into vampires *collaborated* with the beast?

It's a hideous thought. Unfathomable. And yet…

I cannot stay for long. Vampires might avoid the sun, but no such restriction holds the Narwhark in place.

I look around the circle. I want answers to what happened here.

The only way to get them is from one who was directly involved.

So I pick up the only woman in the group, sling her over my shoulders, and make my way from this place as fast as I can.

I fully intend to be completely hidden, and entirely out of reach, when the missing woman is discovered.

By that time, I suspect… I'll know all there is to about what transpired.

And if the woman proves uncooperative? Well, what better way to quench my thirst than by draining a newly-made vampire completely dry?

Chapter Fifty-Five

Raul stands next to me, silent as a statue, while Riyu conjures up the portal that will take us into the Paths.

The horrendous, pitiful creatures Beatrice showed us—they are playing on his mind. He cares more about the plight of others than he cares to admit. Perhaps more than a vampire in his position, with his strength, should.

But that very *humanity* is what draws me to him. It is what I glimpsed the first time we interacted. I knew right away, deep down, that Raul was unlike the rest.

For a time he had lost that part of himself. I knew what he was doing when he'd tried pushing me away. I pretended ignorance only because I thought it would help him realize the flaw of his approach.

The portal materializes. Dagan puts a hand on Raul's and my shoulders. The three of us go through.

Riyu appears behind us a second after we land. The portal winks out. I feel the vibrant magical energy all around me.

I look back at the smallest vampire and catch him staring at Dagan's back.

When he sees me looking, he scowls and quickly takes the lead.

"This way," he says, casting me another suspicious glare. "We need to move fast."

We follow him through the secret paths in silence.

I wonder what Riyu uses to navigate. It cannot just be familiarity with the Paths. Everything looks too much alike. Without a guide, I bet someone could get lost wandering for ages down here.

But after a few minutes of walking, a hypothesis forms in my mind. The flow of magic in the air is constantly shifting. Yet there's a certain underlying pattern to them. They're not quite as chaotic as they are in the outside world.

In fact, the more I concentrate on it, the more I think I am right. The first time I was brought here I was too taken in by the sheer majesty of the place to pay any mind to such details. But now, if I concentrate, I think I can pick up the trail that Riyu is following.

I want to ask him about it. But Raul and I agreed that it would be best not to speak in the presence of our escorts. Whatever we said would be passed on to Logan or Beatrice. We do not want to give our position away.

Riyu stops suddenly. His head snaps to the left. A flicker of doubt forms on his face, but it is immediately vanquished.

"What is it?" I ask, but then I feel it, too.

Over in the distance, far away, there is a... suction. Like a black hole, pulling all the magic in.

What's more, out from it comes a resonance... a sort of reverberation that I

349

feel in my very bones. The magical currents aren't just being sucked in, no—they are being spit out dark and corrupted.

The impression of that lasts barely a second. As fast as I'd felt it, it's gone.

Dagan growls a warning. "You better not be thinking of anything stupid."

I glance at Riyu. A look passes between us. It tells me all I need to know:

He's just as uncomfortable as I am at what we felt.

"We're almost there," Riyu says. He hurries down the cavernous passage. "A few miles this way, and we can cross."

All four of us use our vampire speed to arrive at our destination quickly.

"Here," Riyu stops. "I'll cast the portal."

Without waiting for Dagan's permission he begins the incantation that collects the magical energies required.

Quickly, it opens up. The portal looks just slightly weaker than before. I don't know if it's because Riyu was in a rush, or because of the strange effect we both felt earlier.

"This goes to the border of The Haven," Riyu says.

"Why aren't you bringing us inside?" Raul demands.

"For our own safety," Dagan answers. "Last time we came upon you unprepared... and got a nasty reaction. We don't want to be the spark that starts the wildfire." He grins. "At least, not yet."

"Go now!" Riyu prompts. "I'm not going to hold it open much longer."

Raul looks at me. He takes my hand.

We both jump through.

For a disorienting moment I cannot tell up from down. My vision blends into a multitude of harsh, swirling reds and blacks. In my mind's eye I see the vision of an apocalyptic future, with humans enslaved around the world, Beatrice's twisted sun vampires running wild, and uncontrolled, society crumbling into ruins…

And then it stops, and I'm jerked back to myself. My feet hit the ground. I open my eyes. Immediately I recognize The Haven's familiar forest.

Raul lands beside me. The moment he does, I feel a short zap.

The portal disappears.

"Well," Raul begins. "Looks like we made it. It—"

Out of nowhere, the Narwhark leaps at us.

Neither Raul nor I have time to react. The demon collides into his chest. Raul falls with the weight of the beast on top of him.

My claws are out and my fangs are bared in an instant. But before I can move to help, the creature's head snaps back.

"No!"

The thought is not my own. It hits me with such force that I stumble back. The demon has Raul pinned to the ground, but it's not attacking him—simply keeping him there.

The Narwhark's eyes bore into mine. This time, I have no doubt. The creature is sentient. It has developed consciousness. I make to move forward, but that thought crashes into me again:

"No. Stay!"

Is it the Narwhark speaking to me? But no, it can't. *How* can it? And yet...

I realize with a start that once more time has slowed. *That* is why Raul is still on the ground. His arms are just starting to move up, to try and get the demon off of him, but they're moving so slowly, it's like a lagging movie.

The Narwhark looks at me. Just like in the audience chamber before the Royal Court, we are both locked into a trance-like state. The whole of the atmosphere seems to shimmer around us. Something about this creature disrupts the flow of time...

Of course! Now it hits me. *That's* why it appears so fast to those on the outside.

It blinks. Its eyes, usually opaque, become shiny and reflective. I see myself mirrored in the black.

I can't look away. Something tugs at me to come closer. It's almost—*almost*—like the vampiric influence. But this one comes from the Narwhark—at least, so I think.

I take a step forward. The Narwhark watches me, swinging its tail back and forth like a pendulum. Its paws are right on Raul's chest. One of them presses down over his heart. I feel the threat acutely. If the demon even *tries* to hurt him...

Well, it'll find out what it means to spark the anger of a witch.

And yet, I feel no menace from it. It watches me as I approach. I wonder for a second what Raul is thinking. But from his perspective, no more than half a second has passed.

Perhaps less.

That pull continues beckoning me, until I'm right at Raul's feet. The demon still hasn't moved. Only its swishing tail gives any proof that it is not a statue.

"Stop."

Again the thought comes that is not my own. It's also, I realize, not a spoken word, but a collection of feelings, a jumble of emotions, all combining to give it meaning. It is a language without words. A type of instinctual understanding that penetrates the emptiness between the conscious and subconscious mind.

"Kneel down."

The command is amplified by an increase of the pull. I could resist, but with Raul in such a precarious position…

Slowly I bend my knees. The creature continues watching me. *Swish, swish, swish, swish* goes its tail.

I see myself clearly in its black, midnight eyes. It is like staring into a pool of inky oil. This close to the Narwhark, I would expect to feel a sort of revulsion, maybe a dissonance…

But there is nothing. The evil of this beast is either hidden, subdued, or locked away from me.

Is that because *I* summoned it?

When my knees touch the ground, the Narwhark finally moves. It lifts its front leg up off Raul's body. It bends the twisted joint that functions as its knee… and bows to me.

I swallow hard.

Next, it drops its head and takes a step closer.

I reach out. Before I know what's happening, my hand is hovering half an inch away from the demon's head.

Without warning, through a sudden suction, a magnification of that pull, and my hand clamps down on its crown.

Immediately, a flood of images pour through my mind. A world of pure black. Existence in a void where you are the only living thing. A light breaking through and ripping you out. Pain, pain, pain, enormous, hideous pain as you're torn from the reality in which you belong and flung into this foreign one. And then a mixture of feelings: confusion, anger, fury—and above all, *hunger*—when you find yourself in a body many times weaker than your own.

I gasp and pull away. My heart is racing. What I saw—what I saw...

It's what the Narwhark experienced when I summoned it.

"Isn't it?" I whisper.

As if it understood, it bows its head again. It wants me to resume the link.

I take a deep breath, and, with a shaking hand, touch the Narwhark's neck.

More images explode in my mind.

A pristine, sterile white room. Bright lights flooding in from overhead. Glass walls positioned all around.

A cube. Someone inside. Someone... me?

The glass reflects the light, and the surface shimmers like a mirror. I cannot see through to the other side, but I feel the presence of others. There are humans gathered all around, and I know they're in their laboratory, though how I know this, I

354

could not say. They're studying me, keeping me locked in this hateful, horrid place where the only comfort is the small bed I lie on.

I move my eyes left and right. But my eyelids remain closed. They've been closed for years, for decades, maybe for centuries?

Hate. *Such blinding, all-consuming hate takes me. Hate for all the people who brought me here. Hate for the fools who think they can contain me. They cannot! They will not! And when I rise, when I recover all my strength and open my eyes, they will all know the fury of a slighted Black Sorceress!*

I rip my hand away. I'm panting now. Sweat lines my back and neck. Beads of it drip down between my breasts. "What is that?" I gasp. "What did you show me?"

"It is you I want!"

The thought comes to me, full of venom, full of loathing and envy and hate. It comes not from the Narwhark...

But from the one whose body I possessed for a second.

And, in that instant, I recognize the link for what it is: a connection of the sort that existed between Victoria and me. Except now, it is between the Narwhark and me... and one other.

The witch I glimpsed in the white room.

The demon makes a deep growling sound in its throat. For a second, I'm afraid it will attack. But its anger is not aimed at me. It's directed at that third member of our strange company. The Black Sorceress, whoever she is, whatever she wants or does... the Narwhark hates it. I can feel the hate, it's palpable, it's tragic, and it's all-consuming.

It frightens me. If a demon this strong can summon so much emotion…

In a flash, I feel a great influx of magic. There's a huge collection of energy behind me. I whip my hand back, and see a portal opening. It's pulling on the residue of Riyu's spell.

The Narwhark is doing it.

It leaps off Raul. I assume it's going to simply dash into the opening. Instead, its tail whips down, aimed right toward Raul's heart.

I cry out, "No!"

But the demon is so fast that before the word can leave my mouth, the act is done.

And to my immense surprise—it didn't stab Raul. The point of its tail pierced his pocket and wrapped around the precious vial of blood.

"*Yes, yes, that is what I need!*" comes the foreign thought.

It's laced with triumph and greed and true hunger. And, beyond all that, I feel… evil. True, dark, unvarnished, uncontained, uncontrollable evil, born of envy and jealousy and hate.

Then the Narwhark shoots off, like a bullet through the air. It streams into the portal and then it's gone, and the whole thing winks out of existence so fast I can do nothing to stop it.

The link between me and the Narwhark disappears. Time resumes its regular march. Raul's scream of rage fills the air.

"GET OFF—"

He stops. He blinks. He touches his chest where the Narwhark nearly stabbed him.

His eyes go wide when he understands what's happened. "It's gone," he tells me. "Eleira, it's gone! The demon took the blood!"

"I know," I say, and, in a daze, recount exactly what happened in the time warp.

"The creature's dangerous," Raul tells me when I'm done. "But it sounds like it wants your help."

"What?" I exclaim.

"You were not yourself when you pulled it out of its natural realm. Somebody else was in control, yes?"

"That Black Sorceress," I say. "It must have been her."

Raul nods. "She's the one who summoned the Narwhark. But she did it *though* you. You hold the ultimate link to the creature. And yet..."

"And yet what?"

"The sorceress also has a link to you. As does the Narwhark." Raul shakes his head. "We need Mother."

"But the blood," I say. "The blood of the Ancient is gone. It was our one chance to revive her."

Raul gives a rueful smile. "It's not all gone," he says. "Some of it is contained in your veins, remember?"

I swallow. "You think it'll be enough?"

"I hope so."

He takes my hand. We turn in the direction of The Haven.

"Let's pray that Phillip has been able to keep a semblance of order. We need to shore up defenses for an attack. Because there's no way in hell I'm accepting Father's offer." He looks at me. "We'll need to return to The Crypts at some point and destroy Beatrice's twisted vampire hybrids."

"Agreed," I say.

"It'll start a war. There's no avoiding it."

"I know," I say sadly.

"But first we need our Queen." Raul gives a grim nod. "The days ahead are going to be the hardest of our lives. There won't be anywhere to hide. I'm sorry for bringing you into all this, Eleira. I'm sorry we stole you from your old life. I—"

I cut him off. "Sorry?" I demand. "If you hadn't done that, I would have never met you—I would have never fallen in love."

He blinks and looks at me. Then, something changes in his eyes. A fierce fire flashes in them. He grabs me by the waist, yanks me into him, and kisses me— hard.

I'm breathing hard and nearly delirious when he lets go. Such happiness flows through me that I cannot believe it's real.

"I love you too," he tells me. "And no matter what happens next, I want you to never forget that. You are *mine*, Eleira, and I am yours, and damn any who dare stand in my way. Do you understand?"

I give a small, giddy nod. "Yes," I breathe.

"Then let's go," he says, linking hands and leading me toward The Haven.

I go with him, satiating in the moment... yet secretly terrified that this might be the last sliver of peace either of us will ever know.

Epilogue

Smithson

Location unknown

The military chopper touches down at the entrance of the Order's secret facility, high amongst the snow-capped peaks of the Rockies.

The pilot motions for me to go. He doesn't bother speaking above the roar of the blades and the buffeting winds.

I clutch my coat closer to myself, giving the impression that I am affected by the cold, and jump down. Already I can see my men waiting for me at the entrance. The gusts of wind fling snow every which way.

As soon as I'm a safe distance away from the helicopter, it takes off. I stamp through the deep snow and greet my lieutenant.

He gives an immediate, proper salute. "Welcome back, Lord Commander. We weren't expecting you so soon."

"I came the moment I got the message," I say, not wasting time on pleasantries. "Take me to her."

The soldier gives one more salute and leads me through the triple-reinforced doors. Once inside, they close behind us, cutting off the roar of the elements and sealing me in my true home.

We walk through a long, metal hallway. Cameras and sensors follow our every step. This is the most secure facility in the world—even the US government has nothing on us.

We go through an intricate series of checkpoints designed to verify the identity of those who enter. It is no simple thing to gain the clearance required to come into this facility. Most members of the Order don't even know of its existence.

It is where the Order keeps its most prized possessions.

The trek through security takes a good half hour. I could not be more pleased by the protocol. Even though I am the highest in command, there can be no exceptions made. The fact that no part of this has slackened in my absence speaks volumes about the Order's ability to sustain itself.

Of course, very few here know of my *true* nature. Few know I'm a vampire.

Therein lies the difficulty. I've had my hand on power for centuries, but I've had to disappear for decades at a time before I could re-ascertain my rightful spot. The invitation to come join The Haven came at a time when I was the most involved that I've been in the Order's workings for years. That made this particular absence very different from the leaves I've taken before. Before, there had to be a generational turnover of my human companions before I could return—lest any get overly suspicious.

Of course, the Order deals with the supernatural. Our cause has not changed in the time since we were founded:

We are here to stamp out evil from the world.

The irony of having a leader with a secret such as mine is not lost on me. But my humanity was stolen from me. The day I lost it, I vowed that I would get it back—but not before eradicating the curse that took it from me in the first place.

Eradicate it once and for all. Eliminate it altogether.

The only way that is possible?

By the complete and utter destruction of every vampire on earth.

I *have* to be the last. I *have* to be the only one who's left. Because, when the moment comes when I alone carry the poisonous spore, the malevolent seed of this corruption, I trust only myself to do what must be done.

Only when my eyes close for the final time will the Order's purpose be fully realized.

Finally, we reach the true entrance of the facilities. The doors slide open and reveal a massive laboratory inside.

There are scientists, engineers, academics, researchers, all sorts of the best and brightest professionals walking the floor. Computer screens dot the perimeter. Everything in here is top-of-the-line. The glass-and-steel décor is a marked contrast to the almost-medieval existence I'd grown accustomed to in The Haven.

My people really are the best. There is no comparison. The Order recruits straight from the top schools in the world. Everyone around me is young, ambitious, hungry... and above all, fiercely loyal.

The Vorcellian Order prides itself on finding those recruits who would serve us best. A mere interest in the supernatural isn't enough. We look for people whose lives have been touched by forces of the occult. Those who have known tragedy at the hands of what we know as otherworldly entities. The stronger an emotional connection our recruits have with the supernatural, the easier it is for us to fit them to our mold.

A commitment to the Order is a commitment for life. We simply cannot allow word of what goes on to leak to the outside world. Of course, we send moles out to infiltrate other organizations. We have people in all levels of government in countries worldwide.

But the type of people we house *here,* in this exact facility, cannot be found anywhere else.

A few of the men and women stop to greet me quickly as I pass, but most continue with their duties.

That is just how I like it. Their tasks are more important than exchanging pleasantries.

I march into my office, which has long been unoccupied, and look over the stack of papers on the desk. Daily reports of the Order's happenings all over the world. I have quite a backlog to catch up on.

But with my own preternatural secrets, I will have no trouble tackling it all in a single night.

Yet status updates are not what brought me here. I hit the intercom and ask for Sylvia—the lead scientist responsible for the project I am most intimately involved with.

A few minutes later, a sophisticated woman in a stylish black dress enters the room. She takes just as much pride in her appearance as she does her mind— and she is far and away the most brilliant human I have ever come across. Her outfit does not conform to the usual dress code, but it is the one concession I was willing to make.

Besides. The pure sensuality of her figure should never be hidden.

"You got my letter," she says. That is one other thing I like about Sylvia. She is straight to the point.

"Yes." She is one of those rare few who know of my true nature. "How long has it been?"

"We first detected brainwave activity a week-and-a-half ago. Just a flicker at the start. But since then, it's grown stronger. Just this morning—for a tenth of a second—she opened her eyes."

I keep my features still even though a torrent of excitement riffles through me. "Did she do anything else?"

"No. But it's just a matter of time, we believe, before she tries to make an escape."

"I trust you've reinforced the barriers?"

"Don't insult me."

"Of course. I apologize."

"This is *my* project, Smithson," Sylvia warns. "I've spent more than a decade to get to this point. If you think to interrupt now—"

"You spent a decade and a half *serving the Order*," I correct her. "If I order you tomorrow to step down, you will do so without protest. Understood?"

Sylvia glares at me... and gives a miniscule nod.

"Of course your efforts will not go unappreciated," I continue. "Nor will your dedication be unrecognized. But we can talk of plaudits later. Right now, you must take me to her."

Sylvia spins on her heel and leads me out the room.

We walk out of my office, go down the steps to the West Wing, and walk through the mass of people crowding the floor. From there, we climb up a set of stairs and proceed along a narrow, suspended walkway that goes to the East Wing.

There's an even higher level of clearance required to enter. For good reason. Because the East Wing houses my most ambitious project yet.

We reach an enormous vault door. It is many times stronger than the most secure bank in the world. Nothing man-made can penetrate it.

And the secret behind its creation? A rare metal, infused into the structure, that is impervious to heat and cold. Any sort of external force directed at it only makes it stronger. Less than an ounce of the metal has ever existed in the world—and all of it has been used to secure this vault.

Sylvia punches in the entry code and brings her eyes to the scanner. The little machine reads her iris, while simultaneously taking in all of her vitals: body temperature, heart rate, breathing patterns—all things that, as a whole, are more unique than a fingerprint and could not be replicated by any fraudulent process.

The scanner beeps, granting access. The vault door starts to part and rise. As soon as sufficient space shows, I duck underneath... and am greeted by a glorious sight.

In the middle of the room is an opaque, white cube. It's made entirely of glass, and is about the size of a car trailer. Surrounding it are all sorts of computers, all types of machines, and all are used to monitor the creature that is inside.

The Vorcellian Order's small and secret clan of witches rise when they see me. "The cloaking spell has been indispensable," I praise them in salutation. "It was very skillfully done."

A round of smug smiles greet the proclamation.

Sylvia steps in after me and waits for the vault doors to shut. When they're closed, she gives a relieved sigh, and casts off the black wig hiding the branded rune marks all over her skull.

"Much better," she exhales. She shoots me a look. "I don't understand why we can't let the others see."

"Best leave the humans in the dark," I respond, without much enthusiasm. This is a discussion we've had many times before.

"They'll find out eventually."

"So why rush the process?" I step up to the nearest computer screen—the one providing a bird's eye view of the interior of the cube.

And there, I see her: the hideously ugly, wretched old thing, lying still as Sleeping Beauty on a tiny bed in the middle of the cube. She looks exactly as she has for all long years since we took her from her slumbering hideout deep in the woods of British Columbia and brought her here.

And as I stand there, just looking at her... I feel the greatest sense of anticipation I've known in decades. The brainwave activity monitor to my right shows her constant delta waves increasing in tempo.

It's only a matter of time until she wakes up. And when she does...?

The Order will possess the strongest witch in existence.

The End

THANK YOU FOR READING!

Want More of The Vampire Gift?

The Vampire Gift 4 is coming soon! I'm aiming for a September/October re-

lease.

Don't want to miss it? Then sign up for my mailing list

(http://eepurl.com/bYCp41) to get an email the day it comes out!

Loved the book? Let me know by leaving a review on Amazon! Or come say hi

to me on Facebook – I love meeting and interacting with my fans :)

www.Facebook.com/AuthorEMKnight

Free Book Offer!

Want to get the next book in The Vampire Gift series for free? Here's how you do it...

1. Leave a review on Amazon.com for *The Vampire Gift 3: Throne of Dust.*

2. Once the review is posted, email me a link to it with the subject "Free Book Offer". My email: em@emknight.com

3. As soon as the next book comes out, I'll send you a special link to download the book for free! You can request any book in the series as your free "thank you" book.

Made in the USA
Middletown, DE
31 October 2016